Praise for Peter Orner's

MAGGIE BROWN & OTHERS

One of the Best Books of the Year

New York Times Book Review • *Chicago Tribune*
O, The Oprah Magazine • *Kirkus Reviews*

Long-listed for the Simpson / Joyce Carol Oates Prize

"It's been apparent since his first book, *Esther Stories*, that Peter Orner was a major talent…His exacting prose casts an elegiac and autumnal glow…You know from the second you pick him up that he's the real deal. His sentences are lit from below, like a swimming pool, with a kind of resonant yearning that's impossible to fake…He has that gift (Keats saw it in Shakespeare) of 'negative capability'—in part that passive yet electric ability to submerge himself in the thoughts and emotions of a wide range of humans…Orner can do anything."

—Dwight Garner, *New York Times*

"There are forty-four stories in this collection, and they are all marvels of concision and compassion. Pick it up. Trust me."

—Bethanne Patrick, *Washington Post*

"Orner writes words that don't disappear...At the same time, these stories never seem confined to the pages on which they appear. Though set in different eras, going back to the '60s, as well as in different time zones, they float over and under each other, their recurring characters cutting across time and space... *Maggie Brown & Others* is so full of brilliant, reverberant lines—and cuttingly funny ones as well—that they are like critics' popcorn: You can't stop citing them... Writing doesn't get any better."
—Lloyd Sachs, *Chicago Tribune*

"There's a beautiful drifting quality to *Maggie Brown & Others*, a sense of being invited inside a roving, kaleidoscopic mind—reluctant to generalize, tender, astute, with an eye for both comedy and heartache—and adopting its rhythms as your own... 'Lighted Windows' is the title of the collection's second section, but the phrase might apply to the whole book. Peter Orner is a wonderful guide, training our gaze from window to window, where we find reflections of ourselves even as we glimpse the inscrutable, captivating lives on the other side of the glass."
—Elizabeth Graver, *New York Times Book Review*

"Orner writes with a combination of sincerity and self-awareness. He takes a subtle tone of empathy toward his characters' ambitions by acknowledging how simultaneously unremarkable and wrenching their lives feel... The book is in its totality most vividly reminiscent of Raymond Carver."
—Antonia Hitchens, *San Francisco Chronicle*

"A master of flash fiction tosses Chekhov and Carver into a blender, adds a dash of Catskills wit, and serves up an effervescent cocktail conjuring sunset beach strolls and marriages on the rocks."
—Hamilton Cain, *O, The Oprah Magazine*

"This collection's forty-four powerful tales express Orner's talent for crafting captivating character sketches that read like memoirs...Readers will sympathize with Orner's characters and identify with their all-too-human frailties."
—*Publishers Weekly* (starred review)

"The stories in Peter Orner's *Maggie Brown & Others* feel eternally human, less like they've been written and rather like they've been drawn by patient hands from an ancient aquifer of memory, longing, and soulful knowing."
—Adam Johnson, author of Pulitzer Prize winner *The Orphan Master's Son* and National Book Award winner *Fortune Smiles*

"Peter Orner is an extraordinary writer, and *Maggie Brown & Others* was a deep pleasure to read. His stories teem with life and energy, and unfold with a kind of soulful grace he has made all his own."
—Adam Haslett, author of *Imagine Me Gone*

"Orner has a sharp eye for absurdity and a discerning ear for dialogue...Insightful, rueful, and often humorous, this collection holds a mirror to contemporary life and gives the reader much to reflect on."
—*Kirkus Reviews* (starred review)

"Orner writes simultaneously heartbreaking and witty stories."
—*AV Club*

"It's unusual for a writer of such great detail and originality to still have so much heart on his sleeve. I didn't realize how I'd missed actual feeling in our celebrated younger writers until I fell onto Peter Orner and these sublime new stories. I may not go back."
—Thomas McGuane, author of *Gallatin Canyon*

"No one captures the inner lives of vanished places and people like Peter Orner. Radiant, funny, full of wisdom and heart, his vibrant portraits pulse with authentic energy and are as perfectly tuned to his characters' idiosyncratic speech as those of Grace Paley."

—Andrea Barrett, author of National Book Award winner *Ship Fever*

"To read Peter Orner's stories is to live simultaneously in so many lives: the reader's memories intertwine with the characters', the characters' dreams resurface in the reader's. People we have loved and lost, people we have encountered and missed—they wait for us to rediscover them in Orner's stories. This book, exquisitely written, is as necessary and expansive as life."

—Yiyun Li, author of *Where Reasons End*

"Orner is a master of the aphoristic short story. The forty-four concise and stinging tales in *Maggie Brown & Others* express a full spectrum of caustic observations, nuanced emotions, and life-warping predicaments…Orner writes with a heady blend of gravitas and wit similar to that of such kindred short-story virtuosos as Deborah Eisenberg, Andre Dubus, and Gina Berriault, while expressing his own edgy empathy and embrace of everyday absurdity."

—Donna Seaman, *Booklist* (starred review)

"One of the best contemporary writers working today: his characters are indelible, his focus small and piercing, his insights moving…all with his special sense for truth, character, and wistful realism."

—Emily Temple, *Literary Hub*

"Peter Orner has the unique ability to invent fully-formed, vibrant characters within the shortest of stories...His characters are unapologetic and complex, holding guilt, fear, and love... Orner presents the character's entire inner world—and it's all done in just a few pages...He builds these stories carefully—full of nuance and a special kind of lightness—and hands them to us on an assorted platter."   —Jeevika Verma, *Ploughshares*

ALSO BY PETER ORNER

FICTION

Last Car Over the Sagamore Bridge
Love and Shame and Love
The Second Coming of Mavala Shikongo
Esther Stories

NONFICTION

Am I Alone Here?: Notes on Living to Read and Reading to Live

AS EDITOR

Lavil: Life, Love, and Death in Port-au-Prince
Hope Deferred: Narratives of Zimbabwean Lives
Underground America

MAGGIE BROWN

&

OTHERS

PETER ORNER

BACK BAY BOOKS
LITTLE, BROWN AND COMPANY
New York Boston London

For Katie, Phoebe, and Roscoe

AND

In memory of James Alan McPherson

Copyright © 2019 by Peter Orner

Hachette Book Group supports the right to free expression and the value of copyright. The purpose of copyright is to encourage writers and artists to produce the creative works that enrich our culture.

The scanning, uploading, and distribution of this book without permission is a theft of the author's intellectual property. If you would like permission to use material from the book (other than for review purposes), please contact permissions@hbgusa.com. Thank you for your support of the author's rights.

Back Bay Books / Little, Brown and Company
Hachette Book Group
1290 Avenue of the Americas, New York, NY 10104
littlebrown.com

Originally published in hardcover by Little, Brown and Company, July 2019
First Back Bay trade paperback edition, July 2020

Back Bay Books is an imprint of Little, Brown and Company, a division of Hachette Book Group, Inc. The Back Bay Books name and logo are trademarks of Hachette Book Group, Inc.

The publisher is not responsible for websites (or their content) that are not owned by the publisher.

The Hachette Speakers Bureau provides a wide range of authors for speaking events. To find out more, go to hachettespeakersbureau.com or call (866) 376-6591.

ISBN 978-0-316-51611-2 (hc) / 978-0-316-51612-9 (pb)
LCCN 2019930556

10 9 8 7 6 5 4 3 2 1

LSC-C

Printed in the United States of America

Contents

At that moment it all seemed extraordinary to me
and made me want to flee from it and yet remain forever.

—Isaac Babel

I

Come
Back
to
California

Come back to California, come back to California
every mapmaker, every mapmaker is pleading.

—Jack Spicer, "Letters to James Alexander"

The Deer

When she was a kid, she watched a mountain lion chase a deer into the lagoon at low tide. She'd been riding her bike on the path along the edge of Murch's farm. The deer ran out so far into the water that the mountain lion turned back to the shore and vanished into the trees. An hour later, the deer was still stuck in the mud. The tide began to roll back in through the channel connecting the lagoon to open water. She was only a kid, but as she watched the deer out there alone, she knew almost right away that this was something she'd carry the rest of her life. Later, she heard that a tourist, seeing the deer in the lagoon from Highway 1, had called the fire department and begged them to do something. The assistant chief said, "What do you want me to do about it? Go out there with a boat and get kicked in the head? Call the DNR." The lagoon, the waves, the motionless deer. It made no sound, or at least none that she could hear from where she was sitting as it waited, or seemed to wait, while the water rose, covering its legs and then rising higher.

She'd sat on a wet log and watched. The damp seeped through her pants. The wind began to blow inland from the ocean. No, it wasn't really happening. Even then it was more like an image, fixed, not a breathing deer out there in the water. So much of what she remembers became lodged this way. Something occurs, in the motion of the present, but it's already over. Because even then, even as she watched, she was already moving away from it, already thinking how years from now she might tell someone about this. Someone who's never seen this lagoon. The wind began to blow harder. The sun had long since fallen, but there was some light left. When she couldn't watch anymore, when she picked her bike off the ground and rode away, the water had reached the deer's chest, and still it had not moved.

Fowlers Lake

Fowlers Lake is out past the national forest campground, about nine miles or so from McCloud, California, off Route 89. It's not a lake; it's a swimming hole, a place where the river widens out. Somebody built a crude dam there fifty years ago. We call it our lake, our mountain lake, and it's so cold you can swim only in August, when it's hot enough outside. Sometimes in July, maybe a week or two into September, depending on the year. Billy and I liked to go out to Fowlers in the late afternoon when the sun was just about to drop beneath the tops of the trees. The place was usually less crowded with campers by then and we could pretty much have the lake to ourselves. I read a philosopher once who said heat and cold are pretty much the same thing, that their contraries are mirrors. Whatever the hell he meant, he never swam at Fowlers. Heat, isn't it amazing how it vanishes? It's so heavy when you're in the thick of it. As soon as the sun began to drop, no matter how hot the day, the shadows always brought a sudden chill, and that was the exact moment we chose to swim.

It was a Wednesday, and the parking lot was empty when we got there except for a pregnant woman with a flat tire and no spare. She said she was from Shasta City and that her boyfriend wasn't answering his phone. There's no reception out at Fowlers. She must have told us that in order to seem less helpless.

Billy, who was an expert on everything, said the rim of his truck's spare wouldn't match the rim of her little Mazda. Otherwise he'd lend her a tire. Instead, he offered to drive her to McCloud, where she could get some help or arrange a cab home to Shasta City. She could leave the car and deal with it tomorrow, he told her. The rangers would wait a couple of days before they ticketed her for overnight parking. Would she mind, though, waiting a half hour while we swam?

She didn't say yes or no. She just smiled. She looked only at Billy. She was pretty far along, maybe seven and a half months. She stood there the way I've seen other pregnant women stand, with her feet pointing a little outward, for balance, I guess. We figured okay, so we dove into the water and fuck it was cold. And you couldn't warm up a little out of the water anymore because the sun was already farther down past the trees and the whole lake was in shadow. But as Billy said, that's when your body has no choice but to acclimate fast and become fishlike, no longer dependent upon the sun for survival but on the water itself, which is only, Billy said, as cold as your brain permits it to be. This load of total bullshit was weirdly right. Freak that he was, Billy sometimes made sense. And the more I swam around, the more I got, if not warm, something, yes, maybe a little fishlike, fishish. We didn't talk, Billy and me. We didn't touch. We just splashed around in our own worlds for a while because that's what you do if you're going to stay in that water at all. You've got to concentrate. Hard to imagine what we must have looked like to her. She wasn't a kid. We found out later she was thirty-two. It turned out there really was a boyfriend in Shasta, just no evidence that she'd tried to call him. Apparently, she didn't even own a cell phone. She was sort of a hippie that way, the boyfriend told the police later. She was against phones on principle.

She'd spread a blanket on the little patch of rocks that passed for a beach and watched us. That's what I remember and that's what I told them after, that she was just sitting on the rocks on a blanket, watching, holding her stomach in front of her like you might a large bowl. We may have ended up swimming more than a half hour. It could have been forty-five minutes. It might have been closer to an hour. Once we got going in the water, time was different. And a late-August day, even the shadows of it, drags on forever. Anything was possible. Maybe I'd finally fuck Billy. Maybe I finally wouldn't. He never pushed his case, though I know he ached, and sometimes his puny hard-on would win out against the cold and push against his shorts like a ruler. We were considered smarter kids, college bound. There weren't that many of us our year. Maybe I was thinking about Billy, about yes or no to Billy. Or maybe I was just breaststroking around, looking at the light, thick green and yellow, how it merged with the gray-blue lake water and made everything…the only word I can think of is radiant but that's not right. It's too loud. There was something stealthy about the light that didn't call attention to itself. It was glowing, but not in a showy way. We were still swimming, still trying to stay ahead of the cold, knowing that getting out would be worse because now there was hardly any sun at all behind the trees. So, all told, it probably was longer than a half hour.

We checked the Mazda, thinking maybe she was lying down in the backseat. Billy knocked on the door of the porta-potty. We didn't know her name, so we just shouted, politely, into the woods like we were calling for a teacher: "Excuse me, miss, we're ready to go now. Miss, we're ready to go! Sorry for the wait! Miss?"

Billy jogged up to the road to see if she was up there waiting to hitch a ride. She wasn't there, but that's what we figured, or Billy did, anyway, that she'd gone up to the road. The next day the boyfriend reported her missing, but the story wasn't in the Shasta and Redlands papers until two days later. That's when Billy and I went to the sheriff's office and told them what we knew, which wasn't much. We said we'd told her we'd give her a lift and she didn't wait. Her car was still in the parking lot. Teams searched the woods for three days running. Divers searched the lake. But the working theory has always been, and it's been almost eight years now, that she got tired of the waiting and ended up hitching a ride on Route 89.

My own small thought about the whole thing, for whatever it's worth and it's not worth much, since it won't help find her, wherever she is, is that when we got out of the water she was still there, still at Fowlers. That she was somewhere on the edge of the woods, looking at us, hearing us call for her, but for some reason not answering. I never mentioned it at the time because what good would it have done, since they were already searching the woods around the lake? What happened to her, I say, happened later. When Billy ran up to check the road, that's when I felt her eyes on me. I stood there in a bikini and cutoffs, teeth clacking, and I knew she was still in the woods watching me through the trees. Miss! We're ready to go! She'd been watching us swim. Maybe she noticed me toying with Billy? Maybe she envied the fact I could still toy? God knows maybe whatever made her refuse to answer had nothing directly to do with me. I've just never been able to shake the certainty that she would have done just about anything other than ride in a car with me to McCloud. Billy, yes; me, no. And maybe there's something to this. That one refusal may have led to another refusal and that whoever she accepted a ride from, if she accepted a ride at all, had no choice but to let her be and drop her somewhere. Somewhere—or a stop on her way somewhere—she'd always wanted to go, she just hadn't known it until she got that flat.

Tomales Bay (Emily)

From the kitchen window she watches the fog lift. She often wakes early and waits for it, this moment when the vague gray curtain rises and there it is, the bay and the mountains beyond. She always feels, as she does now, exalted, but at the same time unworthy. She grew up in the Midwest, where beauty is filched in glimpses. As a kid, in winter, she'd walk down the street to the edge of the bluff and look out at the lake through the leafless trees. She'd watch how the waves would push the shards of ice forward, as if trying to unload the burden of them onto the beach. A kind of grace. Still, nothing like this. The bay, the mountains, this fog, thick and smoky. *Behold thy beauty.* All hers now, this view from the top of the ridge. But that didn't make it any less somebody else's dream, this house, this kitchen, this big window. She'd always considered it a kind of arrogance of the rich to imagine that there was one place on earth destined to be yours and only yours. Neil says they can move anytime. Say the word and we'll go, he says. And she knows that if she were to call his bluff he'd do it, he'd sell. For her, he'd sell anything. But then he'd drag this house around in his head. What would be the point? Why not stay?

Still, there was no getting around the fact that the Polaroids of his dead wife on the wall in the kitchen unsettled people. When her sister visited from Madison, she took Emily aside and asked, "Why don't you make him take those down?" She told her sister that she did it for his children. "You know, so they can still come home to home? You know what I mean?" This explanation was only half true, and she knew, of course, that the four grown-up kids, in their twenties and thirties, would certainly have understood if the pictures came down and were shoved into a drawer. And it wasn't as if Neil hadn't offered. A number of times, he'd offered. No, she'd actually demanded that the pictures stay up. She didn't expect her sister or anybody else to understand. She'd never spelled it out to anybody, including Neil, but there was something about being a permanent guest in her own house that felt right.

Last Thanksgiving, when the children had all come home (and one girlfriend, one husband, a couple of grandkids), she and Neil had made an enormous spread—homemade cranberry sauce, a small mountain of mashed potatoes, a turkey they'd slow-cooked for eleven hours—and everybody'd had a good time, and she'd felt not only tolerated, but welcomed, even loved. The following morning she'd slept late—not slept, stayed in bed with a magazine—because, again, this was the house they'd grown up in. She *did* want them to feel like they could come home. But when she had, at last, come down to the kitchen in her robe, the chattering, the jokes, the laughing, stopped immediately, only for a moment but enough to horrify them with embarrassment and remorse. They all spent the next hour or so trying to make up for it, forcing her into every reference. She'd searched in vain for a silent way to say, Please, please, I get it. There's no need. *All your years here.*

She'd stood there in the kitchen, gripping her coffee, pleading with them with her eyes, but they were too busy frantically including her to even notice her anymore. And yet there must have been something inside each of them, even if they didn't admit it to themselves (after all, didn't they want their father to be happy? after so much heartache, didn't he deserve to be happy?), that found it galling. She wasn't a whole lot older than Neil's oldest daughter, which didn't scandalize anybody, this was California, but there was no getting around the cold math. The house would be hers. Not soon, but soon enough. Their dead mother smiling on the wall. The photographs have faded over the years in the sunlight so that they've begun to look like X-rays. Didn't that ghost on the wall demand loyalty?

How could she blame them? How could anybody blame them?

An old boyfriend once told her that she had a way of using magnanimity as a weapon. That wasn't exactly a fair assessment at the time. She'd dumped the boyfriend soon after. Still, she'd been intrigued by the possibility and hadn't, ever since, put it past herself. That kindness itself can be wielded. That love itself—

She drinks her coffee and watches the light above the bay, now green, now pink. Neil will be up soon. They'll both sit here and look out the window together. Isn't this the way of it? You stray, you stumble; somehow you find yourself on a ridge? Was that why she told him to leave the photographs on the wall? Because she'd won a battle she hadn't known she was fighting?

Neil's retired. Now his job, with a tool belt and great aplomb, is fixing things around this ramble of a house. Her job? What does she do all day? She works from home, writes marketing copy. But she'd told the old busybody up here on the ridge, his beloved neighbor for decades, the one who told her how pleased she was to see such joy and light back in Neil's life, that she was working on a memoir in the shed.

"You know, Catherine lingered for years, it was beyond dreadful."

"Yes, I—"

"She died in the house, you know."

"Yes, Neil—"

"What's your book about, if you don't mind my asking?"

"I'd rather not say."

"I absolutely respect that."

"Thank you."

"Certain things one must keep to oneself."

"Yes."

Neil certainly found himself a young one. Says she's writing a book. Who's not? Who's not writing a book is what I'd like to know.

Out back there's an orchard that predates the house. It's August, and huge yellow apples, an ancient variety, one you could never hope to find in stores, have begun to drop off the gnarled trees.

Naked Man Hides

Everybody knows this. Sometimes you lose everything, including your clothes. I must have taken them off at some point after the crash. I can't remember. I must have felt hot. How else to explain why I took off all my clothes? Helene came to jail the next morning and showed me the paper, and we even laughed about it, at first. Above the fold: NAKED MAN HIDES AFTER CRASH. They'd never given anybody much of a reason to buy the *Independent Journal* before. I should get a cut of the sales. Helene said she hadn't come to bail me out this time. I said, "When have you ever?" That's when she started to cry. She wanted me to understand what I'd become, as if I didn't know it. She thought shoving a headline in my face would help me see in black and white what everybody else saw. Not just our kids, my parents, her parents, my sister, but everybody in San Rafael. You went to college to end up here? I told her if I had any shame left I'd yank it out of my throat and stuff it down again. Helene threw the paper on the floor and stood up and knocked on the little window to let the guard know she wanted out. She stooped, picked up the paper, and left. Maybe she'll paste the article in one of her scrapbooks.

They brought me back to the cell, and I sat there and trembled, for hours. It was hell, of course, but it's also a little like having the chills when you've got the flu. You're grateful because that seizing your body's doing helps keep you warm. I'd gone from so hot to so cold. Must have been hours sitting there. I remember at some point they tried to give me lunch. I couldn't look at the food. Same later on with a dinner tray. Before lights-out, they brought in two new guys. Because I'd been in there alone, I'd taken the single. These two got the bunk. They each took a long piss and went to bed. At eleven, they turn the lights down, not off completely, and I sat there in what passed for darkness. You know how your eyes adjust to the light there is. I looked across the cell, which was maybe seven by nine, and saw the two sleepers, both of them wrapped in white sheets up to their necks. The fat one was on the bottom. He was a stranger to me. I'd seen the skinny one around town. I was still shaking, but like I say some part of me almost half enjoyed it. There was a blanket I could have pulled around my shoulders, but I didn't. Amazing what our bodies are designed to take. Helene says I'm looking at five to six on a good day, if the judge got laid the night before and had some waffles for breakfast. Eight to ten, at least, if he didn't get much sleep and was suffering from an upset stomach. Possession of a controlled substance, driving under the influence of said controlled substance, driving under the influence of another controlled substance, unlawful taking of a vehicle, reckless driving, fleeing the scene of an accident, indecent exposure, failure to follow a lawful order, resisting—

"It was your car, Hennie."

"How was I supposed to get to work? Who was going to pick up the kids? In what?"

But what I'm trying to say is that while I was watching those guys sleep, just two guys snoring, coughing, gurgling, moving around, changing positions, trying to get comfortable on those slack mattresses, I felt something, let's say, beyond my immediate predicament. My mother once took me and my sister Francie to a museum. We were in Chicago visiting cousins. An Egyptian museum. What it was doing in Chicago, who knows, but there were these mummies in glass cases and I remember how I pressed my nose against the glass and stared at the wrapped-up body of a woman and wondered what she'd make of me, some ten-year-old—what, almost two thousand years later?—snooping on her infinite sleep. My nostrils up against the glass. You know how it makes you look like a pig? I was doing that. Oink, oink. I wanted to get as close as I possibly could. I whispered hello to her head, to her old head wrapped in that yellowed burlap—was it burlap they used? Hello? Francie asked. Who are you talking to? And I said, Who do you think I'm talking to?

It was like that with these two guys. I was only trying to get close, to establish a little camaraderie across the chasm. Do I make any sense? Except with these two I didn't need to move toward them at all. My two fellow fuckups asleep in white sheets. I didn't need to move an inch. I swear, from my bunk, I stroked their faces without needing my hands. The skinny one had stubble. I felt it grow beneath my fingers. The fat one was clean-shaven, his face slicked with sweat. And I thought, Holy fuck, we're not dead. Together. As in not dead yet. Think of all the years we will be. Our bodies turn to caramel. You with the tiny sprouting tendrils of facial hair. You with the sweat-wet cheeks. Together at this moment, I thought—don't laugh at me, Hennie—we are not dead. You think this isn't a net positive?

Reach

The way a door gradually opens on a windless night when you're alone in a room. That's how she described how she came to understand, to know slowly but all at once, that he wanted her, that the last thing he wanted was to want her, but he wanted her, my God did he want her. He was a journalist and critic of some renown. Nobody reads him anymore. She said that for a number of years he'd been gradually losing his sight. It was almost completely gone by the time she met him. He'd put the word out that he needed someone to take dictation. He'd promised his publisher a last book about growing up poor in India. The aimless London years. The move to San Francisco in the late '50s. His improbable rise to relative fame as an unlikely chronicler of the counterculture. She told him he'd never intended to finish it, that the whole exercise was frivolous. He'd grown up poor, he said. That's novel? *The mass of humanity lives a world away from a hot bath.* Simone Weil, she knew the score.

He'd written, he told her, about flower children because they made him laugh. Spent my life trying to get clean and these kids can't get dirty enough.

He's long dead now. But she told me that, recently, while examining her face in the mirror, it was as if she caught a glimpse of his opaque brown eyes.

They'd meet at the Mechanics' Institute on Post Street, in his little office down the hall from the chess room and the silent chess players. A table, stacks of oilskin typing paper. That paper, she told me, smelled like new soap. His half-empty bookshelf. He was always giving her his books. The typewriter, its ink-stained keys. A curtainless room. The dust, how it was ever present, like tiny drops of dry rain in the stab of afternoon sunlight. She remembered how he listened to her when neither of them was speaking. Her feet shifting on the grainy, never-swept floor, her clicking tongue, what he called her girlish sniffles. When he was too tired to dictate, or, as he put it, spew, he'd ask her to read to him. Often it was Faulkner. He'd sit back in his chair and listen to her and let the great man lull him, sentences with so many clauses they'd climb the walls. Occasionally he'd stop her.

See? He's your crazy drunken Uncle Billy until he's not. The sober truth was almost more than he could take. He was drunk when I met him. This was at the tail end of his folly in Hollywood. Not sloppy drunk, polite drunk, cordial but utterly off his crock. Lovely man. The interview was a bomb. He didn't tell me a thing. He just sucked his teeth and nodded. The only time he wasn't drunk was when he was working. Drinking was the only way he could turn off the sentences. He didn't tell me that. I must have read it in Blotner's biography. The only thing he said to me was, "Is it as hot as they say in New Delhi?" And I said, "Sir, I've never been to Delhi."

Go on, go on, please, and pardon my blather—

He'd done it while she was reading. Without leaning forward he'd reached across the table with one long arm and placed three nervous, twitching fingers on her clavicle. She told me she didn't need to react. He retreated like a startled crab. The feel of her skin, her bone, was shocking enough. She'd been wearing a low-cut V-neck blouse. How could he have known? He'd been prepared to meet only fabric, not skin. She'd stopped reading for a moment and watched him. This substantial man, this winner of prizes. He didn't attempt to explain himself. She'd let him dangle, her finger holding her place in *Light in August*. And now, she told me, all these years later, his minor prominence forgotten, his books long out of print, she imagined pulling him close, letting him do what he wanted, which couldn't have been much. Only to touch her. Is it always a choice between love and pity? Back then she'd felt neither. Is there nothing in between? His eyes, the way he didn't move his head, not because he couldn't see her but because he could. He saw her with everything he had left.

The Case Against Bobbie

Was embezzlement of her demented mother's bank account. There wasn't any question of fact. She'd drained it. Someone from the nursing home must have tipped off the police. The day after the story appeared in the *Light,* she walked to town in the morning like she always did because the old Mercedes that had belonged to her late father no longer ran. It sat in her driveway; sometimes you'd see her in there taking a nap, the front seat reclined. Every morning she sat in the park and waited for Smiley's to open. This was when the bar still opened at nine. (The new owners sleep in.) I'd already be there, sitting on a bench with a cup of coffee reading the paper, but willing to listen in case she was in the mood to talk. If Bobbie was in a good mood, she'd interrupt me and tell me another story about her father, who'd once been a well-known film director, and her mother, who'd been a concert pianist. The house on Lilac was long bought and paid for, though God knows, she'd say, they'll pry it away from me eventually.

The day after the story broke, she didn't want to talk. Who would? We sat together without speaking. I went back to reading. Who am I to judge anybody for stealing? After a few minutes, though, she told me that the night before she'd had a talk with her father's ghost. You know, like in *Hamlet,* she said. Her father asked her—no, demanded—that she go and kidnap the child, or, no, the grandchild, a grandchild would do the trick even better, her father told her, of one of the studio execs who'd fleeced him back in the '60s. "Kidnap a kid," Bobbie said. "Like Lindbergh's baby. Lindbergh was a horse's ass, but he didn't deserve that, or at least that little boy didn't. You ever see his picture? The little blond boy with the fat face? I said, 'Papa, I love you with all I've got left, but I'm not a kidnapper, I don't even have a ladder.'"

I laughed. Bobbie looked across the street at the bar, which was still closed. There were some mornings, for Bobbie, when getting from eight forty-five to nine took more than an hour.

Eventually they dropped the charges. Her mother, the concert pianist, had left her estate to Bobbie, so while it was still technically theft because the mother was absolutely still alive, the DA in San Rafael probably decided that a jury might not convict, given that the money would be Bobbie's soon enough anyway. It wasn't good precedent, but you had to pick your battles. And as far as the town felt, most people thought, Why shouldn't Bobbie have the money and not the far-bigger thief in this case, the nursing home? Bobbie didn't gloat. She'd sit in the park in the morning like she always did and try not to look at Smiley's. She started to read the paper again. She never bought her own. She'd ask to look at mine because the last thing Bobbie would do would be to walk into John's and buy her own paper. Another morning, a couple of months after her mother died—so we all knew that she was either flush with cash, or at least would be soon—Bobbie told me, without preface, "She always thought her hands were ugly, that they were too plump. That's why my mother played Bach so fast, not that anybody could see them that far away in the dark."

An Old Poet
Is Dying in Bolinas

A lesser-known Beat poet. There were others like him. Unfamous names who made the Beats the Beats, scrawling in dirty notebooks in cafés, typing in unheated North Beach apartments wearing gloves with the tips of the fingers cut off. You can still see his face on the wall at City Lights. He's standing in a photograph, in a row of poets, behind Ferlinghetti and Ginsberg, hardly recognizable because he still had a full head of hair then. He'd come to California from Minneapolis and found poetry and women. In the City Lights picture he's wearing a ferocious grin. He's a foot soldier in Ginsberg's army of jesters. He'd kill for poetry, sure. But, honeybaby, wouldn't it be more fun if we just fucked for it? By the time I came to know him, he was still smiling. He smiled all the time. I believe he was one of those rare birds, a truly happy soul. I used to see him in the bar, when he could still walk, shuffling around, dancing by himself. He'd lived off poetry and the many women who'd come and gone over the decades. More off the women than the poetry, he'd be the first to say. The women who'd come and the women who'd gone. In and out of his little one-room cabin up on the Mesa. The place smelled of mold and rot, old books and unwashed sheets. His eyes don't quite work anymore, but still he lies in bed holding a book over his face. *What else are my hands good for?* He doesn't write anymore, either. Thank Eros he still has filthy dreams. A man who used to write ten, twenty, thirty poems a day.

Sometimes, even now, a line will emerge out of the fog of morning:

The only defense against man's envy is not to be enviable.

Who said that? Did I say that? Why not? Now I can say I've said anything. Friends, Romans, countrymen, lend me your toes— and he'll laugh till his ribs hurt. He'll take pain over emptiness. Every night an old friend, his neighbor from across the road, sits beside his bed and reads him to sleep. Every once in a while, she pauses and says, "Aren't you weary, Henry? Would you like me to stop?" And he answers, "Yes, it is. Isn't it wonderful?" And when he's alone, those long hours he's awake and waiting for the dawn to creep through the windows, he listens to the ocean and considers the total uselessness of sleep when there's no body beside you. He never had much talent. He'd always known it. Ginsberg once said, Don't worry, Hank, you got a poetic face.

And he thinks about how they used to call out. How when they approached his cabin, they always, always, before knocking, called out his name.

Pacific

After Andre Dubus's "At Night"

She sat calm and motionless in the living room while they worked on her husband upstairs. There's something so assuring about these people who tromp into your house out of the night. She'd always been a socialist and saw these men, and this one woman who's in charge, with their dark blue uniforms and heavy boxes and imperturbable faces, as physical proof of the ultimate (potential) goodness of government. She knew them. It wasn't the first time they'd come. Nor was it the second.

She sat in the living room amid their work. He was a sculptor; she was a potter. When people asked what the difference was, since they both worked with clay, she'd say, "The stuff I make is useful." And this was true. She made bowls. He made heads. Both of them always had day jobs. She'd been a librarian; he, an accountant.

The day jobs were a front.

On weekends, when they were younger, they'd attend craft fairs all over northern California. Sonoma, Napa, Solano, Contra Costa, San Joaquin. A few times they'd driven up to Humboldt. Once all the way to Oregon. They'd set up a card table and a couple of umbrellas. What better way to see places we wouldn't normally see! That's what she always told the children as she gently set unsold piece after unsold piece back into the trunk of the car.

She'd have to call them in the morning and tell them. Maybe not tomorrow morning, but soon. She sat in the living room, hardly listening to the commotion in the bedroom. She'd heard it all before. What fuss over a failing body as if it weren't designed to ultimately fall completely apart. To disintegrate. She gazed at their work in the half dark. The work of their hands. The rest of the world, she knew damn well, including their kids, thought them both a little bonkers. This room, the bedrooms, the kitchen, the bathroom, the front stoop. There was never enough room for their work. New pieces crowded out old pieces, heads and bowls, heads and bowls. After they retired, it was as though they'd been spurred on by a kind of delirious compulsion. Not to stave off anything, but simply because they'd had the stamina to go on working. Let it not make sense.

The kids, of course, would have to figure out what to do with it all.

"Ruby?"

It was Lucinda, the chief.

"Yes, dear?"

"Fred's medications, do you happen to—"

She recited them one by one by one, a litany, a chant.

The past few years they'd begun to shrink. In town, people said they'd become almost identical. This is often said of elderly people, but even she had to admit that in their case it was almost uncanny. They'd become dead ringers for each other. Same height, same wobbly gait. Really, from a distance, you couldn't tell one from the other.

The dog died. The other dog died. Still, every morning they walked across the sewer ponds, through the fog, doubled back to Overlook, and wandered up Ocean Parkway to the place where the road crumbled down the bluff. You could stand there two hours; you could stand there five minutes. The Pacific didn't give a hoot about time. It would eat a year for breakfast. Is that why they'd always been so drawn to it? Is that why, still, they came and stood at the edge, day after day? Its blessed indifference?

The Going Away Party

He left a note on the kitchen table. On the note, he'd drawn a map that directed where on the ridge, near the dam, they could find him. The children were still very young. The little girl was four. The boy only five months. His memory of his father would be shaped by other people. The girl, though, would probably retain glimpses of his face, scraps of his voice. Some said it was selfish, monstrously selfish. Two kids? Others said that once he decided he must have been in such a hurry to get it over with he couldn't possibly have known what he was doing.

They hadn't been in town long, maybe a year. He worked over the hill, so we saw him only on weekends. It wasn't that long ago. Hard for me to believe, but the truth is I've already forgotten his name. Her name, though, was Mel. Or at least she called herself Mel. She painted and taught art in the after-school program. We'd begun to invite them to parties. They were friendly, distracted by their kids like we all were. He was a little shy, maybe, but gracious enough to laugh at inside jokes about our town that weren't funny, especially if you were new. We must have bored him to exhaustion. Mel was more outgoing. She'd joined the mothers' book club and had even offered to host meetings at her house. We figured they'd be around town for years. We figured we all would. Why wouldn't we? West Marin County. Paradise on earth if you can keep affording it.

Her parents came to stay afterward. They were from Indiana. Kind and stoic, they'd left their jobs—and their lives—and immediately driven to California from Fort Wayne, a day and a half without stopping. The father would sit with the little girl for hours, giving voices to her dolls. After maybe three or four months, Mel bought a small camper. Her father helped her hitch it to the back of what had been her husband's truck.

There was a kind of going away party. It was in the morning, a breakfast party. A bright day. Kitchen chairs had been carried out to the parched lawn. Her mother met us at the gate, declaring that she'd made her famous pancakes and that we'd have to shoot her before she would give up her recipe. She put her hand to her mouth. The little girl gave tours of the camper for all the other children, who promptly jumped on the mattresses until somebody's mother shooed them out of there. Because that was a home now and you don't just go into somebody's home and jump on the beds. Her paintings were all bubble-wrapped and stacked in rows in the garage. They were going into storage. She'd come back for them, she said. Where she was heading she wasn't exactly sure. First, she'd visit her brother in Boise. It was the beginning of summer. She still had time before she had to figure out school for the little girl. A new start—Mel laughed—a clean slate, the open road. I remember how she pushed her hair out of her eyes when she didn't need to. That gesture with the back of her hand even though her hair wasn't in her eyes. And we believed her. Why shouldn't we have believed her? Wasn't it possible? The interstate, the two kids, the little camper with the beds—

On the Floor, Beside the Bed

An ex-outfielder for the San Diego Padres, two seasons in the majors, mostly on the bench, but everybody in town referred to him as the guy who played for the Padres. He didn't seem to work. He drove a tiny car, one of those old Honda Civics you could pretty much hold in the palm of your hand. What is it about big guys in small cars? Like big guys with small dogs. An attempt to say, I don't see myself as you see me? His dog, though, wasn't small. It was just mean. And who's ever heard of a mean golden retriever? This one was vicious. His wife was ponytailed, small, friendly. We never saw her in town. She must have taken the bus to a job over the hill. And the only time we ever saw him was when he was driving too fast on our dirt roads. Who knows where he was driving, because we never saw him in town, either, but he drove that Civic like the pickup it wasn't. You saw him coming, you jumped in a ditch. Soon mow you down as look at you. He was a menace, but there were worse menaces in town. And there was the fact that he'd played for the Padres.

One night, late, we got a call to his address. Over the radio, dispatch said a thirty-eight-year-old male fell out of bed. Arm injury. Lacerations, possible broken bones. They lived in a one-and-a-half-room cabin up on the Mesa, off Agate Beach, up from Jack's Path. A bedroom and half a kitchen. When the three of us got there, his wife was holding the frothing dog by the collar. He was on the floor beside the bed, groaning. She was wearing a tank top and pajama bottoms. Her feet were bare. That dog would have taken a chomp out of any one of us. We scooted by, those raging teeth lunging for our knees. She managed to lock the dog in the closet and got down on the floor and held him, or as much of him as she could wrap her arms around. She asked if she was in the way. Macy said no, she was fine, he could work around her, not a problem. If she helped calm the patient, all the better. I handed Macy the ears and the BP monitor. Macy told Dante to do a C-spine.

The ex-ballplayer shouted, "Not my back, my arm."

Macy kept his cool, told him it was protocol with any fall to do a C-spine. His wife moved over a bit, and Dante, on his knees, slid the collar under his neck. His vitals checked out fine. There was a small, old bruise on his left arm, but no open wound. Macy asked if he thought he'd broken anything. The ex-ballplayer said how the fuck should he know. "Did you hear any pop?" Macy said.

"I heard a pop, yeah."

And he started moaning louder. He tried to lift his head, which was now collared. Dante gently pushed it back down. We'd seen this act before. His wasn't even an especially good performance. The dog was trying to eat his way out of the closet. You could see his teeth gnawing under the cheap door.

Macy gave me a look and I went and scoped out the bathroom. It was clean, smelled nice. Flower-scented air freshener. I wondered if she'd cleaned it before we got there. In a bottom drawer I found a pile of empty pill bottles, the labels scratched off. I came out and gave Macy a shrug. We're not cops.

Macy asked the ex-ballplayer if he wouldn't feel more comfortable on the bed. "My arm!" he shouted. "Can't you see? I'm in pain here. I need something, all right?"

And she held him, this enormous guy. I'm sometimes struck by how people who don't look like they'd fit together actually do. Macy was polite, all business. He told him we were only EMTs. "Or the two of us are." He upped his chin at me. "He just helps. Talk to the medics. They'll be here in fifteen, twenty—"

"Look, I'm telling you I need something."

"We don't even carry aspirin anymore."

"Fuck you. Fuck every inch of you."

Not just physically but how people fit together period. I'm talking about the assumption of other people's realities. I read somewhere that we brood when we're alone, we act when we're together. As in act in a play. But his wife wasn't acting, at least she didn't know she was acting. Or maybe she was a better actor than he was. She had a shy, fearless face. This was nothing. Him shouting, a cabin full of strangers in the middle of the night? You should see how he is when we're alone.

I was a volunteer, nobody important to the scene. I carried the five-minute bag for Macy. I filled out the yellow sheet, though the chief complained that my handwriting was too small. She said I wrote like an ant. I held open doors. Sometimes, I helped roll out the stretchers. Or I'd go out and scout for the ambulance in case the medics got lost, which happened sometimes because not all our roads are marked, and GPS, forget it.

Someone once told me the Pacific scrambles the maps.

Mostly, I watched. Mostly, I was invisible, hardly there at all. Two o'clock in the morning, I'd get out of bed and walk into people's worst moments. You think I wasn't thrilled? One night a former professional ballplayer with nothing to show for it but a dank rental, a piece-of-shit car, and a nasty dog in the closet. They got evicted a few months later, took the dog, and left town. But he had her, her thin arms around him as best she could. The two of them still on the floor. He was done with it now, weeping. She clung, *Baby, baby.* We waited on the medics.

Stinson Beach, 2013

He goes with his ex-wife and kids to the beach and there's a calmness, an easy silence, between the few words they say to each other. The kids dig ruts by the edge of the water. Sammy's on her stomach watching those weird little bugs that bounce backward. He rubs her back with sunscreen. She didn't ask but doesn't recoil, either. He hasn't touched her back in three years, maybe four, since during that last year they'd hardly looked at each other. His hands linger longer than necessary to make the creamy whiteness disappear, and still she doesn't say anything, and he thinks maybe she's not watching the bugs anymore and has fallen asleep. Skin he knows and doesn't know, a kind of alien familiarity he couldn't explain with words. Why? What's simpler than remembering—not remembering, seeing, rubbing—a mole on a left shoulder blade you'd forgotten all about? And he remembers something else, his hands still rubbing her skin, something she once said, not at the end but earlier, years earlier than the end, before it went wherever it went. What if we're ordinary? And his response was to laugh. Us? And now, with the years having piled up, even the kids hardly argue, perhaps too afraid that this rare moment will vanish into the blue air. They're quiet, digging in the sand, though his older daughter, at nine, believes she's too old to be digging in the sand and would have said so had this been a normal day. And the younger one isn't hungry and she doesn't need to go to the bathroom. None of that. It's as if they are both holding their breath at the edge of the water.

Sammy murmurs something.

"What?"

"Gmnec?"

"What?"

"Get my neck?"

Not a question, an order, but shaped to sound like a question, which was Sammy all the way, except now he was happy to oblige, and he wonders, as he slicks both his palms down the contours of her neck, whether love sometimes comes down to this, orders posed as questions and how we react.

She's remarried now, to the very decent Doug. She found him online. He knows how to change the oil himself and is very kind to the kids. "Rugrats, backpacks, your dad's here!" Doug shouts whenever he comes to the door.

Her shoulder blades are still shaped like the prows of row-boats.

Above Santa Cruz

I remember the nights in Santa Cruz as darker than nights other places. I'm sure this has to do with my state of mind when I lived there. Even so, I remember that I could feel just below the surface of the town's smug self-satisfaction an undercurrent of seething resentment. It had, I believe, to do with money. How a number of people in and around Santa Cruz had unimaginable amounts of it while everybody else, including people with good-paying jobs, or what used to be considered good-paying jobs, like professors and chiropractors, were living paycheck to paycheck. And yet there seemed to be this unwritten edict that those who had somehow managed to hang on were expected to fall to their knees every day and kiss the ground for the privilege of living in Santa Cruz. It is true. The beaches are wide, are glorious, but this sort of obligatory genuflection cuts to the bone. Not that I spoke to a soul about any of this. I lived in a shoebox off Soquel Avenue for ten months, and aside from my students, who'd vanish so fast after class I'd be left standing there wondering if they'd been there at all, I don't remember having a single conversation with anyone. As an adjunct, I was so far down the food chain I didn't exist. I'd go and get my hair cut, I was so lonely for some fingers.

They weren't paying me enough to live, but I had to sleep somewhere. For the first two weeks of the term, I stayed at the Capri Motor Inn. The drain was clogged, and every time I took a shower, I'd stand ankle deep in water that reeked of urine. I hoped at least it was my own. I'd lived in worse places. The room came with a mini-fridge and microwave. But that year I had hopes. I was teaching at a genuine accredited university. I answered an ad on Craigslist for a cheap, one-room rental. It was up in the mountains, near a place called Bonny Doon. Sounded cheerful. Bonny Doon, a place you could dance to. For some reason, I drove up there at night. The darkness around Santa Cruz is heavily populated. You never knew what your headlights were going to pick up on those mountain roads. Around one curve, I lit up a couple humping, happily, violently, on the edge of the trees.

It turned out to be a room in a mansion on an old estate. The house, which I learned later dated back to the Roaring Twenties, was dilapidated and had been chopped up into multiple apartments. On the side of the house was a sagging veranda and an empty, cracked swimming pool. I found a door, not the front door, there didn't seem to be a front door anymore, and I followed a set of handwritten signs to "the office," where I met a high-heeled, sunburned woman who introduced herself as Charlene. She opened a cabinet and, after some deliberation, chose a key, my key. I trailed behind her along dimly lighted hallways that echoed with odd thumpings. We passed room after room. In the shadows of half-opened doors were men. Men in white T-shirts and saggy underwear. Men cooking dinner. Men standing not quite in their doorways. Men who coughed. Men who cleared their throats. Men grinding their plates clean with a fork. Charlene called the room an efficiency, and there may well have been a hot plate and small refrigerator, but the light in the room, like the hallways, was so diffuse I couldn't make much out. A single low-watt bulb dangled from the ceiling.

"Is there a bed?" I asked.

"Is there a bed? Didn't you read the ad? The room comes fully furnished. Is there a bed!"

The carpet underfoot was damp and squishy. If there had once been a window, it had long since been covered over with a piece of plywood. "Not all our tenants are on public assistance," Charlene said. "I've got a restaurant manager and an ex-lawyer."

Though I could hardly see a thing, I'm certain that I watched tiny bits of Charlene's skin flake off her face and float slowly to the carpet. I felt myself falling toward her without falling, if this makes any sense. I stood there blinking, only wanting to kiss her to stop her from disintegrating.

It may have been then that Charlene told me factoids about the estate's history. When it was constructed, how many rooms. That it was originally built by an actor named Robert Montgomery. That he was Elizabeth Montgomery's father. That the estate stayed in the family for a few decades before falling into ruin. Until now! She said in the last incarnation, before the new owners divided it up into these cute apartlets, the place was a group home for folks with (mild) psychiatric disorders. "Some of the residents have stayed on, and I have to say you aren't going to meet a nicer bunch of guys."

"Wait," I said. "Elizabeth Montgomery from *Bewitched*? Samantha?"

"Right," Charlene said. "She grew up here. Such a beautiful woman. You know she was Jeannie, also."

"That was Barbara Eden," I said.

"Are you sure?"

I nodded sagely.

Few things I'm sure of, aside from who played Samantha and who played Jeannie. One wrinkled her beautiful nose, the other slept on a couch in a bottle. My life and reruns after school—

"But Elizabeth Montgomery was in something else, right? What was—"

"The Lizzie Borden TV movie," I said.

Charlene shouted, "Now, that was creepy!"

"My mother is from Fall River," I said.

"Where?"

"Fall River, Massachusetts, where Lizzie Borden—"

"Took an ax!" Charlene shouted.

"Forty whacks!"

For a moment, we both shared the ecstasy of those whacks. *And when she saw what she had done*—be honest, who hasn't wanted at some point to swing an ax at someone and then at someone else?

"Elizabeth never came back here after she got famous," Charlene said. "Usually how it goes, you know. Why come home if you don't have to? I only mention her because, like I say, she's an interesting factoid."

I didn't tell Charlene that in the '60s and '70s my mother was sometimes stopped on the streets of Chicago, she looked so much like Samantha on *Bewitched*. I've come to see that other people are immediately bored by what you consider an amazing coincidence. Elizabeth Montgomery, who could have been my mother's twin (and who also played Fall River's own Lizzie Borden in the movie!), grew up here, in this house, and now look, look, here I am about to move into a room in the same house! Isn't that insane?

Not really.

But seriously, you should have seen my mother when people stopped her on the street. Hell, she was prettier than Elizabeth Montgomery, a lot—

"Why don't you take a few minutes to get a feel?" Charlene said. And she left me. I didn't see her walk away. She just vanished from my field of vision. You know how it is? When you're so alone even the corner of your eye can no longer hold your latest scattershot desire? No quick, dry kiss, no sudden clutch. I remained standing, motionless, for a long time under the bulb that gave so little light. And I remember thinking, Right. Yes. Eventually, I'll wash up somewhere. Why not here? And there are nights, still, when I wake in the dark and I'm in that room in the mountains above Santa Cruz, in that warehouse of men coughing and cooking their dinners.

The Apartment

After his divorce, he moved into a complex out by the 101 in San Mateo. He'd been awarded half the furniture, and, unable to choose what he wanted to keep, what he wanted to sell, and what he wanted to put in storage, he ended up stuffing it all into a one-bedroom apartment. He lived among towers of teetering cabinets, tables, lamps, crates of records, houseplants on top of couches, loveseats, recliners, bureaus, his grandfather's old desk—years of accumulation stacked and scrunched together. He told himself, in the beginning, that he wouldn't spend much time here. This was a temporary stop. He'd find a bigger place. He'd only sleep here, and not even that, if he could help it. This proved optimistic, and he found himself spending more and more time in the apartment. He dated a few times, but after two, three years, nothing had come of the four or five women he'd taken out. Not a revelation and yet, still, he thought a lot about the way time moves. He found he could sit down in one of the few chairs that wasn't piled on top of other chairs, and hours could go by without him noticing. He wasn't sleeping, he hardly slept anymore, it was something else, a kind of absence during which entire weekend afternoons could be swallowed whole. He began to see it as a talent, this ability to obliterate hours without moving.

The complex had a pool, and one Saturday he went down there with the vague notion of burning off a few calories. The pool was too small for laps. He tried anyway. Three splashes and he'd reached the other side. He kept it up. Three more splashes, end, three small splashes, end. When he'd done this thirty times (he kept count), he stepped out of the pool. He hadn't brought a towel. She was lying long-legged in one of the lounge chairs reading a magazine. Had she been there the whole time, watching this odd display? Of what? It couldn't have been called swimming. He stood there, dripping. But she smiled at him, over the magazine.

"Forgot my towel," he said.

She tossed him hers. And smiled again, wider, with more teeth. A smile of second, third, even fourth chances. Only he wasn't close to what she'd been hoping for, not that she even knew anymore; she just knew it couldn't possibly have been him. She'd had in mind some jaded swashbuckler, a traveler, someone who'd been around awhile, maybe a long while, but was still game for one last crazy romp, the sort of guy who might say, *How about Melbourne? How about we leave in two hours for Melbourne? I was there in the eighties doing a photo shoot, it's a bit run-down, but quaint in its way—*

"Pool's as big as you," she said. She hadn't meant it the way it sounded. He was paunchy. He was more than paunchy.

"You should see me in a bathtub," he said.

That night, at Moon's, he told her about his divorce, and she told him about hers. It was like trading war stories. All divorce stories are the same. And as in war stories, it's not about the combat, but the emptiness. She had two college-aged kids: a daughter at Santa Barbara, a son who'd recently dropped out of SF State to become a drummer.

"Good for him," he said.

"We'll see," she said. "He's got to find a new place to practice.

Now he drives out to a warehouse in Fremont at three in the morning."

He told her his wife had always wanted to wait for a time when they were in a better financial position to have children.

"I'm sorry," she said.

He took a chance and looked directly into her eyes. She closed them. The light was no good at Moon's, but he could see she was wearing purple mascara. Every once in a while, the fact that he wasn't anybody's father lurked like a dull ache, a phantom limb.

"For the best," he said.

Convenient that they lived in the same complex. It took the pressure off somehow. His friends, his family, considered him a failure, he knew, not a spectacular failure, a mundane, run-of-the-mill failure, and yet here he was with this woman, Judy, in the passenger seat of his Mazda. The novelty of having a person next to you. Months, years, you drive around alone, and suddenly somebody's breathing next to you.

His place, she'd said, because her daughter was up from school for the weekend.

"Shit. You weren't kidding."

"A lot's going into storage."

"Uh-huh," she said.

He turned off the lights. The two of them squeezed their way along the narrow alleyway between the heaps toward his room.

"One thing you should know," she said. "I have sleep apnea."

"Sounds good."

"It's a disorder."

"I've got flat feet, really flat. Basically, I walk on pancakes. You could pour syrup—"

She shut him up with a kiss. No, he wasn't anybody's definition of a catch. He didn't have great skin. He didn't have great teeth. So fucking what? Maybe because the problem of bodies was a little easier now? You bungle around, eventually you fit together. Or you don't. If not tonight, another night.

Wine helped.

Something—an electric space heater? a toaster?—slid off the top of a pile and nearly hit them. It fell to the carpet with a twang. A pair of ski boots followed, one thud, another thud.

"Don't move," he said. "Avalanche precaution."

She kissed him again. "You want something to happen," she said. She was still a little woozy. "In your life, you know what I mean?"

"Yes," he said.

"Nights are hardest. And you wait, and you wait. For what?"

"Exactly, for—"

"And then in the morning it's morning. The light is back in the trees again. And I think, Really, another one? I'm not talking about going to work. Though there's always work. Some days I even like it. Other days I feel like there's not enough of it. Because I'm not tired enough for the night, you know?"

"I know, I know."

"But it's like your morning never met your night. Like it has no idea how dark it gets."

"Yes, yes."

"And maybe that's not such a bad thing," she said.

"Right," he said. "Maybe it's—Listen, I hear voices."

"Who doesn't?"

"I'm the voices. I wake up and hear somebody speaking and it's—"

They reached his room.

And it was as if they crumpled into each other as they fell together to the carpet, groping, pulling, squeezing, unfastening—

And later, weeks later, how many he couldn't have said—time being different now—he'd remember this, how after the two of them did finally stand and make their way to his bed and stretched out on their separate sides, with only their feet touching, he listened to her, awed by the noises she was making. Every breath a death struggle, her neck muscles straining, as if just about to drown, she crashed through the surface of the water at the last possible moment.

II

Lighted Windows

I'll never forget how impatient I was—
I see it would be easy to go mad with love.

—Maeve Brennan, "The Springs of Affection"

The Return

In the last year of his life he got back in touch with his sister. This was in 1987. Never in person, only on the phone, and there was no anger in his voice anymore, only a kind of calm, if not joyous, evenness, though what he seemed to want most of all was to listen, to hear Janice talk about the years when not only their parents were still alive but Stevie also. At first he apologized, saying it must be hard to talk about Stevie. She said to be honest Stevie was only a flicker now. "Sure, I see his grin, I see his chipped front tooth from that bat you swung at his face. (How is it possible that you only nicked his tooth?) Stevie...Stevie...If not for the accident he'd have stuck around home just like I did. Maybe he'd have married one of those tall Hoyne sisters. Remember them? The oldest never did marry. Tina Hoyne's still around. She's a branch manager at the Key Bank. If not for ordinary bad luck, Stevie would be a mile away from where I'm standing right now." She paused and let that hang there for a couple of moments before saying flat-out what the silence had already said. "It was horrible what happened to Stevie, but it was you we were robbed of, Frank. Not Stevie, because Stevie never would have left us if given the choice."

She waited, certain he'd hang up, but he didn't. He was still there, and for a while she listened to him wheeze. "I'm not asking you to explain," she said. Yet she had the feeling he was about to. His voice cracked, but he couldn't muster any words. How to even begin? How to stuff all the years into a few words? But wasn't this the frightening thing? You could. In two, three, four sentences you could jam fourteen years, easy. She almost asked him right then where he was, and he might even have told her, but what would it matter now? She knew this was some kind of last lap, a tying up of a single loose end in a life where so many loose ends had scattered. A few phone calls to a little sister.

She knew there were ways, without too much difficulty, to have the calls traced. Alan was always going on about this, that all they had to do was contact the phone company, or the police, who would contact the phone company. But Janice said if Frank wanted her to know where he was, he would tell her. "He's not my brother, he's a voice, and hardly even that. Why make more of it than it is? He wants to listen, I'll talk." A few memories always seemed to satisfy him. He usually called just after dinner. He seemed to always know when dinner was over. Alan said this was definitive proof he was in the eastern time zone. She told him to shut up with the Agatha Christie crap.

"We used to play tea party," she told Frank. "You remember? One time you raised one of the little cups with your toes, and I swear you reached all the way to your mouth and pretended to drink out of it. I'd never been so amazed. I kept saying, Do it again, do it again." She wasn't even sure whether it mattered if anything she said had any basis in truth. The toes story might have been more recent, something Alan did with Holly or Val when they were tiny. But he seemed to like it, seemed to believe it had been him who'd been so dexterous. He almost seemed to laugh, or at least grunt with a little happiness. From then on, she told him anything that popped into her head. She could take any story she heard yesterday at work and turn it into some common memory. Like the time the couch spontaneously combusted. That was something someone read in the paper. The less related to anything that had actually happened the more he seemed to believe it, as if what he wanted above all was to hear about an alternate past life, one he could imagine without experiencing a kind of vertigo.

As a kid he'd been in trouble a few times. Nothing very serious. Busted a couple of times for pot. Another time for shoplifting. But it was his anger. Nobody could really pinpoint why it started. The night before he took off, he and their father had had a fistfight in the backyard. About what she no longer remembered, but she still retained an image of the two of them out there in the dark, not saying anything, just lunging at each other. Shirtless? Were they shirtless? Why does she remember them shirtless like two old-time boxers? Her mother said it was just a tussle. That was the word she used. A tussle. Only a tussle. Her mother blamed the drugs. The drugs, the drugs. She said he'd vanished into New York City, a bus ride away from Ohio but another continent. New York, where lost souls went to get even loster, her mother said, and there was a kind of comfort in knowing he'd had a destination, that he'd known where he was going. That maybe he had friends there. It was 1973. Her father said he probably never got farther than Akron. They've got drugs in Akron, don't kid yourself. Lot of drugs in Akron.

Months into it her mother would wake up just before dawn and sit in one of the wicker chairs in the den and moan. Stevie. Now Frank.

The first time he called, he'd had to introduce himself. And there was something uncertain about the way he said "Frank" that made her think he didn't go by the name anymore. That he was only "Frank" for the purpose of this call to his sister. Her mother moaning in the predawn light and she remembers part of her, a lot of her, wanting to leave so her mother would moan

over her, too. Nobody seemed to appreciate that she was still in
the house. That every morning Janice went down to the kitchen
to make the coffee that she didn't even drink. The years piled up
as years do, and they adjusted to his nonpresence, to his being
somewhere out of their sight. Somewhere concrete, not abstract,
eating, sleeping, waking up—

High school. College. Work. Alan, the kids. The kids growing.
Work. Mom and Dad passing away. First Mom, then Dad, seven
weeks later. And Alan says there's no such thing as dying of grief.
Alan, you oaf. We all die of grief. And then, a few years later, the
calls after dinner. The voice out of the darkness wanting to listen.
Not to talk, not to explain.

"You know you have two nieces."

"Of course I do."

Not asking names.

"Val has your nose."

That almost-laugh, but less like a grunt now, less a sound
trapped in his throat.

"Hope not, for her sake, hope she doesn't."

And she could almost see it, him opening his mouth to almost
laugh again, him alone in a room. He would have to be alone
in a room because she never heard another voice or any other
sounds at all. This ruled out prison, Alan said. He must live in
some after-prison place, a halfway house—

Shut up, Alan.

Only his labored breathing, only his occasional words.

And then the calling, which even at its peak was only maybe
twice a month, stopped for good. And all she could think about
for months was whether the room he'd been calling from, the
room where he must have slept, was heated.

Two Lawyers

A couple of lawyers talking, Chicago, 1982. It's February. They're sharing a small table at a crowded deli across the street from the circuit court at Twenty-Sixth and California. Dave Pfeiffer and Arthur Blau. "And so maybe ten minutes before the sentencing," Arthur says, "the guy turns to me and says, 'I'm going to run over to the deli to grab a turkey sandwich.'"

"Right," Dave says. "Must have been pretty hungry. What was he looking at?"

"Worst case," Arthur says, "five to seven. Possession with intent, plus a twink of a weapons charge. There was a penknife on his key chain."

"You knew?" Dave says.

"Yes and no," Arthur says.

"Right," Dave says. "How could you know for absolute certain what's in another man's mind. Even a client, especially a—"

"Exactly," Arthur says.

"How long's it been?" Dave says.

"Four months," Arthur says.

"Hear anything?" Dave says.

"Not a peep," Arthur says.

"Who's the judge?"

"Antonia."

"What'd she say?"

"Threw a fit. 'Absconded? Your client absconded?' Like he was the first fugitive in the history of Illinois."

"Married?" Dave says.

"Indeed," Arthur says.

"And?"

"Wife says last time she saw him was the morning of the hearing."

"Believe her?"

"She's more pissed than the judge," Arthur says.

Both men laugh, slurp their coffee. As usual the place is jammed with attorneys, clerks, cops. The sandwich guys are roaring. I got a BLT up! Turkey club, no lettuce! A lone judge, Collier, sits in a corner munching a bagel, the *Sun-Times* open before him like the Holy Word. But his eyes are closed as he chews, as if he's listening to music only he can hear. Judges are isolated figures, planets around which lawyers revolve.

"Who's the bondsman?" Dave says.

"Nelson Junior," Arthur says.

"Nelson can't find his ass with both hands. You think he'll make it?"

"Don't know. Maybe. Quiet guy, never said much. When he did talk, he whispered. Polite to me, to the judge, to everybody. Seemed like he was taking the whole deal on the chin. I could have gotten him a year and a half with probation. Fucking penknife."

"Tricky," Dave says.

"Right," Arthur says.

"Whole new life."

"Possibly."

Dave and Arthur. Old friends for years, but the kind of friends who knew each other only through work. Weeks might go by without their running into each other. Yet when they did, they'd always fall right into talking. And their talk amounted to one long conversation about the peculiar nature of practicing law in a world with so little sense of order. The phrase "practicing law" itself was comical. Like it was violin or piano. Aside from the court calendar, chaos knows few boundaries. Not that either of them especially craved order. It was inside the cracks in the havoc that they honed their craft. Neither Dave nor Arthur could ever remember the other's wife's name or the names of the kids they each knew, vaguely, the other had. They weren't that kind of friends, and maybe this is why it was such a relief when they saw each other. No outside chitchat required. No unnecessary entanglements. No shared sorrows. They were a couple of soldiers in suits, reconnoitering during a pause in the action.

"You hear Kowalski's not on the take anymore?" Dave says.

"He got religion?" Arthur says.

"Word is he's so rich now he can't be bought."

"Maybe that's how you get religion."

Old friends, loyal friends, criminal defense attorneys of the solo practitioner breed. They'd never been part of a firm. They were like similarly overweight leopards hunting alone—the image doesn't quite work, but the point is they were solitary predators—and yet, when one of them couldn't make a pretrial hearing, the other filled in. If Dave was heading to the jail and Arthur had a client there, too, Dave would deliver Arthur's message. Attorney Blau says sit tight, he's coming to see you Thursday. In the meantime, don't tell your life story to your cellmates because any one of them might have grown state's ears, okay?

Both lawyers had spent the good part of two decades doing midlevel stuff. Drunk driving, assault, drugs, drugs, drugs. Occasionally either Dave or Arthur would take a murder or a rape case to trial, and when that happened the other would hold down his friend's calendar until he got out from under the trial.

Dave and Arthur were considered by their peers, and the judges they appeared before daily, as solid, if somewhat interchangeable, professionals on a small scale. They were lawyers. Not great lawyers, decent lawyers. They got paid. You could do a lot worse than Dave Pfeiffer or Arthur Blau. You want it free, call the public defenders.

In June of the year the client took off like an eagle for a turkey sandwich in the sky, Arthur dropped dead of a coronary while jogging along the lakefront in Evanston. He'd just turned forty-nine. Dave couldn't help but think it goes to show you about exercise. Arthur's wife called Dave's office from the hospital.

"What can I say?" said a voice.

"Pardon me?" Dave said.

"What can I say?"

"Who is this?"

"Liz. Arthur Blau's wife."

"Is something wrong?"

"I'll say."

At the hospital Dave took Liz aside and told her he'd take all of Arthur's pending cases and explain the situation to his clients. "I'll hold down the fort, collect all the fees, and take as many cases as I can. I'll petition a judge to reassign the others, which under the circumstances shouldn't—" She was tall, taller than Dave, and had a kind, bewildered face. High cheekbones. Dave had a sudden notion, where it came from he wasn't exactly sure, that although she was especially bewildered at that moment, for her, bewilderment itself was a near-continual state. If ever there was something he understood. She wasn't looking him in the eyes. It was as if she'd chosen to focus exclusively on his left ear in this difficult moment. Dave completely forgot whatever it was he was trying to say. He remembered that Arthur had once mentioned, offhand, that his wife was a therapist and that to her all defendants were innocent because whatever they'd been driven to do could be explained by the damage done to them in their childhoods. What had Arthur said she'd said? Fewer jails, more... what was it? Ice-skating rinks?

"What are your plans?" Dave asked.

"Plans?" she said.

"I mean with the body."

"Oh. Yes," she said. "The body. Years ago, Art said he'd rather be cremated than stuffed in a hole in Skokie."

She stopped. They stood in the crowded hall looking at each other. Nurses hustled by in sensible shoes. And Dave thought, There are people who are alive, and there are people who aren't, and at no time in his life had this dividing line been so starkly defined.

"Did he have it attested?" Dave asked.

"What attested?" she said.

"His desire to be cremated. Did he have it—"

"He said it under his breath at my mother's funeral."

"There's no will?"

"Not that I know of," she said. "How do I—"

"I'll check with the county clerk. Who's the attorney?"

"You. Arthur said you were—"

"Me?"

"You."

She was clearly making this up, which struck Dave as—no other word for it, inappropriate as it was under the circumstances—joyous.

"Is it what you want?" Dave asked.

"What?" she said.

"For him to be cremated."

"You're asking me? I last saw the man at breakfast. He said the coffee tastes like plastic. He thought something might be wrong with the coffee maker. I said the coffee always tastes like plastic, you're just noticing it now?"

She looked at him differently this time. Her eyes opened slightly wider, and somewhere in there, he could have sworn, she was laughing, not happy laughing, but Jesus H. Christ laughing—

"Cremated," she said.

"I'll take care of it," Dave said.

"Do they have viewings at such places? I mean before? The children will want to see him."

"Oh, the funeral home will—"

"Yes, a funeral home. I've got to call a—I feel a little woozy."

"No! Consider it…" Resisting a gallant urge, he just trailed off.

He thought of her—nearly a year he thought of her. He avoided the deli out of loyalty, as if the bellowing sandwich makers could see into the pit of his soul. But you stare at a phone enough, for that many mornings, that many afternoons, a certain point you pick it up.

"Liz?"

"Yes?"

"It's Dave Pfeiffer."

"Who?"

"Attorney Dave—Arthur's friend."

"Oh, Arthur's friend."

"Right," Dave said. "I just wanted to follow up. Check in. If there's anything you need. Any loose ends I can attend to?"

She was silent for what felt to Dave like a long time. He cupped his palm over the phone so she wouldn't hear his breathing, which was now panting. He listened to her not answer. This was familiar turf. He'd always trusted silence. Hours could go by at home and he wouldn't say a word. To his family he'd become a piece of furniture. At work, he spent much of his day listening to people. There are, Dave often told himself, glib lawyers and quiet lawyers. If there was any secret to Dave Pfeiffer's limited success it had to do with his knowing when to keep his mouth shut. Judges rewarded him for it. And it instilled confidence in clients. When confronted with his placid face, they often spilled out the one thing they'd been holding back, the one thing he needed to know.

"No," she said. "I can't think of anything I need."

So much for that. Dave, obliterating any semblance of strategy, shouted into the receiver: "Liz! I want to take you to dinner! Liz!"

A beat, then two. She said she wasn't in the mood to go out, but "Yes, dinner." She hung up.

A few baffled minutes later he called her back.

"When?"

"Tonight," she said, and hung up again.

His old friend had lived out in Evanston. He'd known this, of course, but he was unprepared for the opulence of the house. A large yellow-brick near mansion, big yawning windows. Only old money lived this close to the lake. Arthur never gave that off. Maybe it was hers? And hadn't she had that look in the hospital? What look? Like she'd never lacked for anything, but since she had no idea what she wanted, the not-lacking had never been especially a boon. Dave remained motionless, rooted to the front walk. From every window there was a light. He wanted to turn and run the hell back to his car.

The front door opened. "Oh," she called out. "Flowers."

"Flowers?" He said it like the word made no sense. As if he wasn't holding a cellophane-wrapped bouquet from the Dominick's. He watched her watching him and thought of his flab, his rumpledness, his guilt, his unhappiness—his atrophied love for his wife, Ellen, who at this moment was probably at home reading, as she often did this time of day, near dusk, with the light off in the family room. Twilight, she called it. Dave would come into the room and try to turn on the lights.

How can you see to read?

The dark hasn't caught up to my eyes.

You always say that.

Just let me be, Dave, would you?

Helpless, he stood on the walk holding flowers. And yet later, after dinner, as she held the same hand that had held the flowers and gently led him up the carpeted stairs, it wasn't just that it made sense, it was that it couldn't have happened any other way, as if the two of them were enacting some strange and perfect ritual of grief. Each time she passed a light switch, she swatted it off. Room by room the house darkened. At dinner, they'd hardly spoken.

"And the kids?" Dave asked.

"Sleepovers," she said.

The bedroom was large as a hotel suite. Her fingers were slightly damp in his palm. They stood there, and that's when she began to talk to him. About where she was from, about how she'd met Arthur, about their years together, happy years, dull years, about how after his death she tried to immerse herself in work, how she took on more clients, how every day, for hours, she listened to people talk and talk.

"Everyone's so bottled up, you know? I'll be sitting there in my office and listening to someone going on and on about their relationships—that's mostly what people talk to me about, of course, their *relationships*. Such a ding-dong word. Why 'ships'? Why not just 'relations'? And I'll think, It's the talk that's weighing them down. That if they could for once just get out from under it, they'd be cured—cured of what, who really knows—but at least they'd be a little lighter on their feet. The talk, though, just breeds more talk. I know I sound ridiculous. I've been doing this—what?—nearly twenty years? And suddenly, I think, it works, the talking, it works. Or at least it could work. If it weren't so inexhaustible."

She sat on the bed and took her socks off.

"Shouldn't there be a point where you could truly drain yourself of it? But maybe talk is the only truly inexhaustible resource there is. And I get paid to—I'm giddy. But you know, your clients, they must talk a blue—"

"Yes and no. My clients don't talk so much about their relationships."

"Is something wrong?" she said.

"I'm worried I'm crushing you."

"I'm not glass."

"Liz," he said. "Liz."

"Don't think I didn't love him."

"Never would I think—"

"Not all the time," she said.

"Who could?" And he heard himself groan with such unexpected pleasure that he apologized.

"Don't—" she said.

Eventually, they slept. But it wasn't really sleep. It was groggy murmuring, incoherent conversation, and squeezing. When Dave did get up, an hour before dawn, and groped around for his things, he could find only one shoe. *Liz,* he whispered, as if her name alone could help him find a renegade shoe in the pale dark.

Padanaram

Y ou don't talk it away."

"I'm not talking anything away," he said. "I'm existing."

A doomed trick, to come back to a place they'd once been happy, as if the location truly had anything to do with it. But, she thought, it's all we have, all we ever have, this possibility of return, which might be another word for faith, though faith is what she felt she no longer had much right to have—and look, here she was, faking it. Faking it was the only way she could keep the visions away. When you think there's going to be great change and it doesn't happen—what else is there to do but fake being who you once were? So here they'd returned, to this speck of a New England fishing village outside New Bedford.

"The beach?" he said. "How about the little public beach that had those broken chairs? Remember?"

And so they walked, silent, the three blocks to the ocean, and she was relieved to find the chairs gone. They sat on the grass, and he talked about real estate. How it always comes down to real estate. "They'll ruin this place, too. They've half done it already. Fishing village? Are you kidding me? All I see are yachts." He liked to rail against the rich—the looters!—and his hatred was as genuine and heartfelt as his desire for the money he could never seem to get ahold of, much less hoard. He made no attempt to square the contradiction. She loved him for his open-faced, full-throated hypocrisy. Hating what you wanted seemed perfectly natural to her. Now he was blaming the disappearance of the old broken chairs on the rich, how they were always trying to improve what didn't need improving, thereby ruining everything they touched. For her part, though she didn't say it out loud and was hardly listening to him anyway, the loss of the chairs signified a difference between last time and now, and she was grateful that the chairs at least respected this by making themselves scarce, removed by the malicious rich or not.

"Would be nice," he said, "to break some more chairs and leave them here."

She looked at the water, at the bobbing sailboats, at the thing that looked like a floating doghouse. That *was* here last time. She almost pointed it out to him but thought acknowledging it might make it vanish, or at least look different. An old boat with a little shingled roof moored out there in the bay beside the sailboats. It made no sense. She was grateful the broken chairs were gone while at the same time relieved the doghouse boat was still here. There you had it. You want it to be different; you want it to be the same. Of course, there was still time. The odds were against them now, or her, rather—she was forty-one—but of course there was still time. And what she'd gone through happened to other women every hour of every day. Nothing unique about it. She'd miscarried (what man came up with the terminology? missed connection, misadventure, swing and a miss!) once before, in her early thirties, and then she'd been relieved. Then, there'd been no grief whatsoever. Grief, she thought, is situational, like everything else. Location, location, location, she could hear him saying, except that now he was on to something else: where to have dinner. She half wanted him to notice the doghouse boat on his own, half didn't. Is this the root of my problem? Chronic opposing wants? Yes, there's still time, and yes, they'd try, but can't a person mourn even when the reasons are lacking? There's something so ruthless about optimism. The damp grass began to seep through her sundress. Later this same afternoon, at the little hotel next to the yacht club, they'll undress, and their fucking will be a distraction, a welcome one. She always enjoyed hotel sex because to hell with the sheets. She always left a good tip on the night table. Now it also would allow her to express her rage at him—yes, at his talk, his constant, futile, unceasing river of talk—but at God, too, an entity, an idea, she hadn't thought much about until now. Now she practically believed in a him. A great big man-sized eyeball in the sky watching your every move made sense. The Lord giveth, the Lord taketh away.

He can't make up *his* mind, either.

The boats bobbed in the water, and the arm of shoreline sheltering the small bay curled inward.

"You're not in the mood for fish?" he said. "How come? Last time—"

Later, at least, she'll moan loud enough to scare the Sunday sailors.

My Dead

Her name was Beth. We didn't know each other. We took her car and headed to Missouri from Chicago. I remember that by the time we'd gone a few miles south on the Stevenson, we'd already run out of things to say. But for some reason we both decided, without spelling it out, not to push it. Nothing was going to come of this, and it was all right just to let the silence be and listen to the radio. We were on our way to a séance she'd heard about from an old high-school friend. Beth had grown up in a small town southwest of St. Louis, and the séance was being held nearby, at an abandoned air-force base.

A couple of years out of college, I was waiting tables at Ed Debevic's. The shtick at Ed's was to be rude to the customers. Tourists couldn't get enough. They sure as hell didn't come for the food. It was billed as an authentic Chicago experience. Eat an overcooked burger, get insulted. *Hey, lardbutt, stuff more grub in that trap and your stomach's gonna go kapow.* And I'd say this stuff in exaggerated Chicagoese. Suburban born, I couldn't pull it off. My tables came away disappointed that they hadn't received the full-on Ed's treatment. Also, I was a crap waiter to begin with. I'd forget waters, put orders through late, drop plates.

Beth wasn't a tourist. She'd come for lunch with a couple

of girlfriends to celebrate her birthday. I said, "You're my fifth old maid today. This is a restaurant, not a nursing home. I'm kidding." On her way out she wrote her number on a napkin, handed it to me, and demanded, in front of her two friends, "Call me." One nice thing about Ed's was that it encouraged patrons to be uninhibited as well. That was the goofy religion of the place.

A couple of nights later, over drinks at a bar on West Roscoe, she told me she wasn't the kind of person who ordered people to call her. Something about my face had said that I needed to be told what to do. And that's when she told me about this séance near St. Louis. Did I want to check it out? If we left right away, we could probably make it. The fact that we both had work in the morning only made it more spontaneous and awesome. We headed out into the night, exalted, until, like I said, our conversation dried up before we were even out of the city. It was as if the intrepid adventure were already over, and now we just had a shitlong ride ahead of us, which we did.

When I woke up, we were already past St. Louis, and Beth had turned off onto a narrow two-lane highway that cut through a forest. We drove another hour and a half before we reached the base. As per her friend's instructions, we ditched the car beneath a stand of trees. Beth didn't need any help climbing the fence. She practically leaped over it, and I had to sprint to catch up with her as she strode along the ghost streets, past rows of empty barracks.

"What's the hurry?" I said. "Everybody's already dead."

No answer.

When we got to hangar 32, the séance had already begun. About a dozen people were standing in a circle holding hands. At the center of the circle was a flowerpot. Two people unclasped their hands to allow Beth and me to join. A bearded guy in a black watch cap was mumbling with authority. I admit that at first I found the whole thing mesmerizing. Coming upon this group in the darkness of that enormous hangar, the man chanting, the single flame throwing shadows onto the corrugated walls. There was something weirdly sacred about it all, and I thought, Right, if you want to commune with the dead, of course what you have to do is drive across the night to Missouri.

But after half an hour, forty-five minutes, I began to understand just how fucking cold I was. Mid-March and I hadn't dressed for it. You want to dress lightly on a first date to demonstrate how free and easygoing you are. The dude was still mumbling, and I waited for something, anything, to happen, while softly stamping my feet on the crumbling pavement to warm them up. I was about to whisper to Beth, whose hand I was holding, Yo, why don't we go to a Waffle House and get some fucking breakfast? when somebody new began shouting, "Marina? Is that you, Marina?" Then other people were speaking, too. "Larry, tell your sister I'm onto her games." "How many years did you think you could hide in plain sight, Ramon?" Even Beth got into it: "You never loved me, not a day, not an hour, not a second of a single minute—"

Everybody was speaking at once, and I had trouble discerning individual words in the chaos of voices. And it was ridiculous, it was beyond ridiculous, but it also wasn't. Shouts in the dark. Maybe that's the best we can do to reach beyond ourselves. I tried to join in, too, but I could sense none of my dead, and I couldn't, for the life of me, think of anything to just spout out. So I bought it, but at the same time, by that point, I was just trying to live through it, I was so cold. Then the candle went out and our leader broke ranks and swooped down to relight it, but his lighter jammed. Everybody stopped speaking and we all began patting down our pockets for a lighter or matches. But our leader shouted at us, "No! Don't break the membrane! Rebond!"

We never quite got back on track after that. The collective

spirit or belief or whatever it was escaped from us, and, though our leader mumbled for another half an hour, only a few people spoke up. The guy next to me, a guy I'd been holding hands with for almost two hours without getting a look at his face, actually made a joke. At least, I thought it was a joke. He said something about the temperature of coffee in hell. I laughed out loud. No one else did. That pretty much ended it. Before we left, Beth went up to the leader and gave him a kiss on the lips that wasn't a friend's kiss, not by a long stretch. In the car, I asked her who she'd reached. She said she didn't want to talk about it.

"So you and the leader dude—"

"That was nothing. Okay?"

We settled back into the silence of the drive. No radio now, just the drone of the engine, which you don't hear unless you listen for it, and then it's there all the time. It was getting toward dawn, and the dark was giving way to gray. I've always loved that early morning gloom. I was about to say as much, to try to chip away at the silence, when I noticed that the car had begun to drift into the oncoming lane. Beth had fallen asleep. I don't know why, but instead of grabbing the wheel, I seized her shoulder. She woke up but didn't seem to realize what was happening and immediately stomped on the brakes. We jolted forward, skidded, and stopped. Headlights were approaching out of the gray. I had time for only one thing. I opened my door, got out, ran off the road into the trees, and waited for the headlights to slam into Beth.

They didn't. The other driver saw her in time and fishtailed around her and stopped. For a few moments, everything was still. Then I heard the birds in the trees. I walked back out to the road. The guy rolled down the window of his truck. He looked at Beth in her car; he looked at me. Then he drove away, as if a couple of idiots having some lovers' spat wasn't worth anything he might have mustered up to say. My door was still open. Beth was calm, motionless, her hands still gripping the wheel.

When something happens, for better or for worse it's happened. It has a before and an after. Maybe you can talk about it. Maybe you can't. But what about something that almost happens? What almost happens repeats itself. I've come to believe this as a kind of personal gospel. We're stopped in the opposite lane. I see lights emerge out of the gray. I open my door and run. I leave her in the car to die every time.

Untitled

They chose the ugliest part of Rome. Maybe they thought it would make it all seem less out of a movie. No beautiful backdrops. She knew a lot about architecture. She said Mussolini had built EUR in the '30s. He wanted the district to be majestic, she said, but not in the way Rome already was. He wanted to assert that greatness would now, and forever, be sought in the future—not the past. That worshipping the ancients was for cowardly nostalgists. Il Duce sought intentionally anti-bourgeois architecture that would actively subordinate the individual to a grander collective cause. No, "collective" was the wrong word. He wanted, she said, to engender a kind of new worship, one where people would begin to see themselves in a new and heroic light through architecture...He wasn't listening.

EUR was falling apart by then. This was the early 2000s. Government office buildings, once white, now were dirty-looking.

"It really is hideous," he said. "Brutalist."

"No," she said. "Brutalism came later. A lot later. This is functionalism. Or maybe rationalism? I forget which."

It was late morning. They were lying on a patch of dry grass by the Metro station entrance, watching people saunter by on their way to work. No one is ever late for work in Italy. And they were in love; they almost couldn't believe it. They couldn't stop talking about it. To talk, really talk, about it, they'd have needed a year, maybe even two years, of near-constant conversation, but as it was they only had an hour, at most.

They were both with other people. They hardly touched because that would have been almost too hard to take. It was enough to lie side by side on a patch of scratchy grass by the Metro station entrance in EUR and try not to think of the future. She always had a cold. She said it was allergies, that everything in Italy made her sneeze. *I look at something and love it—Keats's grave—and I sneeze.* She wore leather shoes with straps and brass buckles. Like shoes Rumpelstiltskin might wear. Lying there. The two of them. They had year-long fellowships. Every morning they woke up in separate beds with different people. Roman mornings. The old ladies shouting, the pink light, the laundry stretching from window to window. Side by side on the grass by the entrance to the Metro. To Italians on their way to work, they were invisible. Tourists had been part of the Roman landscape for how many centuries?

She rubbed his knuckles with her fingers, and he said, "I wish I could say something original about time."

"Forget it," she said. "Bold lover, never, never canst thou—"

Twelve years later, they meet in a hotel room in a city unfamiliar to both of them. The room looks out upon a parking lot and an office building across the street. It's the middle of the day. He begins to close the curtains, but she says, "Nobody can see in with the glare, and even if they could, who cares?" It's awkward and fumbling. They know each other and at the same time they've got no idea who the other is. Skin to skin, they're ridiculous. Far worse than if they'd been strangers. Lying in the hardly tussled sheets, they begin to talk instead. That's better. She tells him her daughter has an imaginary friend, a poltergeist.

"Mine," he says, "has heart-to-hearts with the vacuum cleaner."

"The poltergeist is named Queenie," she says. "And she lives in the closet in one of her old shoes. A living presence that's dead. She's very adamant about this. That Queenie is dead but that Queenie sees in the dark, that Queenie remembers things. You're supposed to say I look amazing. That after a couple, three kids—"

"I already did," he says.

"You're supposed to keep exclaiming it as if it's some kind of miracle."

"I exclaim, I exclaim."

"Fat and old."

"If this is fat and old," he says.

"People don't do this anymore," she says.

"What?"

"Meet in motels."

"They don't?"

"It's completely passé. It's past passé. Also a little gross. Not as gross as I thought it would be, but—"

"This is a Marriott Courtyard," he says.

"You never saw a therapist?" she says.

"No."

"Helps."

"I don't want to talk."

"I'm not talking about this," she says.

"I know."

"Helps to get out of your own head. You of all people."

"You told me that before," he says. "You have any Tums?"

"What?"

"My stomach, it gets—"

"You used to want to talk so much. You craved the talking as much as anything. More so—your guilt, you talked a lot about your guilt. You were guilt's desperado, agonizing daily—"

He kisses her again so he doesn't have to say anything else. Her lips less unfamiliar now, and she moves her mouth toward his—no, jams, beautifully, beautifully she jams her mouth into his—

He pulls away. "Those shoes," he says.

"What shoes?"

"With the buckles. Like a pilgrim's shoes, you don't remember—"

"No."

Maggie Brown

That year I drove a battered '79 Corolla, my brother's old car, and collected parking tickets. I had an eight o'clock class. Even with a car I was late. I'd shove the bright orange tickets into the glove compartment along with the expired condoms and the map of the Upper Peninsula, where I hoped to disappear one day without a trace.

I had a roommate who'd come to Michigan from Dix Hills, Long Island. Flegenheimer thought the Midwest was a quaint experiment. An interlude before he assumed the helm of his father's sanitary-supply business. He said there wasn't a shithole in New Jersey where they didn't install the broken towel dispenser. Flegenheimer also told me that because I had out-of-state plates (Illinois) the Ann Arbor parking gestapo would never track me down. "You're home free, man, park the fuck away." And I remember driving to Sociology 202 with my left arm out the window, sweeping away the rain because the windshield wipers didn't work, and looking at all my fellow citizens stomping down the sidewalk with their umbrellas and their backpacks, and wondering senselessly what I'd done to deserve this exile. Why wasn't I out there in the rain with everybody else?

In February, they towed me, Franco Magocini and his twin

brother, Joseph, the local towing duo. It wasn't my first time meeting them. But now they refused to release the car without a notarized authorization from the Ann Arbor Police Department that I'd paid at least three-fourths of the violations. That's three-fourths plus a storage fee of forty dollars a day. There was a sign. STORAGE: IT'S NOT A FEE, IT'S AN ASSESSMENT. Franco did the towing, Joseph the accounting. They weren't identical, but both wore the same yellow snowsuit.

"What the hell is this, parking at the Ritz?"

"Listen, kid, I've got vehicles to displace," Franco said.

I sold them the Corolla for $175. Joseph said he'd take care of the paperwork and have my slate wiped clean. Franco reached deep into his yellow suit and pulled out a sweaty twenty, told me to go buy myself a steak at Myron and Phil's out on Zeeb Road.

"How am I going to get there?"

"For ten bucks," Joseph said, "my brother will take you anywhere, so long as it isn't past Dexter or north of Washtenaw."

Maggie Brown was around then. She liked the whole bit about the car. It was worth the Corolla to make her laugh. She liked it when I chewed my lip and talked like Franco. This was before she dropped a hit and a half of acid and disappeared to follow the aging Grateful Dead to Hamilton, Ontario. Maggie Brown was her first name. She was from Montgomery, Alabama. Her great-great-great-great-grandfather owned slaves. Not that many, she said. This was her nod toward going to college with a bunch of sanctimonious Yankees. She played the cello in the university orchestra. Her accent alone burned a hole in my lower intestines.

On our first night together she undressed me slowly from the shoes up. We were in her room on East William. She left the lights on. Her bed had no sheets. That mattress like striped pajamas, like the uniform of some sad old convict. Her cello case loomed in the corner, an elegant beast. When she unbut-

toned the last button on my shirt, Maggie Brown looked me
over, stared me down, and bit me so hard in the stomach I bled.
I've hardly been alive since.

A few years ago I saw her at the Minneapolis airport. She
looked right at me, didn't know me from Adam, and marched
onward. Maggie Brown in a business suit. One of those sleek,
purposeful rolling suitcases trailing after her like a well-trained
dog. You end up forgetting the people you shouldn't and remembering the people who've forgotten all about you. For me
what echoes, what reverberates, what I often relive and relive,
are those times that were cut short, times so fleeting they hardly
even happened.

That week in February, for instance, when Maggie Brown disappeared into Canada and I slept on her porch in a sleeping bag
until she returned home at three in the morning, passed out in
the arms of a skinny Deadhead in a Dr. Seuss hat.

"She your girlfriend?"

"I'm not sure," I said.

He looked at the sleeping bag basketed at my feet. "Lose your
key?"

I shook my head.

"Well, shit." He picked up one of my shoes. "Mind if I?"

"Not at all."

"Hold her a sec?"

She felt lighter than I remembered. I dove my nose into her
smoky hair and stood there with what I can only call a weird sort
of triumphance. The Deadhead knocked out the front window
with my shoe, cleared the shards with his hat, and climbed into
the apartment. When the front door opened, I handed Maggie
Brown back across the threshold and went home to the dorm.

In spring, I began walking. I'd skip class and wander down
State Street in the early afternoons. I'd take a left on Packard
and head out of downtown until I reached the '50s-style neigh-

borhoods of north Ann Arbor. Ranch houses, open windows, curtains lilting sexily in the late-March breeze. I lusted housewives who weren't home, who were probably at work. It was that brief time, the early '90s, when there weren't any housewives. I fell in love with open garages, all that beautiful equipment stored away. Old boots, basketballs, storm windows. Garden hose, miles and miles of garden hose. It wasn't loneliness; it was a numbness I was trying to prick so that I could feel something. I'd walk with my hands in my pockets and greet the citizenry. The elderly men in hats walking long dogs. The sashed eleven-year-old crossing guards who kept the intersections safe after school. I'd greet them all, dogs included, with a subtle nod of my chin, as if I'd been roaming those crumbling sidewalks my whole life. I thought about getting a job. Instead, I took a bus to Ypsilanti and bought a cheap gun. It wasn't much to look at. It had a plastic handle. The bullets, though, were impressive. I found that walking around with a gun in your pants is very different from walking around without a gun in your pants.

I switched on the overhead light. One of Flegenheimer's large, hairy feet was hanging over the side of the loft.

"Fuck you been?" he murmured. "Shut the light, fuckhole."

I didn't say anything. I just stood there and stared at that hairy tarantula foot. That Chewbacca foot.

"I said shut the light."

That overhead light, its buzz. I noticed that fluorescence doesn't seem to create shadows.

"Yo, fuck's the problem?"

Above all, Flegenheimer hated silence; it completely freaked him out. Curious how simply not talking can throw even the most confident bastard off. Flegenheimer didn't go to class. He didn't own a single book. He slept and went out to the bars, Charley's, Rick's, and back to Charley's. He delivered life lessons and commentary from the top of the loft. *You fuck and you get fucked. Fuck and get fucked, around and around and around. Any questions?* I was a complete bafflement to him. Even the city of Chicago rang no bells. A Jew not from New York? *What'd your grandpa do? Rub some* rah-rah *at Ellis Island the wrong way?* Flegenheimer wore his fat with the same sort of swagger that he wore his gold chains. Girls in sweatpants were incessantly knocking on our door. I'd answer, and their faces would drop. "Jeremy's not around?"

"Shut the light," Flegenheimer said, "or I'll kick your face in."

Only the dead can sustain it. That's the amazing, awe-inspiring thing. We, the not-yet dead, can never hold the silence. Sooner or later we'll talk. Sooner or later we always, always talk. Flegenheimer stretched his foot out, flicked it at me, but he couldn't reach my face. And I stood there with that foot, that hirsute foot reaching, flicking—

We used to talk, Flegenheimer and me. He didn't need books. He wasn't that stupid, not that stupid at all. If I ever run into him in the airport, I wonder if he'll remember me.

"The crossing guards," I shouted. "They wear orange sashes and they guard the streets with their very lives, the little heroes!"

He'd fallen back asleep. I stood there in that buzzing, aching fluorescence. I liked Flegenheimer. I may have even loved him, and so help me God in the spring of 1988 in Ann Arbor, Michigan, I pulled that toy-seeming gun out of my waistband and aimed and thought long and hard about blowing his foot clean off his ankle.

In May, Maggie Brown held a solo recital. She sat alone on a stage amid a crowd of music stands, awkward skeletons, facing all directions. She wore a sleeveless black dress, and she looked almost miniature with that big cello between her legs. Until the music. I wish I knew now what it was. There were programs, but I wasn't the sort of person who might have noted what was about to be played. Whatever it was, it was sudden and frantic and shrieking. Then it went low. Long stretches of deep, somber tones followed again by more streaking jabs, Maggie Brown's elbows flinging. I felt every note—high and low—in my groin. But her face: placid, detached. It was as if she weren't even in the room, as if the music had nothing to do with her and the present moment, as if she knew, but it didn't concern her, that this music, her music, would continue to reverberate in some forgotten head long after she quit playing and sold the cello, or donated it, or just left it somewhere because it was too expensive to keep lugging around.

I studied the sparse audience, ten or twelve of us. Parents, a few professors, five or six old ladies from town here to pass the time with some free music, all of us sitting on rusty folding chairs that squeaked if you moved an inch. One lone professor type, a couple of chairs away from me, couldn't help it and began to squirm in his noisy seat. He was bald, fiftyish, and wearing an ill-fitting cable-knit sweater. I watched him trying in vain to silence his chair, and I thought of Maggie Brown's hands on my throat, her knees on my chest, and how once she sent me naked into the kitchen for a glass of water and then locked me out and laughed from the other side of the door as I stood there on the cold linoleum, my balls shriveling to peanuts. *My great-great-great-great-grandpappy owned slaves, but none of them were related to Rosa Parks! That's what you tell your hairball fucker of a roommate? Liar! Falsifier!* I backed up and charged at the door with the full intent to break it down, and even as I bounced off it, I had a premonition that my life would always, one way or another, feature me trying ineffectually to break down doors I'd only just been locked out of. My bald neighbor? Professor Sweater? Even if he'd known I existed, that we were kinsmen, he didn't have any comfort to spare. His forearms tightened as he gripped the bottom of his chair as if he worried he might float away. I wanted to jump in his lap to weigh him down. To feel that rough sweater on my cheek. Maybe only the stranger we will become can save us from ourselves. But we never meet. We remain separate in our squeaky chairs as the music, Maggie Brown's music, moans slower now, slower, slower, never stopping.

The Roommate

Spring semester, sophomore year, I moved out of the dorm and into an apartment on South Forest with Eliot Birnbaum. I hadn't known him very long. I envied the books he read. He was an English major who refused out of principle to read a single assigned text. I'm going to let these clods choose my books? On his own, he'd read *Ulysses* twice and now read only work in translation. It was Eliot who urged me to read Sartre's essay on masturbation in order to liberate myself from the tyranny of sorority girls. And it was Eliot who told me to copy. To take a great piece of work and write it out, word for word, in my own hand. Thereby, Eliot said, I might dupe my brain into the fantasy that creating such a work was, physically, at least, within the realm of the possible. Muscle memory fools the brain. He said, of course, the idea took, as its point of departure, Borges's "Pierre Menard."

Who?

Dude wrote Don Quixote, again.

I've got no idea where Eliot Birnbaum is today, or even if he's alive. I've tried the usual ways to find him. If he's out there, he's not making himself known to people who once knew him. Even back then he mostly wanted to be left alone. About a month after

I moved in, Eliot holed himself up in his room for two weeks with *Finnegans Wake*. He'd surface, holy text in hand, only to go to the bathroom or slurp cereal or open a can of corn, pour it into a bowl, add some butter, and shove it in the microwave. He'd stand there for two minutes and read until the ding. Then he'd disappear back into his room. A week in, I knocked on his door and said, *Finnegans Wake* isn't a translation.

Through the door, Eliot said, "You think rendering sleep into English isn't translation?"

"Even Borges called it obtuse and totally unreadable."

"I'm over Borges."

"You want to get a pizza?"

One afternoon when I came home from classes, Eliot accused me, with cause, of eating his Raisin Bran.

He was a small, muscular guy with curly black hair and long, also curly eyelashes. Lurking under the lashes, two unblinking bloodshot eyes. In another era he might have been one of those matinee idols with a serious, pouty look. Smart girls, especially, threw themselves at Eliot.

Another night, when I came home late, he said I'd used his mouthwash, that I'd sucked his Scope straight out of the bottle, which was also factually true.

"Who'd do that?" Eliot said.

No, I hadn't known him very long, but in the little time I had, he hadn't been greedy about his stuff. In fact, in the beginning, he often gave me things, and not just books. He gave me a new backpack because he didn't like the color. He gave me quaaludes. He gave me a weight-lifting belt. I'd heard that he was rich, that his maternal grandfather had founded Wieboldt's, a defunct department store everybody, for some reason, remembers. He let me drive his Saab whenever I wanted to, which was often. He was the kind of new friend who trusts you right away on a hunch. I didn't deserve it, obviously, but I was happy to take his stuff and drive his car. And his apartment beat the dorm.

"Seriously, what kind of person uses someone else's mouthwash?"

I shrugged.

"Are you drunk?" he said.

"Drunk?" I said.

There was more to it than that he was merely mad (and he was definitely mad); he was also completely incredulous. He'd thought I was one person, and now here I was being somebody else. The sort of person who'd swig someone else's mouthwash right out of the bottle. And yet at the same time, the whole thing seemed to go beyond me, as if Eliot were staring in disbelief not only at an intoxicated roommate but at an entire human race capable of such atrocities.

"You need to get a grip," I said.

That's when Eliot smiled at me, his normal smile when he hid his teeth, and bowed at me. Not knowing what else to do, I bowed back. He bowed again; I bowed back. This went on for a while. Like we'd become a couple of Oompa Loompas. Then Eliot withdrew, slowly, back into his room.

I didn't sleep much that night. Eventually, I got up and crept to his door. His light was on; Eliot's light was always on.

"I'll replace the Scope, all right? I'll run over to CVS right now. Okay? You need anything else? Pack of condoms? Detergent? Halloween candy?"

In my screwball memory, which, as always, is egged on by an equivocal sense of guilt, as well as mournful impatience to get to the sad crux of any story, it happened directly after the mouthwash incident. But it had to have been at least a few weeks, maybe a month, after, because I remember that, at last, Ann Arbor was getting warmer. Girls had finally begun to emerge from the cocoons of their thick coats. And during those weeks, Eliot and I must have existed in the loud and unique silence that is shared only by people who live together but are no longer speaking. When every door closing, every pot lid clattering, every ping of the microwave, is amplified deep in your skull. I can't quite remember. I just know that the days must have passed. And in those weeks, we must have slept, ate, and sometimes gone to class, or at least I did.

So it had to have been into May when Eliot swallowed a bottle of pills and had to have his stomach pumped. He checked himself into the hospital. He never told me one way or the other, but he must have changed his mind. Some vision caught his sleepy eyes before it was too late?

By the time I went to see him, they'd already moved him upstairs from the ER and into a regular room. He looked older, more distinguished, even more brilliant, because he hadn't shaved in days. He was sitting in one of the two visitors' chairs and had his feet on the other one. His bed was made. He wasn't reading. He didn't take his feet off the other chair when he saw me.

"You must be tired," I said.

"That's actually funny," he said.

I stood there. The only available place was the bed, and sitting on it didn't feel right.

"Need any books?" I said.

He shook his head.

"Malcolm Lowry? I got a nice *Under the Volcano* at Shaman Drum—"

"No books."

* * *

I lived in Eliot's apartment until after finals. I remember now that our building had a name, Rockwell Gardens. The words were chiseled above the front doorway arch. A touch of grandeur for a place that had no grandeur left. Before they chopped it up into student apartments, it must have been a desirable address. It was partially hidden by straggles of ivy and reminded me of the House of Usher. Poe's story was one of the ones I'd copied out by hand. Most houses and apartment buildings don't, as a result of the weight of their own stories, implode into incestuous dust. Poe's do, bless that drunk lunatic. No, most buildings, unless somebody comes along with a crane, just sit there. For decades, no matter what happens or doesn't happen inside, they just sit there. Drive by Rockwell Gardens today, and it will still be there on South Forest in Ann Arbor, students rushing in, students rushing out.

And there will still be a garden out back. When I lived there, the garden was overgrown but retained some of its old beauty. There were once carefully manicured shrubs, still holding their shape, and the remnants of a stone walkway beneath the dirt. And I remember there was also a defunct fountain with a little boy standing in the middle. That he was aiming his little wiener at the pond actually seemed natural. Water must have flowed through it into the pond back in the day. A sculptor with a sense of humor or a creep, who knows? The garden was separated by an alley from the sorority parking lot, and when the weather was good, after Eliot left, I sat out there with my fellow penis holder and half studied for exams, half listened to the Tri Delt girls as they laughed and got into and out of their cars. The laughter of spring and warmth and newly bared legs. What is it about sorority girls and laughing? Who told them the world is such a party?

Allston

W e were still in our twenties. She was already married, a weird novelty. My first clash with that specter: husband. Society's great, dull bulwark. We met, of course, at someone's wedding. She was a friend of the bride's. I was an old roommate of the groom's. The husband hadn't joined her. I'd come alone also. We were both in the wedding party and had been assigned to walk down the aisle together, arm in arm. She wore a lemon-yellow dress. It was my first time in a tuxedo. We got drunk and happy and a lot drunker and a lot happier.

As you do at a Chicago wedding in July, we ended up in Lake Michigan. I think of the dark water, that glorious floating, her dress like a little parachute blooming. Stumbled back to someone's room, hers or mine, I wasn't sure. Woke up to the open blinds, afternoon light. On the floor, the sandy wreckage of our respective uniforms. We'd missed breakfast. We'd missed brunch. We'd missed the bride-family-versus-groom-family softball game. The bride's mother was pounding on the door. Bridesmaids are indentured servants, serfs. Groomsmen get drunk. She needed to be in more pictures. Day-after pictures, married pictures! More door pounding. Didn't she have the schedule? Didn't she know they were taking the day-after pictures at three sharp? The photographer's on the clock. Must have been her room. Easy to say now that we were in our twenties and didn't have a clue. Fact is we were already making plans.

"Remain here," she said.

"I'm rooted to these sheets," I said. "Where are the sheets?"

I slept. She came back a couple of hours later and fell asleep next to me in her clothes. At some point I woke up and gave an impassioned speech about fate and destiny to the hotel-room ceiling. I toasted Mr. Conrad Hilton for bringing us together. She slept through it. She was small and blond and wore big glasses. When she was awake, she laughed a lot. She already had a master's degree. She spoke Basque to her grandmother. She subscribed to the *Utne Reader.*

I lived in Boston. She lived in St. Louis. She worked for an accounting firm and traveled a lot. Three months later she came to Massachusetts for work. I remember this. Walking very slowly, as slowly as possible, down the corridor toward her hotel room. I got down on my hands and knees and crawled. She must have felt my presence because she opened the door and saw me and laughed and got down on her hands and knees and crawled my way. Had it not been for a startled maid and her big cart of sundries, we'd have torn each other to nothing out there in the corridor.

Things get hazier. The single bed in my dog-meat apartment in Allston. Her putting lotion on her feet. A walk in Boston Common. Couple of milkshakes at J.P. Licks? A rented car and a drive down the Cape to a bed-and-breakfast. How easily she laughed. A kindness in her always-wet eyes. Tears waiting all the time, though I never saw them drop. Her braininess. The fact that she paid with her corporate credit card because she knew I had no money.

I was working at the Cambridge YMCA on Mass Ave, in the after-school program. I played Ping-Pong and yelled at kids.

And I was writing short stories. She read a couple of them and laughed, though I can't imagine I was trying to be funny. My aim was extreme solemnity. I wanted everything, even then, to be a dirge. Everything delighted her. The clam shack by the Bourne Bridge. Boiled clams were fucking hilarious. Drinkable embryos! At one point, in the Common, I showed her the statue Robert Lowell wrote about in "For the Union Dead." I stood in front of Colonel Shaw on his steed, his men marching beside him, and announced: "Come and live with me." I watched myself gallant. So I worked in day care. Did this mean I couldn't be a tragic hero?

"In Boston?" she said.

"Technically I live in Allston, which is an independent entity."

"So, it's a neighborhood?"

"Yeah, but sort of more. It's hard to explain. It's a little like Kosovo."

"Or Vatican City."

"Exactly. Allston's just like Vatican City. Only we got more liquor stores."

We walked on, hand in hand, swinging arms. I wasn't going to press the issue; what was obvious was obvious. I remember the silence of the drive back from the Cape. I remember milkshakes. I remember walking backward, again, doing a little backward shimmy, down the same hotel corridor as she stood at her door like an actress, wagging at me with her index finger. A beckoning and goodbye at the same time.

Two weeks later she called. Her husband, she told me, was on the line as well. They both had something to say. She wanted to make clear that there wasn't going to be any more to this. That we'd had our time together. She had no regrets. Did I understand? No more phone calls at work, no more letters. The husband spoke up: "You all right with this?" His voice was pleasant and considerate. "Look, it's cool. I know she's awesome." She laughed a quick laugh but stopped. She asked if I wanted to say anything. I said I didn't think I did.

Part of me wants this to be a sad recounting, not a pathetic one, but I see I'm failing. I'm trying to stay close to the facts as best as I can remember them, but facts disintegrate. For days, weeks, I mourned around the city. I rode the T and read. I went to work. I shouted at kids to line up for snack. "If you guys don't line up, there will be no snack, period." At night, in Allston, I considered the nature of self-pity, how it's not unlike masturbation in the sense of how satisfying it can be in the short term. And the long term is just a linked chain of short term after short term. Then I'd die.

A few years ago I found myself teaching, briefly, in St. Louis. This was at Washington University. (It's neither here nor there, but my mother had long thought that my life would have turned out better if only I'd been accepted to Wash U for college. She was quite proud that I'd made it there at last as a contract lecturer without health insurance.) I thought about calling or sending a message. All I had to do was reach out to my old friends and ask how to get ahold of her. But it felt more like an obligation to a defunct emotion than something I actually wanted to do.

Still, I thought, maybe I would run into her buying groceries, or we'd both be pumping gas on the same island. We'd go to a café and I'd sit across the table and listen to her talk. I'm always interested in the way people edit the details of their lives, the way they compress all the years into sentences.

Ineffectual Tribute to Len

After graduate school I hung around another year and drove a cab for Iowa City Yellow Cab. The cab was a boat, a Chevrolet Caprice wagon. I could have put a mattress in the back and lived in it. I didn't hate the job. I'd sit in the Kroger parking lot and read. If the dispatcher radioed and I liked the sound of the call, I took it. If I didn't, I went on reading. My indifference didn't make me popular with Ovid Demanaris. I once asked him, over the radio, if he'd ever read Ovid, and he said he didn't answer personal questions. "He's got some real smutty stuff," I said. Dead air. I didn't have to drive a cab. I was broke, and the only money I had was the play money left over from my student loans. Now I can't pay them off with real money. Still, I wasn't a cabdriver. I was a grad student, an ex–grad student, pretending. I'd sit in the parking lot and read. Occasionally, I'd drive somewhere, pick somebody up, and drive them somewhere else.

In front of the Deadwood one late night, 2:30 a.m., I earned a few chops picking up blitzed undergrads. When one of them puked in the back of the cab, I hit the brakes and ordered them all the fuck out.

"But it's fucking February, man, it's fucking Iowa."

"Out."

That made me feel like a cabbie. And I used to take calls out to an encampment along the river west of town. People there didn't live in tents or refrigerator boxes but in full-on shacks constructed of scrap wood and sometimes even a few bricks— it was a small, functioning village. Nearly impossible to find. It wasn't on any map. You had to bumble along a series of rutty dirt roads south, then head north again, before you could go west that close to the river. It may have been a derelict property, or maybe it was a kind of no-man's-land in a flood zone. Ovid would put out a general call. "Anybody want to pick up some ancient freak out by the river?" If nobody took it, he'd recue his mic and say, "Ornery? How about getting off your pampered ass?" The freaks weren't that ancient, maybe in their mid-fifties, but most of them had lived so many years outdoors—in Iowa. Their faces were perpetually red from frostbite. In winter, the tall bare trees hid nothing and blocked no wind. I'd trek out there and stop in the center of that scattering of hunkered, makeshift houses and wait and see who jumped into the cab. More often than not it was a grocery run. A woman who called herself Birdy once squeezed my forearm—Birdy always sat in the front seat alongside me—and invited me to shop with her at the Kroger. Nobody had requested my presence in a long time. We were both in need of company. I remember she bought a single loaf of bread, cottage cheese, and some chocolate. The fare must have been double the cost of the food.

Another night a guy having a bad trip started bouncing on the seat so hard his head bashed the top of the cab. His girlfriend was passed out next to him, but every time he bounced she'd wake up and shout, "What? What? What?" She had a pretty snub nose and was wearing sweatpants. Neither of them could tell me where they wanted to go. So I drove in circles, mooning over the girl in sweats, until the guy came down enough to drop them at the bus station. Mostly, though, I sat in the Kroger parking lot and watched the shoppers push their carts out of the swinging doors and listened to the sound of those wobbly wheels struggling across the potholes in the pavement—and went back to reading.

Then, in February, it was always February that year, just as I was about to leave for my shift, Len called from Chicago. He'd been calling a lot that winter. He liked hearing stories about the cab. He thought now that I was becoming hard-boiled, I'd have something to write about aside from being a lonely horndog.

"How many horndog stories can one person write?"

"Lots," I said.

But that night Len said he wanted to talk in person.

"When?"

"Now."

"You're four hours away. It's snowing like all get-out. I don't have a car. And I have to work."

"You got a cab," Len said.

He'd been my boss at a summer camp. He was one of those people who pop up randomly and change everything, and you can't imagine any story of your life, lame as it might be, told without them. Len was one of the first people to notice something, anything, in me. It was only a summer camp in Wisconsin. How to express the significance of the place and of Len in particular without sounding ridiculous? My job was to entertain rich kids from the suburbs while their parents went on vacation. But for Len, after so many years working in psychiatric wards (good training for any administrator, he'd say), camp had become a kind of gracious calling. Part hippie, part drill sergeant; his mission was to instill in us that rich kids or not, these noxious little fuckers were, at their core, human. If, by the end of the summer, we could make them a little more so, we'd have accomplished something. "Because don't forget these world inheritors will go forth into the universe and become

CEOs and heart surgeons and white-collar criminals. Imagine, my kittens, if they were a tad more decent, a smidgen more compassionate. Imagine!" Len would stand before us during staff meetings in the push shack and exhort, his protruding stomach lording atop his skinny legs. His wild, shoulder-length hair, chaotic beard, and big white teeth. All camps have their characters, and our leading man was Len. There was something of the werewolf about him, and even when he said something completely banal, like "We work hard so we can play hard," I'd think, Yes, that's it, that's the key, why hadn't I thought of that? "Seize the day," Len would say. "Set yourself up for success, gentlemen." He'd raise his monstrously thick eyebrows. And the whole time he'd be sucking on one of the cigars he kept in a constantly replenished stash (along with the bourbon) in the bottom drawer of a desk so strewn with the junk of summer—flippers, softballs, Frisbees, confiscated candy, confiscated porn, spent cans of Off, bags of charcoal—we never saw the top of it. Smoking was forbidden, except in the trees behind the rec hall, but Len's loyalty to camp was so strong that even when he was breaking the rules, and he spent his days breaking camp's rules, it was his way of respecting—loving—the institution for instituting the rules in the first place.

And on days off, Len would take me and a few other carless counselors to gamble at the casino in Bad River. It was from Len that I learned how losing all the money I had could be not only a full day's entertainment but also honorable in itself. The least you can do for a Chippewa, Len would say, is hand over a lousy twenty-five bucks, no? What'd they give us, Wisconsin, Minnesota, North Dakota, Illinois? Canada? I stole my own cab and drove across I-80 through the snow.

Len may have been HIV positive for years before he finally became so frail he had to be hospitalized. He never told me this; I put it together later. When he called, Len always made a point to say he had non-Hodgkin's lymphoma, which was probably technically true. Because camp was always—always—on his mind. It wouldn't have done to employ a man with AIDS (no distinction would have been made at that time between being HIV positive and having the disease itself), not at a boys' camp in Wisconsin in the mid-'90s, no matter how much of a beloved character of an assistant director he was. For years, he'd felt the need to hide it. *If I only had Hodgkin's, whoever this asshole is. It's not having Hodgkin's that's really fucking things up.* Now it no longer mattered, at least as far as camp was concerned. He was done. He'd never get back up north. The summer before the winter I drove the cab to Chicago was the first one Len had missed in eighteen years on staff. He called me to relive past summers. Not the specifics, because all summers were the same. That was the point of camp. You didn't go up to camp because anything new ever happened. You went to camp because history repeated itself. The lake will always be too frigid in June to put the docks in the water. But how are you going to put the docks in if you don't get in the lake? And always some joker who shows up in a wet suit will get howled right off the beach. The camp dog, not the dead one, the new one, will always bite a nurse from Scandinavia. A stoned junior counselor from Kansas City will always, always, hit a tree in front of Saul Q's, and Saul Q will always run out of his cabin in his tighty-whities and squeal about how the drug culture's ruining camp. Totally ruining it! And years ago, before anybody's time, there will always be a kid whose name nobody remembers who drowned off the point. Pulled down by a mysterious current having something, who knows what, to do with the camp's shady past as an illegal logging operation.

The drive to Chicago took hours longer than usual because of the heavy snow and ice. By the time I pulled up to Rush–

Presbyterian–St. Luke's it was three thirty in the morning, and I found Len drinking coffee and shooting the shit with the security guard in the lobby. Gone the potbelly, gone the crazy hair. The man was gaunt.

"What?" Len said. "You drive from Tashkent?"

He introduced me to the guard, an old man with an abnormally big head and a bushy mound of curly hair. Reminded me of Henry Kissinger.

"Ted," Len said, "this is a grad student. A grad student, this is Ted. You ever met a grad student before, Ted?"

"Never so up close," Ted said.

Though he was still wearing flimsy hospital slippers, Len had decked himself out in his old camp clothes: fleece jacket, camouflage pants, and, slung across his now-skinny shoulders, his red Duluth pack. A couple of years ago, cleaning out the basement, I found that red pack in a puddle of water. It had been lying there so long that when I knelt to pick it up, the thing came apart in my hands.

"I thought I was supposed to break you out of here," I said.

Ted guffawed. "He tried to give a hundred bucks to every nurse on the floor. He tried to give me a hundred bucks. I told Daddy Warbucks here he's free to come and go. He wants to be locked up, he can call the 12th District precinct captain. And besides, I told him, the hospital only steals direct from insurance. Or is it the insurance that steals direct from—"

Len slugged the dregs of his coffee and shouted at me, "Lead the way!" And he bolted out the door into the night. I shrugged at Ted and followed. Fat chunks of puffy snow were still thumping down. Gingerly, Len moved toward the cab, watching his step, but even in this new slowness, there was the old sense of half-baked purpose.

"Where're your boots?" I asked.

"Camp," Len said. "My boots are at camp. In the closet of the

Big House, second floor, the cedar closet—you want to know something else?"

"What?"

"The guard back there."

"Yeah?"

"He's a Ted, but he used to be a Trish."

"That guy?"

"First sex change in the history of Indiana. You don't believe me?"

"Head like Henry Kissinger," I said.

"More like Kissinger's mother. Imagine. Henry Kissinger had a mother. And Ted told me he'd rather be Ted, but there are a lot of days he still gets as sad as Trish used to get on her worst days. Wrap your brain around that, master's degree. Does this hearse have heat?"

"Barely."

"Keys?"

I wish you could hear the sound of Len's voice, which in its heyday was a combination of chuckle and growl. And he always spoke a little under his voice, as if to pull you into a common conspiracy. That night, as we crept through the snow—now Len drove like he walked, with timidity laced with determination—up and down the unplowed streets, his voice was so hoarse there were times I couldn't hear what he was saying. We drove through the dawn before ending up at the White Castle on West Madison, where we must have had at least thirty of those little square burgers between us for breakfast. Then Len drove himself back to Rush. He died a month later. I took the bus back to Chicago for the funeral. I'd been fired from Iowa City Yellow Cab. When I brought the cab back to the garage the day after that last night with Len, Ovid Demanaris said I was lucky he wasn't pressing my balls in charges. I gave him two hundred of the three hundred dollars Len had stuffed in my shirt pocket, which satisfied

Ovid because it was equal to the amount of cash I might have grossed that night had I been on the job (a figure I couldn't have grossed in two weeks of dreams) plus the wear and tear on the car, because, Ovid said, based on the mileage, I'd driven to hell and gone.

Len would have thought the funeral a complete hoot. It was a full-on camp reunion. He was fifty-one.

As much as Len talked, and at camp he talked and talked and talked, I always thought that at root, beneath the ceaseless cascade of stories, exhortations, bullshit, sayings, advice, encouragement, teasings, there was a silence. He rarely got personal, and when he did, it had more to do with something he wanted us to understand than something he wanted to tell us about himself. Len's sister, his only sibling, had been killed by a drunk driver. He often mentioned her, ineffectually, to scare us off driving wasted on northern Wisconsin's deer-infested back roads. He'd tell us about his father, a born-again Christian and successful trial lawyer who'd once argued (and lost) an abortion case before the United States Supreme Court. But this was only so Len could say that *he,* not the loss of an epic case, had the distinction of being the greatest failure in his father's life. And we knew that in the off-season he worked in various psych wards and hospitals across the Midwest. He said the secret of his longevity in the loony business was that the nuttier he acted, the more the inmates trusted him. They knew it was an act (a lot of *their* act, Len said, is an act), but they appreciated his effort to meet them halfway. Nobody else ever much tried. At Hennepin County in Minneapolis he'd been named an honorary schizophrenic in a solemn ceremony. The entire ward chipped in for a plaque. WE SISTERS AND BROTHERS OF LYSSA, HEREBY PROCLAIM LEONARD CAHILL OFFICIALLY DEVOID OF SANITY. SINCERELY YOURS, DR. MENGELE.

* * *

Though he had only been in Chicago for a few years—he'd moved there for treatment; he'd stopped working in the off-season to save his energy for camp—Len seemed to know every side street on the Northwest Side. As we slunk along through the snow, in that muffled silence, I don't think that Len, sensing the end, was fulfilling any sudden need to unburden himself. That wasn't why I'd been summoned. He knew unburdening wasn't possible. He knew that certain things we carry to the grave, or in Len's case the crematorium. It was more, I believe, about his own voice, hoarse and unrecognizable as it was. Sometimes in order to hear your own voice you need someone else present, even if that person isn't necessarily awake. And I confess, tired out from the drive from Iowa, I spent a lot of that sacred night in and out of consciousness.

—and so somehow I graduate from Lawrence College in Appleton, Wisconsin, in June of what, 1970, 1971?—with a degree in, you guessed it, psychology! Appleton, you know Houdini grew up there, right? His greatest escape was getting the dodge out of Appleton, Wisconsin. Anyway, I start hitchhiking, I've got some vague notion of reaching New York City. I've got about as much clue what I'm going to do in Manhattan as a porcupine in a car wash. One of my rides takes me off course, and I end up in Northampton, Massachusetts—at this point without a dollar. One of those stories, they used to even be true— there was a time when you could be a person in this country without a single dollar. And I start snooping around for some work. I hear they're hiring at Northampton State Hospital. I didn't even know what "state hospital" meant. I'm a kid from Minnetonka, Jesus fanatics for parents, what do I know about state hospitals? I think it's a hospital hospital. I get myself

hired as night attendant for four and a half dollars an hour. At first it was pure drudgery, Cuckoo's Nest sort of stuff, bedpans and force-feeding, doling out meds like gumballs. They taught me how to restrain people with restraints and how to do it without restraints. Believe me, you have a choice, use the restraints. But the long and short is I had an aptitude. I put people at ease. I almost said east. Be a nice thing to put people at east. I told nun jokes, Polack jokes, rabbi jokes, Irish jokes, homo jokes—boy, did they love the homo jokes on the ward—Chinese jokes. Rented an apartment in town and worked six nights a week at Northampton, I learned the regulations concerning shoelaces and nail clippers, I learned the drugs, the -zines, perphenazine, fluphenazine, chlorpromazine, otherwise known as Thorazine, the miracle drug! And yeah, like some kind of bleeding-heart rookie, I thought to myself these drugs never seem to take away the anguish in the eyes of these people. You hearing me? Not anguish, exactly, it was a kind of exhaustion that was beyond being physically tired. That's what it seemed to me then. An exhaustion that sleep could never chase away. And it would have been easier to take if they'd moaned out loud, but they didn't, they only do that in movies; these people on the ward at Northampton were quiet. God, it would have been better had they moaned and cradled themselves and sobbed. The only time I ever saw that was when a relative visited, then they turned up the volume on the batshit. Then they really amped up the bonkers—

"Hey" —nudging me—"hey, you even awake?"

"Huh?"

"I'm asking. You hearing this?"

"Sure, Len. The loons were exhausted, I get it."

Anyway, two, three weeks in, a couple of state troopers from Springfield bring in a kid, wild kid, flailing, kicking, calling the cops cunts and murderers. And I'm excited, I haven't really had a real live one yet. Me and another attendant get him in a jacket, stuff a pill down his throat. Lock him in the padded intake room. The troopers give him a few licks on their way out, but that's it. Eventually, the kid calms down, and after that, he sleeps maybe fourteen, fifteen hours. But the following night, during my shift, he starts up again, and again we've got to restrain him. A doc on duty gives him a shot, and soon he's right as rain, docile as a baby. It was only then I got a decent look at him, and I'm telling you the kid was angelic. He had this golden hair. What do you call it, flaxen? Is golden hair the same as flaxen? Writer? Hello? Anyway, my first thought was, and it would have made my late mother proud: Jesus Christ. The Redeemer's what, a thousand years late, but he's finally on the scene. You think I'm kidding? Later on in my storied career I met a lot of Christs. They haunt the wards. A new guy—and I met some women Christs, too—creeps up and starts blessing you and all that and you know. He cometh again. She cometh again. But this one, this boy, he only looked the part. All he wanted to do was kick you in the balls. But wasn't Satan the best-looking angel? My God, one look at that kid, and I was gone—

Since the year Len died, 1997, I've been carrying around, from rented apartment to rented apartment, a manila folder filled with notes. The folder itself has begun to disintegrate and will soon go the way of Len's backpack. For longer than the eighteen years that he worked at camp, I've been deluding myself that I'm going to make a novel out of Len, the novel I've long been contracted to write for a publisher that alternates between forgetting I exist and sending me threatening emails demanding the return of a long since spent (tiny) advance. He was, as I've said, only my boss at a summer camp, and yet I remain a disciple. My book would celebrate and spread the gospel, far and wide, of Len's irreverent humanism and induce people to run to the nearest casino with no intention or even desire of winning any money. Because I loved the man. The want wasn't entirely delusional. I wanted people who never knew Len to remember him. Does this make any sense?

—broke the lock on the cabinet in the nurses' station and read his file and find out he's been busted for, among other things, jerking off on a city bus in Springfield, Massachusetts, and then wiping his syruped hand on a cop's blue shoulder. Only twenty-two and already pages of arrests, including two for heroin possession, another five or six for weed, bad checks, assault, some more lewd and indecent behavior, which in my opinion should always be in the eye of the beholder, theft (liquor, a watch, more liquor). Also, there was a nonexpunged juvenile record, and I'm telling you I'm reading this stuff like it's biblical, this list of transgressions. He'd been rendered what they called "incorrigible." There was chronic truancy (apparently record-breaking), vandalism, breaking and entering, more assaults, including one with a deadly weapon, another theft, a bike, a stereo. But in the winter of 1971, the kid gets a kind of reprieve, or at least it's not exactly jail time as he's known it before. The judge accepts his court-appointed lawyer's Hail Mary that his client might well be a lunatic, and so he sends Dominic—his name was Dominic—to Northampton State for a minimum four-month observation period, extendable (unlimited) upon a doctor's—

There's a line of William James's I came across years ago. I've never been able to find it again, but the gist of it (I think) is: if you tried to take into account all the heartbreak behind the lighted windows of a single city on a single night, your head would explode clean off your neck. Even if I've muddled the line beyond recognition, which I'm sure is the case, you get the point. I think of it every time I remember that night in the cab with Len. And in Chicago, even at four in the morning, there are more lighted windows than you could possibly imagine.

Nights I'd watch him sleep. He'd finally begin to calm down a little, and we were able to move him from the intake room with its strappable bed to the dorm. And look, I wasn't the only one gaga over Dominic—the whole place, the other patients, the nurses, even the doctors. Everybody was doing him favors. Some people just have that magnetic force, you know, you can't help it, you just get reeled into them. The lights were always on in the dorms, but they were dimmed at night per the rules. I go over to his bed, I just want to touch his cheek while he sleeps, and I do it, and he grabs my wrist so hard I think he's going to pull it off my hand. And then Dom slowly, almost gently, but still with that iron grip, guides my hand down beneath the sheets. I'm watching a spot on the wall where there used to be one of Dorothea's beautiful windows, and I'm telling you, I don't even know what I'm telling you, because you go from zero to sixty, from wanting to touch somebody's cheek to the whole enchilada, things get—

"Enchilada?"

"You'd like me to be crass? What about your virginal heterosexual ears?"

"Who's Dorothea?"

"Dorothea Dix, the great reformer. She wanted asylums to be asylums. An oasis, a tranquil idyll where the disturbed of mind could listen to the birds."

Years ago, in my zeal to prove (to myself) that I was working diligently on my Len novel, I did some research on Dorothea

Dix in the basement of the Boston Public Library. This is what novelists do; they swim through libraries, pore over old texts. Look busy. My scattered pre-internet notes are in the manila folder. She was a woman (I noted) of great accomplishment and incessant activity. One of her assistants called Dorothea "a short woman, incapable of whispering. When Dorothea confessed her sins in church you could hear her two towns over." Of the site at Northampton where she hoped the state would build an asylum, Dix recorded this exhortation in her diary: *"It is, without a doubt, the single most beautiful pitch of land in the Commonwealth. It is not a question of if I shall have it, only when!"*

Dix believed that asylums should be at higher elevations in order to provide patients with the cleanest possible air and serenest possible views. Hence, she ordered the architect of Northampton State to ensure that from every upper-story window it would be possible to see either Mount Tom or the Connecticut River Valley. After the asylum opened in 1858, an orchestra played at every meal from the upper balcony of the dining hall, and the tables were laid with white linen and silver.

—gorgeous flaxen hoodlum, but no dummy, you don't build up a file that needs rubber bands if you're a dummy. No, he had a certain genius, Dom did. Moments of tenderness? Absofuckinglutely. There were lightning-fast kisses nobody would have seen if they'd been looking, and most didn't look, didn't care. On the ward, like everywhere, people have their own problems. Let the hippie orderly stop by Dom's bed every night, what's it to us? And we were surrounded by people, but we were also alone, dead alone, in the middle of that dorm. One night Dom pried open the light box and cut all of the lights on the ward, and that allowed us a few minutes, and holy cow you sleeping motherfuck—

"I'm awake," I said, "I'm awake. He's using you, Len, can't you even see—"

Len stops the cab. I've got no idea where we were. Somewhere off Milwaukee Avenue. It's getting a little light. The snow's let up. There's that after-snow stillness. Only snow can truly quiet Chicago. Every block becomes unrecognizably beautiful. It's been called a somber city. The only time I've felt this to be true is after snow. More and more lights are coming on in the apartments. Len's staring at me in a way that makes me remember my first summer on staff. Two weeks in, Len had summoned me into the shack for what he called shits and giggles. He handed over the bottle, and I took a healthy swig of bourbon. He watched me swallow and then looked me over. It might have gone on three or four minutes, just Len studying my face. I went on drinking the free hooch.

"How's Kevin Friedlander doing?" Len asked me.

"The kid wets the bed."

"What else?"

"He's from Shaker Heights. No, Bloomfield Hills."

"Even a dipshit not paying attention would know that Kevin Friedlander only likes Ping-Pong, that he hardly eats any lunch, and that he flunked archery."

"How do you flunk archery?"

"And that his mother—" Len paused. He dug his hand around in his hair as if he were searching for something alive in there. "You ready to hear this?"

"Sure."

"His mother fell down the stairs, hit her head. Few too many. In the off-season. The kid was the only one home. Poor woman hemorrhaged to death in Kevin's arms."

A month later, parents' weekend, I met Kevin Friedlander's mom, and she was alive and intact, but to this day she died drunk in Kevin's arms, which explained not only why he wet the bed but also why he flunked archery. It's from Len that I picked up the habit of taking one look at someone and trying to imagine the worst thing that's ever happened to them.

In the cab, Len's old voice breaks through, and he howls, "Of course I know he's using me to get the hell out of there. Why do you think I'm pinching pennies—and, yes, stealing from the other patients, stealing! Oh, hallelujah, did I steal from those inmates! And soon I bought a little Plymouth, and when the night came—" Len stops himself short. "It's like I'm telling someone else's life. You ever feel that way?"

"On a good day."

"I'm history," Len says. "And here I am telling someone else's."

Time went by, lots of time, and I made excuses. Every couple of years, I'd take out the manila folder and give it another try. Eventually, though, I lacked the patience, the persistence, the talent, the ambition, the everything—I convinced myself that Len simply couldn't be contained by a novel. Novels, by nature, end, and Len doesn't end. Ah, but—it occurred to me only just the other day—what about a story? The whole time it's been stories. Stories about everything and everybody while "saving" Len for the whole enchilada waiting for me beneath the sheets. All hail Chekhov. If done right, he tells us, a story never ends. A story: lurks. A story, a good story, is just out of reach, always. Wake up in an unfamiliar darkness, in a room you don't seem to recognize. Flip on the light. Nothing there. It's your room again. But didn't you feel a presence in the dark? The presence of someone you once knew? Someone you once loved? All these years I've been deluding myself, carrying around this folder as if one day it would grow covers and a binding. So simple, Len's a story.

Dear Little, Brown and Company:

You say stories don't sell, and God knows I have no reason to doubt you (I've seen the numbers on my story collections and they aren't pretty; I know I'm basically a charity case), but don't you see? It's what Chekhov teaches. The last period of the last sentence of a story isn't a full stop; it's a horizon. It's not about word count or pages. That's a smothered way of thinking. We're talking about the quest for infinity here. Horizons can't ever be reached no matter how many words you lard on a novel. The attempt at closure is inherently dishonest. But a story! One that ends but doesn't end, that's infinity, immortality, right there—and listen, my old buddy Len was this totally amazing, inspiring guy. You should have seen him on Hatfield and McCoy Day dressed as Charles Manson dressed up like Will Rogers. He's dead but not dead, see, he lives, he's still talking and the only way—

—and okay it wasn't even necessary, but I dressed up Dom in an orderly's uniform, light blue scrubs, and we jumped out a first-floor window. I'd cut a hole in the fence. Jumped in the car like Bonnie and Clyde. Bernie and Clyde! Drove straight to the New York border in the corner of Massachusetts and then just kept going until we ran out of gas near Utica. Some motel. First thing Dom did was dig his face in the carpet like he'd never seen carpet before. And we both couldn't stop laughing. And I know I said to myself that if I never see the kid again after today—but even at that moment, I knew I was full of shit—and so I said, Dom, let's travel, you and me. Italy! Dom shouted. The motherland! And I said, We'll do it, I'll find the dough, Italy, the motherland! Is it Sicily, Dom, is that where your people—and Dom turned over on his side and said,

My people? And I said, Yeah, your people, isn't Sicily where—and I've never been able to figure out what set him off, but he stood up and walked right out the door of the room. It wasn't like I hadn't known it was going to happen soon enough, but I wasn't ready, I just wasn't—anyway, he just starts walking across the motel parking lot and down the highway and I'm standing in the doorway, watching—

A few years ago, I was in Fall River, Massachusetts, for the funeral of an aunt. After we buried Aunt Josephine, who'd been so old for so long everybody thought she'd already died, I drove my rented car clear across the state to Northampton. More notes for my manila folder. And there it was. On a hill above Smith College. They'd closed the asylum for good in 1986. I have no idea what I was hoping to gain by looking at a few old brick buildings through a chain-link fence. I desperately wanted the place to mean something. It was, though, a beautiful spot amid the tall trees and Mount Tom and the Connecticut River Valley in the background. Dorothea Dix was no dope. Maybe she figured she'd ride out her influence as long as she had it. She had to have known even then that nobody, not even her richest patrons, was going to pay for an orchestra to play for a horde of psychotics indefinitely.

On an otherwise empty page, I wrote: "Three Adirondack chairs, one broken."

Or maybe the failure of my manila folder, besides patience, talent, etc., etc., has nothing to do with form, long, short, or in between. Maybe it's just a true love story, and like all such stories it will always mean less to the person listening (more or less listening) than it does to the teller. How could it not? Forgive me, Len. How to say this? As I think back on us creeping along those newly blanketed Chicago streets in the cab, I can't help but remember something an old girlfriend used to say to me—no, it wasn't an old girlfriend, it was my ex-wife. It was my ex-wife who used to say it. She'd say that what I sought, what I ached for, what I breathed for, was true love. Except she pronounced it *twew,* like Elmer Fudd would say it. *Twewlove.* She said I was pie in the sky, that my search would never amount to anything because the only *twewlove* that would ever mean anything to me was— by nature—unrequited. I wanted to pine, not love. *Twewlove,* my ex-wife said, isn't love at all.

"And you know what else?" she said.

"What?"

"It's boring as shit."

"What about Chekhov?" I shouted.

"Chekhov died in love," my ex-wife said. "And loved. Olga Knipper loved him back. It was fucking mutual. Nothing *twew* about it."

"But his stories! His stories—"

"He wasn't celebrating unrequited love, he was practically begging his characters, and his dopey readers, to see the stupidity, to understand that their own failure to love was because they loved nobody but themselves. How can you read and read and still not have any idea what he's saying?"

—but I thought, Fuck it, and I ran after him down the highway, and when I reached him, I said, "Dom," and when he didn't answer I tackled his ass. And we were rolling around in the cold dead grass by the side of the road. Whether it was day or night by that point, I no longer remember. All I know is that I started to punch him and

*he laughed—not like the way he'd laughed on the carpet, a laugh
like not only didn't he give a shit now, he'd never give a shit ever—
and so I punched harder—*
  "Hello? Hello? You present? Accounted for?"
  "Mmmm."
  "This is the climax, cabbie."
  "Right, Len, right—"

Or maybe it's even more basic. Len's life beyond camp. Aside
from this one story and a few stray details, I know very little
about it. I never asked. I'm not entirely to blame for this because
in camp theology one simply doesn't exist outside of camp. Since
Len was a high priest, it makes a certain amount of sense that
the rest of his life would be inaccessible to my imagination. A
form of sacrilege to try to conjure him beyond the Big House,
the Little House, the lake, the tennis courts, the point, the upper
diamond, the sand dunes, the casino in Bad River. What we call
the off-season is a netherworld you endured in a kind of fog in
order to make it back to June, July, and August.
  June, July, August.
  That's our calendar. Even if you no longer make it up, even
if you haven't set foot on camp's grounds in years, the calendar
remains June, July, August, because you believe, will always believe, that the time will come when you will return and slide
back into history repeating itself as if you never left and a stoned
JC from Kansas City is about to hand you a joint. So why the cab
ride in the snow? Because he knew he'd been expelled. For good.
From June, July, and August. And he needed to speak, to somebody, didn't matter that it was me; he just needed to speak to
somebody, anybody from June, July, and August. If only the ride
had been longer. Maybe I'd know more about all the heartache,
the decades of heartache that must have followed Dominic, who

in the end probably didn't mean all that much compared with the others Len met later, those friends and lovers who, like Len himself, died too young. Dominic was only the story he chose to tell me that night.

Who's the sucker now—but he still laughed and so I started to beat the shit out of him. I was a little bigger than Dom to begin with, though I'm sure he could have killed me if he wanted to, but he only laughed, bloody teeth laughing, and I just kept hitting—pummeling that face, kissing it, that Christ face, and I can't tell you how satisfying it was to pummel—

A man is walking down the middle of the street, which is what you do in Chicago when the sidewalks are buried by a blizzard. One set of footprints through the untouched snow. We follow slowly behind for a while, as if the man is now the one leading us, somewhere, anywhere. At some point the man stops. Len pulls up beside him and rolls down the window. The man is outlined by snow. He's like a walking chalk drawing. No hat. Ledges of snow over his eyebrows. He's wearing only a thin tweed jacket, with the flaps of his collar up.

"You a cab?" the man says.

"What's it look like?"

"Says Iowa."

"Is Iowa not a state in the Union with full faith and credit?"

The guy gets into the back of the cab.

Len leans over me and flips on the meter. "You're out late," he says. "Or early. Which is it? Late or early?"

The man shrugs and snow cascades from his shoulders. Some nut job from Iowa wants to give him a ride, what's it to him?

III

Crimes of Opportunity; or, The 1980s

Turn left by the old house that used
to be there before it burned down.

—Robert Creeley, "Reflections
on Whitman in Age"

Speech at the Urinal, Drake Hotel, Chicago, December 1980

The urinals, five of them, marble coffins standing upright. I hunched beside my father as we pissed into the fruit and ice. The men's-room attendant my father knew by name— *Evening, Henry. Greet Mr. Henry, Son, and always look a gentleman in the eye*—stood behind us, waiting, steamed towels draped over his forearm.

I no longer remember the exact content of the speech. But I know it was an ode to the faded grandeur of that old stuffed-shirt hotel, that pompous men's room, to Mr. Henry and his flour-white hair and his warmed-up towels, and, above all, to those mighty urinals where generations of Chicago manhood had come to deliver of themselves. To my father the Drake Hotel was a buttress against all that was encroaching after a decadent decade. The '70s disgusted him. People spitting right on the sidewalk, public nudity (not that my father had any trouble with it in the flesh and in fact quite enjoyed it; it was the principle of nudity being acceptable that took all the fun out of it), women lawyers. Women lawyers, my father said, among other contrary attributes, are far too excitable for the law. The law must needs be as fixed, as immovable, as stony faced, as these pharaonic toilets. A longish piss into the crackling ice, into the sliced melon and grapefruit and strawberries, and my father discoursed and I stood there, long out of piss myself, and listened. Chicago was still his city. There may be a lady mayor now (and if there's going to be a lady mayor, let her be a chick as brassy as Jane Byrne), but by God the Drake is still the Drake and the fruit in the men's room urinals is still so fresh you could eat it. This is style, this is grace, and this kind of style, this kind of grace, can't be bought, not with money, new money, anyway, though this doesn't mean you should ever find yourself without money, old, new, borrowed, stolen, embezzled, conned—no greater dishonor in this city, or anywhere else for that matter. Better to be rich and in jail. Better to be rich and dead, are you hearing me? Is this getting across?

And Mr. Henry waits, twin towels folded over his arm.

Visions of Mr. Swibel

For years, first under the old man, and then under Mayors Mike Bilandic and Jane Byrne, Charles Swibel was chairman of the Chicago Housing Authority. A rich real-estate developer, the fox in charge of the henhouse. Yet this was Chicago, and nobody but the reformers much blinked. And who ever listened to the reformers—background noise of a majestic city?

You hear something?

No, what?

I dunno, voices crying injustice in the dark?

Go buy some earplugs.

Through the '70s my father was a rising young lawyer who, among other things, represented the CHA in tort cases. When a resident got hurt at the Robert Taylor Homes or Cabrini-Green or Stateway Gardens and sued the city, my father defended the CHA. Often he argued successfully that though the stairwell was unlit or the elevator out of order, the plaintiff, having lived in the building for such and such amount of time, certainly should have been familiar with this particular hazard and therefore was, at the very least, partially responsible for their own injury. He saved the city millions. And my father, standing in his thirty-second-floor LaSalle Street office, used to tell my brother and me, "If I don't do it, take a look down there at this block of hustlers who will."

So it was a good contract, and eventually my father became personally close to the CHA chief, Mr. Charles Swibel himself. My father revered men of action. And Swibel, who strode around with a tall and wispy head of hair like Liberace and a gold watch that must have weighed twenty pounds, impressed my father as the genuine article. A Churchill, a MacArthur, a Stalin, a Daley. Of course, he knew that mucky-mucks had been accusing Swibel for years of draining the coffers of the CHA for his own gain. But my father was an attorney, a servant of the law. His professional responsibility was to represent clients, and one of his clients was the Chicago Housing Authority. By then the CHA not only was being sued by individuals but was also the subject of massive class actions, and my father was in the thick of it. I remember I'd go to lunch with him at the Standard Club, and the maître d' would approach and say, "A call for you, sir. Would you like to take it at the table?" My father would nod, and a waiter would carry the phone to him on a tray, the long cord snaking behind him like a tail, the receiver resting beside the phone, and you could already hear Mr. Swibel's voice rumbling. My father would pick up the phone and listen until the rumbling subsided and say, "Understood, Chuckie, understood." Then he'd hang up, and the waiter would return and retreat, silently, walking backward, with the phone on the tray. It was an amazing thing: my father calling Mr. Swibel "Chuckie." The man was a kind of subgod, a personal friend of Mayor Daley's. Daley was dead by then, but that didn't matter. He ran Chicago from the grave—he had a switchboard down there and everything—and one of the people he talked to every day was Charles Swibel.

And once he came out to our house in Highland Park. Mr. Swibel actually lived in another suburb, Winnetka, a rich Jew among rich Gentiles (far enough away so that Cabrini-Green might as well have been in Delaware), but Highland Park, just a little farther up the North Shore, where mostly rich Jews lived among other mostly rich Jews, was a bridge *too* far. Hadn't he slogged his balls off to make it to Winnetka? Hadn't his own father washed up in Chicago from the Pale of Settlement in rags? To Mr. Swibel, those few miles north to where Jews still huddled together (while pretending not to) must have been tantamount to slumming it.

Whatever he'd had to say that morning apparently couldn't wait and couldn't be conveyed over the phone. It was Sunday. We were having breakfast. My mother was looking out the window. She was, I remember, always looking out the window in those days, as if visualizing escape.

"There's a car in the driveway," my mother said without interest.

"What car?" my father said.

"A big car."

"A Lincoln Town Car?"

My mother shrugged. "It's a big car, Phil."

"Is it a butter-yellow Lincoln Town Car?"

That my mother didn't tell him to get up and look for himself is an indication of where things stood in our house in the early '80s. She didn't bother to speak to my father any more than absolutely necessary. Words were energy, and she was storing them up for another life.

"What make of car is it, Miriam?"

"It's yellow, but I have no idea—"

My father sprinted up the stairs three at a time. He must have had his suit and tie on in less than forty-five seconds. There wasn't enough time for all of us to be made presentable, but even so my father ordered my brother and me (he knew my mother would silently refuse) out to the driveway immediately. "Just wave discreetly," he said. "Do not approach the Lincoln."

And so that's what we did. My brother and I stood there in the driveway and waved discreetly to Mr. Swibel, or at least to the tinted window that he was purportedly behind. The engine of the Lincoln was purring low. My father, with a humble un-folding of his arm, presented us to the tinted window. It slowly descended to reveal a man in large sunglasses and a bouffant. He lifted a beringed hand languidly in our direction. *Nice-looking brood.* My father approached the car and for a few moments stood in audience before we heard him say, "Understood, Chuckie, understood." But Mr. Swibel wasn't through. He spoke for another five minutes, and then, without waiting for my father to say whether he understood or not, slowly began to back the Lincoln up. While in reverse, Mr. Swibel never took his eyes off my father. I remember being impressed that he could drive back-ward without taking hold of the passenger's seat and craning his neck to look out the rear window. My father stood and watched, mesmerized. Admiration at that level is a form of love, isn't it? A man's got to love something, doesn't he? Mr. Swibel withdrew like the tide, and even after he was gone, my father remained there in the driveway looking at the gravel, at the tracks made by the yellow Lincoln, amazed and bereft at the same time.

The Laundry Room

1. THE LITTLE BUDDHA

When my brother lost the election for sophomore class vice president, he smashed the little porcelain Buddha my grandfather had given him for good luck. The figure had a smoothish belly I liked to rub. When my brother threw him on the laundry-room floor, the little Buddha shattered into so many pieces that years later we were still finding traces of his remains. At night, with the light off, with a flashlight, you could always find tiny specks. Apparently, he was worth a lot of money. My grandfather had brought him back from Tokyo after the war and had been holding on to him, waiting for an occasion to bestow the sacred Buddha upon his eldest grandchild. And when he did, it was with a great deal of solemn ceremony.

A few days before the election, my grandfather, sitting behind his enormous slab of desk, had called my brother and me into his study. My brother must have thought he was getting a Cross pen or something. The little Buddha was squatting in the dead center of the great desk, emanating serenity and wisdom. We'd never seen the Buddha before, and we'd searched my grand-father's drawers hundreds of times. (I was especially drawn to what he called his French postcards, topless women posing like kittens.) When my brother and I were settled and attentive in the two chairs before him, my grandfather stood up, unbuckled his belt, and loosened his pants. Then he sat down again and began speaking what I can only describe as a kind of pidgin Chinese, the voice he used when he tried to read the characters on the menu at Yu Lin's. We laughed but stopped when my grand-father kept making those sounds in that weird high voice. He wasn't kidding. He went on—and on—speaking this language. He seemed to be trying to entrance himself, to reach some kind of fugue state. The whole thing was freaky and unprecedented. My grandfather, a banker, wasn't a playful person. Nor had he ever exhibited much imagination, but there he sat giving voice to the Buddha and bestowing upon my brother, through this se-ries of oinks and dongs and ching chings, the good fortune he needed to guarantee there was no way in Nirvana he'd lose the election.

What we'll fall in love with enough to believe.

Debbie Swinderman was a lock. She was smart, AP this, AP that. Also, she was totally hot, had much-discussed breasts, and smiled at everybody, including losers. She had a platform that included a demand for a salad bar in the school cafeteria. My brother's platform consisted of what? His stance on anti-nuclear proliferation? He put up posters around school: "Save Soviet Jewelry!" which just confused everybody. *And* Debbie Swinderman had an identical twin sister, Trina Swinderman, who, though not as smart (like my brother, Trina was in regu-lar classes), was, of course, equally as totally hot. Trina smiled at losers, too. My brother considered Debbie having a twin an unfair advantage. Debbie had, in effect, not just two per-fect tits to campaign with, but four. Had there been some sort of elections commission, my brother might have registered a complaint.

Instead, he relied on the Buddha. He must have known he was doomed, and yet—how often do we experience the faith of pure belief? Belief's like catnip; once you get a whiff of it, you can't get enough. It makes you loopy. Belief drunkens. It was as if our banker truly spoke ancient Chinese like a native and the little Buddha—

Election day. Debbie Swinderman in a landslide. She strutted across the lunchroom and gave my brother a good-sport hug, in front of everyone, pressing his humiliation into advanced-placement knockers. The lunchroom hooted.

When he got home, my brother charged down into the basement, to the laundry room. I was there. I watched. How he wrapped the little Buddha in his fist, took a running start, and hurled that little fucker—

2. PINEWOOD DERBY

My father built my Pinewood Derby car. He spent a month on it. Our den leader, Mr. Steinhoffer, said making these cars would be a fantastic way to spend time with our fathers but, remember, fathers were not supposed to build the cars for us. It's rule number one, Mr. Steinhoffer said, of the Pinewood Derby. *You* build your cars, with your dad's kind assistance and advice, yes, but you and you alone—

My father gleefully defied this mandate.

"Mr. Steinhoffer says I have to build it myself," I said.

"Steinhoffer?" my father said. "Steinhoffer? Who is this duty-bound Kraut?"

"He's our den leader."

"Den leader?"

"He leads the pack."

"I'm thinking something along the lines of an Alfa Romeo," my father said.

And I, equally gleefully, sat there in the laundry room beside the workbench and watched him. Not because I gave a damn about the Pinewood Derby but because not having to build it with him lessened the contact I had to have with him. As he was concentrating so intensely on his engineering, on the shape of that little slab of pinewood, we hardly spoke. And his design *was* innovative and aerodynamic. My car wasn't like any other. It was flat and sleek, not bulbous. I remember watching my father dig a little groove under the car and insert a small piece of metal so our car would meet the weight requirements.

But the beauty of the car's design didn't make it go any faster. We came in tenth out of eleven cars. The eleventh car was disqualified on account of absence. Nate Sobel didn't show up. Nobody bothered to suspect I hadn't built the car myself. Other cars sped by like nobody's business. It was as if our car had no idea it was in a race at all. The problem, Kenny Ehrenberg said, had to do with velocity. The design didn't allow for the car to gain any momentum at the top of the track because of its lack of velocity. It had a weight on the bottom, I said.

"It's where you put the weight that counts," Kenny said. "You can't just stick a weight in the bottom and expect—"

"Fuck you, Kenny."

My father was a lawyer. What did he know about velocity?

And I remember nearly shouting at Kenny Ehrenberg, as if he'd exposed us. Listen, you blubbery dickwad, we built that car together.

3. MY FATHER OILING HIS GUNS

The laundry room, its cement floor cracked from yearly floods. The single bar of fluorescent light. The string you pulled. The light would flicker and decide either to come on or not; you never knew. The washer that shook the house on spin cycle. Across from the washer, the workbench where my father oiled his guns. There were three shotguns and a little pistol he said had belonged to my great-grandmother. She'd lived in a residential hotel on the South Side. I remember her. She was always lying in bed, staring up at the ceiling. Her helmet of steel hair could have fought in World War I.

My father, brother, and I used to hunt at a club up in Richmond, Illinois, near the Wisconsin border. We were not accomplished hunters. I often tell this. Though the club stocked the fields with hundreds of pheasants, very few lost their lives to our prowess, and those that did just happened to be at the wrong place at the wrong time. But I remember fondly how, after we did manage to shoot one of them, I'd stuff the unlucky birdsoul into the inner pocket of my hunting coat, and the warmth would last so long.

My father kept the guns in a closet behind his suits. Every few months, he'd carry them down to the laundry room to be oiled. He used some special kind of oil. Linseed? And he'd sit at the workbench and regale me, if I couldn't think of a good-enough reason I had to be elsewhere, with the virtues of keeping firearms well oiled. Or for that matter any nonautomated mechanism. You want anything to last? Oil it. I remember how he'd pour a little onto the chamois. The smell, something vinegar about it. And I remember how, as I got older, when I had the presence of mind to inhale anything that came my way, I huffed up that linseed oil because getting high on it helped me, among other things, to endure my father a few minutes longer. This, too, I've said before, though maybe not as directly: I shrank from my father's physical presence. It nearly pains me to say it. Who needs this truth? The man's gone now. It's through, finished. What's the point? Here is where normally I'd say, like a false prayer, something along the lines of: *And my father oiling his guns in the livid laundry-room light.*

As if the image of him in the basement, alone, might absolve me of beating this dead horse to death again.

Miami Beach, 1961

My parents are in a bar. My mother is twenty; my father is twenty-seven. Some local barfly starts something up with a naval officer in a gleaming white uniform. My father was in the army during the Korean War, though he never left the state of Missouri. He loathed every minute of it. Even so, there was something about the brilliance of the officer's uniform that captivated him. Maybe it was the man's Napoleonic epaulets, his beautiful golden shoulders. It also stands to reason that my father had had more than a few drinks by that point. Whatever it was, my father got up from the table he was sharing with my mother and clocked the barfly right off his stool. Mayhem ensues, my mother always used to say, like in a western. Tables are overturned; chairs are broken over heads. You wouldn't think, my mother would say, that you could really break a chair over someone's head, but you can, I saw it in person. The officer and his men whisk the newlyweds to safety out in the street. Valiant father. Beautiful mother in a yellow sundress and a wide belt with a silver buckle. The officer invites the two of them for a nightcap on the ship. And it's on that boat, in the officer's mess, that my parents meet the movie star Ruth Roman, a member of the officer's party. She must have been at least fifteen years older

than my mother at the time but still glamorous in a cavalier sort
of way. She called everybody, even the ship's cat, darling. She
thought my young lawyer father should act. Talk about stealing the show. "Does he always break into scenes like that?" she
asked my mother. "And he wasn't even in the credits." Ruth
Roman drunk, happily drunk—they were all happily drunk—
and she began to regale my parents with stories of Hollywood,
where everybody behaved like cads and everybody, especially
the married ones, went home lonely. My parents ate it up. Their
honeymoon had a headline. Whatever happened to the naval officer, that lost Gatsby in his white uniform? Who knows? Maybe
Ruth Roman married him for a while.

She used to come visit us. She'd be in a play in Chicago. Or
she'd stop in town to visit on her way to New York. She always
took the train, never flew. She said she had enough unnatural
disasters for one lifetime. Ruth Roman had been on board the
Andrea Doria when it was hit by the *Stockholm* off the coast
of Nantucket. My brother and I would beg her to tell us about
it. How she dropped her baby in one of the last lifeboats and
how that lifeboat floated away, leaving her on the deck of a ship
already half swallowed by the Atlantic. "And I shouted to the
waves, Go forth, little Dickie, go forth into the beyond, my boy,
my progeny, good health to you and prosper, and remember,
don't fall for the first tramp that gives you a come-hither in the
tall grass…"

Throughout the '70s we'd see her, and I remember being a
kid on my father's shoulders waiting in the lobby of Union Station, waiting for her to sweep in followed by two or three porters
yanking luggage carts. I'd jump down, and my brother and I
would sprint toward her. My little midgets! She wasn't anybody
famous anymore. Characters, she'd say, I play characters now.
Mistreated middle-aged wives, venomous mothers-in-law. Here
and there, an old-maid aunt with a sense of humor. *You make a*

living how you make a living. But her gestures were still those of a nearly A-level starlet of the '50s. My brother and I used to watch an old VHS copy of a movie, I forget the title, where she plays a gangster's girlfriend who poisons the gangster's oysters. She's in love with a guy from a rival gang or something. The scene where the gangster gags while Ruth Roman swoons in traumatized shock and horror, now that was acting.

By the early '80s, we stopped seeing Aunt Ruth in person, though once or twice she guest-starred on *Fantasy Island.* But the time I'm talking about—those days when she'd stay at our house for a night or two—I think of the preparations. My father would scour the upstairs bathroom on his hands and knees with Ajax. We breathed up that gritty powder for weeks. My father would shout: *Ruthie's coming, Ruthie's coming!* And my mother, who couldn't wait to get out of that house, even she looked forward to Aunt Ruth's visits, maybe because they gave her a taste of what she'd once thought life might hold. When she and her swashbuckling lawyer husband were welcomed on board the USS *Who Knows* on a hot night in Miami Beach.

Ruth and my mother sitting on the back patio in the morning, smoking and laughing as my father slept in, and Aunt Ruth says, "So, this is the suburbs. How dreadful, such beautiful flowers."

And my mother cackling so hard she choked on her cigarette. The blue-gray morning, the tall trees in our backyard—

When my father woke up, he'd come down in unfamiliar silk-looking pajamas, and the three of them would drink and smoke and laugh into the afternoon. My brother and I would make cameos. Aunt Ruth would critique us. Project! Project to the back of the theater!

I have always wondered what was in it for her. Why did she keep coming back to us, year after year? Who were we? As far as I know, neither my father nor my mother ever had an affair with Ruth Roman. That wasn't it. What I'm getting at here is that it may have been one of those rare friendships that was just that, pure and simple enjoyment of one another's company. That's all. You forget such a thing is possible.

Ruthie's coming! Cut your toenails!

It passed, it passed. Maybe laughter always vanishes first?

In September of 1999, Aunt Ruth's *New York Times* obituary headline read: "Ruth Roman, 75, Glamorous and Wholesome Star, Dies." The piece mentioned her appearances in *Champion* opposite Kirk Douglas, *The Far Country* opposite Jimmy Stewart, *Strangers on a Train* opposite Robert Walker, and *Dallas* opposite Gary Cooper. She'd once dated Ronald Reagan. She had a kittenish warmth on-screen. "Few of her films are studied in film schools today," wrote the *New York Times*. "But in their time they made box office cash registers ring like sleigh bells and in 1951 Ms. Roman was receiving 500 letters a week from around the world." The obituary listed her three or four husbands and also retold the *Andrea Doria* story, her only son drifting away into the ocean dark. There's no mention of my parents, but why would there be?

The Language of That Year

The time Mr. Leopardi burst through our always-open front door, shouting gibberish at the top of his lungs. Not words exactly, at least not any words I could make out, because they all ran together. Nobody else was home. I was a sixth grader, up in my room, under my bed, whacking off like there was no tomorrow. My sad, furious, happy ritual. It brought no relief. That didn't mean I didn't live for it. And, of course, I was completely freaked out and thought that whatever the hell's going on in the front hall it's got to have something to do with the private party I'm having up here under my bed. Had somebody been tipped off and come over to bust my ass in the name of common decency? I stopped in midecstasy and listened to that incoherent ranting until I heard the front door open again and Mrs. Leopardi say, "Oh, here you are, Father."

Mr. Leopardi, before he retired and lost his mind, sold cars. He sold my mother our K-car. (Later that year, my brother would total it in Milwaukee.) This was before Alzheimer's became a thing. We just thought Mr. Leopardi was unhinged. Lots of people were in 1982. He'd wander around the neighborhood bellowing in a combination of Italian and English. But that was the first afternoon he'd come into anybody's house, and anyway

I was much too in the throes to make the connection, under the bed with my pants down, more ashamed than terrified, and I was plenty terrified. And even after Mrs. Leopardi came and took him home, I couldn't shake the thought that, whatever he'd been saying, he absolutely intended the tirade for me personally. A message from hell concerning my lonely deviance. A Jew, I still sure as hell believed in hell. It only happened once. But in my memory of that time, it happens often, weekly, me under the bed and every time I'm about to reach the point where my efforts will temporarily pay off, the front door flings open and in charges Mr. Leopardi.

He was a small man with a gaunt face. His eyes were saucered by two half circles that drooped down to his cheeks. He wasn't the sort of salesman to go out of his way to sell you anything on his lot. My mother picked out the K-car because, according to chalk on the windshield, it was the cheapest. Mr. Leopardi just shrugged. It was you who had to prove you were worthy of the car, not the other way around. And just because you happened to live next door to him didn't mean you got any discount. My mother and I got in the car. She asked me if I wanted to "drive," and I reached over from the passenger's seat and wiggled the steering wheel a little and made some growling car noises. I was a little old to be acting this way, but it was the first car my mother bought after the divorce, a moment of great independence, and I had to make a show that I understood the significance. I remember looking out the window at Mr. Leopardi as we drove away, how he stood there with his arms folded, not smiling, gazing at me.

Doesn't this kid have a father?

Also that year, I broke my collarbone playing King of the Mountain at recess. I've never been much of an athlete, but I did reach a kind of pinnacle as champion of King of the Mountain. The game was ruthless, glorious. Elm Place School field, the hill that abutted St. Johns Avenue, across the street from Marcy Feldsher's condo. In the winter, the hill got icy. It's still there. Every time I drive by it, I relive past triumphs. I shoved a lot of bigger guys down that hill. Bob Glickman, Toby Crenshaw, even Michael Zamost once. Because for a time that fucking hill was mine. The object was not just to defend your rights to be on top of the hill by repelling invaders. You didn't just shove. You punched, you kicked, you bit. The point was to humiliate— and maim. When Eddy Loiseau got me in a headlock and kneed me in the groin before throwing me down so hard on the ice I heard my bones crack, I was in such pain I couldn't muster any sounds. Eddy and a couple of other guys carried me inside, dumped me in front of Nurse Kellner's office, and ran like hell. After she found me out there, Nurse Kellner called my mother. This seemed a serious case. Nurse Kellner, God love her, but her medical expertise was limited to ice packs and chocolate.

My mother picked me up and drove me to the hospital. I was, in spite of feeling like someone was repeatedly stabbing me in the neck, somehow able to walk to the car. We drove, I remember, in silence. My mother has always been unflappable in the face of sickness and injury. I'd been knocked around pretty bad, okay, but what else did I have to say for myself? Did I have any new thoughts about the nature of the universe today? How about any insights into what our country, collectively, had done to deserve Ronald Reagan? She didn't say this out loud, and I didn't answer. That's sometimes how we talked. I remember the sound of my mother and me not speaking as she was about to turn left on Vine Street. She was driving another car that day. Because I broke my collarbone *after* my brother wrecked the K-car in Milwaukee. All the useless chronologies I wander around with. My mother replaced the K-car with a used baby-blue VW bug, and I remember as if listening to it right now that the sound of its blinker was direct and forceful, like a loud clock ticking.

Crimes of Opportunity

When I went to make a report, the cop told me it must have been a crime of opportunity. When I asked what he meant, he said there are crimes of opportunity and there are crimes of premeditation. The opportunists are the ones you have to worry about because they can turn on a dime. Less than a dime. Careerists, you know where they stand. Nothing false about a careerist. But an opportunist?

Officer Montez looked down at his shiny plastic shoes as if even the thought of an opportunist made him want to spit on shoes, didn't matter if they were his. We were side by side in the only chairs in the waiting room. These two chairs were bolted to the floor, and so close together that his right knee touched my left knee. I wondered who'd steal chairs from a police station. Our proximity made the conversation not only conspiratorial but possibly, in a different time and place, romantic. Officer Montez turned 180 degrees to face me and said that he spent part of his day doing his rounds, filing nonsense paperwork, and occasionally solving crimes and arresting people, but the bulk of his time, especially his brain time, if I knew what he meant, was spent examining people's faces to determine whether they were opportunists or careerists.

I asked: But what if a person's neither?

Officer Montez's laugh echoed off the walls of the little waiting room.

It couldn't have been a more nondescript room, and yet I still think of it. Once, on a Eurail pass, I went to the Sistine Chapel. I even got down on the floor and stared up at the ceiling until a security guard had a conniption. I thought, This guy's going to report me direct to the pontiff. I remember not a single detail of Michelangelo's frescoes. But I can tell you that the walls of a certain suburban police station in 1982 were the color of urine when you're dehydrated. How in a locked glass cabinet—you know the type of lock I mean? works like a zipper?—were dusty softball championship trophies and public service awards. How in the corner was a furled banner that, if extended (I extended it while I was waiting for Officer Montez to emerge from the bowels of the station), read: CHARACTER MATTERS. The officers brought it with them when they visited schools and delivered passionate antidrug lectures designed ineffectively to scare the shit of out us. *Hmmm, I got to try me some of that.* The ceiling? Chalk-white asbestos, little moonlike craters I wished I could reach so I could run my fingers over the bumps.

Officer Montez handed me a form. Pretty hands, not just pretty for a cop, pretty for anybody, and bright, translucent fingernails. Did he get manicures? Did he wonder if his manicurist was an opportunist or a careerist? As I started to fill out the form, he made notes in a small spiral notebook. He asked me the make and model of the bike.

"Model?"

"Was it a Junior Varsity? Varsity? Continental?"

"It was brown."

"Okay, a brown bike. But a Schwinn, right? All you guys ride—"

"I ride a Huffy," I said. "My parents are divorced."

"Serial number?"

"Serial number?"

"Some people write it down," Officer Montez said. "You know, file it in a drawer with other important numbers, birth certificates, social security cards, that sort of—"

I tried to comport myself like I was the type of seventh grader who would, under normal circumstances, have written down my bike's serial number and filed it in a drawer. I just hadn't in this particular case.

I returned, all business, to my form. *Time of the Incident:* Sometime after lunch. *Location of the Incident:* In front of the Dannon Yogurt, Central Avenue. *Summary of the Incident:* Someone stole my fucking bike.

I looked up at Officer Montez. He was staring into my soul as I sat there like I was the unsullied lamb who'd been wronged. An easy case. A goddamn opportunist right here at headquarters. A plump little faker in Stan Smiths, ready and willing to take the moment a taking presented itself. I considered turning myself in to his virile custody right then.

Officer Montez in his plastic shoes and day-and-a-half-old beard. He'd worked the night shift, and now it was well into the following afternoon, and the man was tired, but not too tired to give a dumbass who'd left his bike unlocked the time of day, and—and—to recognize an opportunist when he saw one. I am grateful for the attention you paid, Officer. Our encounter provided me with some rare clarity.

Eddy Loiseau and I were inside playing Frogger. Eddy was trying to explain to me that the point was not to get hit by traffic, but I got a kick out of watching the frog get run over.

"You're losing. Every time you—"

"I'm good at getting hit," I said.

And outside, someone walking by, just passing the time, maybe whistling a little ditty, minding his own business, and there it was, a brown bike, a Huffy but in decent shape, some stickers, leaning nonchalant against the window. Beckoning him. Or her. Maybe it was a her who stole my bike. Pass it up? So that someone else can come along and take it, or, worse, nobody gets that booty, and the putz who left it unlocked rides it home, no harm, no foul? A gift is offered. It's yours for the pilfer. File charges against another someone like me who happened to be striding down Central Avenue that day, bikeless and able? You read me right, Officer Montez. Even then I was sneaky. Opportunities for thefts and every other sin, I've always done my best to honor them.

In the Lobby

After my parents split up, I went on trips with my father. I didn't have a choice. Vacations were codified in the decree. My brother, being older and already in high school, was exempt from this judicial fiat, so I went it alone. My father was rich then. He didn't die rich. He died without much. That's another story. But, in those years, he considered it almost an obligation to fly off to places most people only read about in magazines.

I'd just turned fifteen when he took me and Cindy Roo to St. Moritz at the height of ski season. None of us knew how to ski, or had any interest in learning to ski, although Cindy Roo may have ended up taking some lessons. She certainly brought a lot of ski outfits. But I wouldn't know for sure. I didn't much care then, and I don't much care now. Still, it's amazing to me that Cindy Roo is dead also. You'd have thought her name alone would have kept her alive forever.

On these trips, my father and Cindy Roo would vanish immediately. I'd hang out in the lobby of the hotel. And the lobby of the Palace Hotel in St. Moritz—where to even begin? First off, it was like a public park, or a public zoo. The lobby was open to anybody and everybody, day and night, an untamed labyrinth, a country of motley sofas, love seats, ottomans, old ladies in worn-out mink coats reading week-old newspapers, small dogs, bigger dogs, card tables with tiny drawers (inside were notepads with scores from card games played during the Hapsburg Empire), grandfather clocks displaying wildly different times, duck decoys, roaring fireplaces, wardrobes, china cabinets, high-back chairs that I could stand on in my socks and not see over the top, bookshelves full of racy (I imagined) French novels, mirrors that were more like black holes than mirrors (when you looked in them you only saw your face in ghostly outline), Siamese cats in baskets, loose, renegade squirrels. And those brass lamps. In every direction on wobbly tables were those green-eyeshade lamps so that the whole place glowed green, nightlike by day, daylike by night. And all of it, every living and inanimate object, belonged there and nowhere else, as if every dog, every cat, every minked old lady, every piece of furniture, had grown up out of the thick black carpet and taken permanent root. And every day I found something I could have sworn wasn't there the day before. Where did this locked sea chest come from? Yet overcrowded as it was with things to investigate, there was a languid paddedness about the lobby, and I'd sink into one of the creaky leather couches, the hair of the cow that had sacrificed itself for my leisure still clinging to it, and sleep to the sweet ping of the elevators.

I remember gawking out the big plate-glass windows, but I'm not sure I ever left the hotel. I was a lobby rat. I ordered Cokes; I ordered sundaes. I ordered fat sandwiches and thick fries and shrimp cocktails and beers. My last name and room number were talismans that opened any door. I'd chat with the concierge, Pascal. All concierges are named Pascal. He never left his post behind his tiny desk that was like my grandmother's dressing table. There wasn't a thing on the planet Pascal didn't know. He never consulted a book or the phone.

He just knew every train timetable from Zurich to Zagreb. What did I chat with him about? The tribulations of a brotherless kid on his own in the Alps. Pascal was well aware of my sort of dilemma. Well-heeled abandoned kids were a subspecialty. And he never scoffed or judged, only commiserated with simpatico eyes.

Unburdening myself to Pascal wearied me. Wouldn't it anybody? I was napping peaceably under an afghan, a plate of coagulating ketchup on the floor beside my shoes being lapped up by a couple of elegant cats, when something pointy jabbed me in the gut.

"What the fuck?"

"You don't ski?"

"Huh?"

"Not even the bunny hill?"

I opened my eyes. Hovering over me was a girl wielding a ski pole. She was dressed head to toe in white but for a big red ball dangling off the top of her white hat. She looked like an elf dressed as an ambulance.

About to prod me again, this time in the nuts, she said, "Do you or don't you even ski?"

"Look, I'm sleeping."

"You came all the way across the ocean to snooze?"

"Yes."

Asinine as this was, it also seemed to make a certain amount of sense to her. I wouldn't be the first person she ever met who flew nine hours to sleep someplace else.

My tab was under the ketchup plate. She knelt down and shoved a cat out of the way, read the name and room number.

"How old are you?" she said.

"Sixteen and a half."

"Right. And I'm Golda Meir."

"Who?"

"You're a MOT?"

"A what?"

"Member of the tribe, dummy."

"What tribe?"

"The Navajos."

"Sure," I said.

"The ancient wandering band of the circumscribed."

"Circumcised?"

"Yeah, I mean that."

"Them, too," I said.

"And you've got your own room?"

I sat up and observed this person in her white ski suit and white hat with a red ball for a long and exhilarating moment. "It's adjacent to my father's. There's a door—"

She took her hat off. Her hair was matted and short like a boy's. Fat rosy cheeks, windblown from skiing all day, slightly puggled nose. Chapped lips. More or less my age.

"But the door locks," she said.

"The door locks."

If only anything in my life since had gone this much without a hitch. It must have been at least a full day before we met up in my sliver of a room next to my father and Cindy Roo's. But hotel time is compacted, a day can be an hour, an hour a few minutes, and in the filth of memory—it happens almost instantaneously after she discerns that the adjoining door locks. That room, narrow and snug as a shoebox. From the bed you could touch all four walls. Above the bed was a rack, like they'd have on a train, where I kept my diminutive suitcase. There was a single round window, a porthole, out of which you could see the mountains. On the wall, a house phone. Claud (her name was Claudia, but she'd shortened it; she said she didn't like an *ia* on the end of anything) told me the room was where the manservant had stayed in the old days.

"Manservant?" I said. "I like it."

"You like it?"

Mornings Claud would clomp out the front doors of the hotel, her skis and poles cradled in front of her like she was carrying firewood. "Au revoir, mademoiselle!" the doorman would shout. Then she'd clomp clomp clomp, her ski boots pounding the cobblestones, around the block to the back door of the hotel and take the freight elevator up to my floor.

The phrase "losing your virginity" is so ludicrous it circles around to being accurate. Except forget the virgin part. Who's unpolluted? Either by our own hand—or, if we're luckier, by someone else's. But to lose. Yes, although in this case, the loss is a gain, and so becomes weight. You end up carrying it on your back. Years pass, and the loss becomes heavier. I'm trying to say that loss in these circumstances is a debt that increases. I'm muddling this. At the time, we fucked a lot. Crazy to think about the hormones of a couple of sweaty barely fifteen-year-olds in a minuscule room with unlimited access to room service. As if all we were was hormones, as if we had no other existence aside from the fact of hormones, hormones incarnate, we bedswam across those four or five days. And it wasn't as though there was anything to learn. How long had our bodies been preparing? Actual experience is a limitation. What we didn't know made us bolder. Those short Swiss days, those mountains, that little porthole window. We also talked. We probably talked more than anything. I told Claud the same things I'd told the concierge. About my emancipated brother and how he didn't give a shit about me so long as the State of Illinois didn't boss his ass around.

Claud would light a cigarette and pop her lips and send smoke rings to the ceiling. "I'm bored," she'd say like an actress. And she'd lie back and smoke and tell me about Tulsa. She said her father was up to his gonads in oil. Maybe that's why he can't find them anymore. And we're not even the richest Jews in Oklahoma. You'd be surprised how many of us are there. The Rabinowitzes are the richest, though they changed their name to the Travises. But you can tell they're Rabinowitzes.

"The noses?"

"Their teeth. All the Rabinowitzes are bucktoothed as horses."

"Oh."

"My mom's sleeping with the concierge."

"Pascal?"

"No, the concierge at the Gran Moritz."

"Pascal's brother Pascal."

"Her name is Karen."

"Oh."

"She does it every year. Not the same Karen."

"I guess that makes me kind of like your concierge."

"Except you don't know anything. Where's the Conditorei Hanselmann?"

"No idea."

"See?"

Horny kids, beyond horny. We were overheated baboons. At first, I remember, I kept my eyes closed. I wanted to feel whatever I was feeling, which was mostly a kind of stoned bewilderment, alone. I no longer had to imagine another body. And yet, I'm not so sure that I stopped imagining. Claud's body was as much in my mind as it was tangled up with my arms and legs. But after a while I did begin to open my eyes. I wanted to meet hers, but though her eyes stayed open, she never looked at me. Whatever position we were in, Claud always found a way to stare at the ceiling. This sounds joyless. That wouldn't be exactly accurate. I think we were both just concentrating so hard, separately, on the pleasure of it. And Claud would never say a word until we stopped and started talking again. She wanted to know all about Cindy Roo, like where my father found her. Did she have a middle name? Was she the prettiest of my father's girlfriends?

"She's the tallest," I said.

"And almost scrawny," Claud said. "She looks like a cadaver except that she goes on for miles. Thin lips."

"Uh-huh."

"And she's pigeon-toed."

"Cindy Roo is pigeon-toed?"

"Do you notice anything? Or does it all just pass by you in a fog? She's his secretary?"

"She's a realtor."

"Ask housekeeping to put on new sheets."

"Okay."

"You need to leave a note. Otherwise, they won't change the sheets."

"I said okay."

"My mom thinks I'm big-boned, which is weird because I'm so short. You think I'm big-boned?"

Right, at first I closed my eyes. I must have wanted to be alone. At first. But then, I remember, I didn't. It was too late. She looked at me only when we talked.

Once, my father called from the lobby. Claud answered and told him he had the wrong room. She hung up. He didn't call back.

For about a year afterward she wrote me letters.

There in the room she'd fall asleep, and I'd sit up against the wall and stare out the peephole at the mountains. Claud told me the Alps were above the tree line. Therefore, they weren't beautiful. She was right. The Alps weren't beautiful. They were bleached, treeless humps with ants streaming down them. And the weather was always the same, bright, no clouds. It must have snowed while we slept. Around four o'clock, when the lifts closed, Claud would put on all her gear and gather up her skis and poles from the corner of the little room and clomp out to the freight elevator. I'd get dressed and ride the regular elevator down to the lobby. After she thrashed through the revolving door, all suited up, skis and poles clattering, that red tassel bobbing on her head, she'd say "Hey" and plomp down next to me on the couch.

1984

Gina Aiello and Danny Fishbein going at it in my mother's bed—Italians and Jews unite! All roads lead to Rome! Next year in Jerusalem!—and Danny forgetting to lock the door, or maybe not forgetting, maybe he left the door open on purpose, and a whole parade of stoners looking for a place to fall down stumbled right into the action. I think that was the party when somebody figured out how to make a pipe out of an apple core. All we had was a dime bag and no way to smoke it. We were about to just dump the pot into a cereal bowl, light it on fire, and huff it up like that when somebody munching an apple said, "Hey, this here fruit has a porous core." And later, this overhappy crew wanders into my mother's bedroom, and Danny and Gina are in her bed, or on top of her bed, maybe they didn't bother with the sheets, and Gina rises up out of the darkness, flicks on the lamp beside the bed, and starts belting out "Maggie May," which whatever you want to say about Rod Stewart is one of the greatest songs ever written by mankind.

Gina was part of the theater crowd. She took any opportunity to perform before an audience no matter how sleepy and disinterested. Danny was one of those jocks who liked to mix it up with artsier kids. And according to one of the more observant stoners in the room that night, he didn't seem to mind the interruption and just stretched out on my mother's bed, his hands behind his head, and enjoyed Gina's singing.

We all did.

This was in the house my mother rented on Laurel Avenue across from the Episcopal church, where we'd moved after my mother, brother, and I fled my father's house with my mother's convertible full of our crap like we were the Clampetts. My father came home that night and asked, Where the hell's my family? Later, my mother said, You should have asked that question years ago.

Danny Fishbein took in the whole moment the way high-school athletes tended to see the rest of the world. Like the rest of us are sort of monkeys to them, but nice, interesting monkeys. The stoners collapsed on the carpet in a drowsy scrum.

And Gina sang.

We're prohibited by Mr. Stewart's management company from quoting the sublime lyrics.

I don't know if Gina ever acted, or sang, when she got out of school. I haven't heard about her since. What difference does it make that it was my mom's bed? Can't we be forgiven for believing she'd go on singing? If only in her head? A group of us was in the backyard trying to barbecue some frozen chicken breasts we'd rooted out of the freezer.

"Asswipe, you got to defrost the chicken first."

Somebody turned the music off.

Listen!

Gina, in my mother's room, the light on, the window open. We held our beers to our noses; nobody breathed.

The Captain

After they arrested the balloon lady, we bought our dope from a man who stood in a doorway on Howard Street dressed as Captain Kangaroo. Red suit with white trim, barn colors, fluffy white wig, the whole deal. You'd drive past him, and if he liked the look of you, he'd nod, almost imperceptibly. If he didn't signal, that was it. Once you were rejected, you couldn't drive by that same night. The balloon lady took all comers. She'd sell weed to nine-year-olds, along with a balloon. The Captain was more discerning. He didn't bother with any sort of front. And the transaction was fast, professional. If you got the nod, you parked whoever's mom's car you were driving on a side street off Howard and walked to the Captain's door on foot. He wouldn't be standing in the doorway anymore, but the door would be slightly ajar. You pushed it open. A little way up the stairs to his walk-up: the Captain. Exact change or forget it. He'd hand you a baggie and that was that. It was so public, so brazen, him standing there in that getup and selling right out of his apartment. Maybe he had it good for a while because he hid in plain sight. Or maybe the cops figured, whatever the guy wore, the fact that he conducted all own his business hand to hand was almost respectable.

This went on for months. We'd drive south to Howard Street, Friday nights. One night, he wasn't wearing his Captain suit. He was standing in the doorway in a bathrobe. No wig, either. And his nod was more emphatic. You could actually see his chin move up and down. Shackenberg parked his mom's Volvo a few blocks away. It was me, Joey Pignatari, and Newt Shackenberg. Joey said maybe his suit was at the cleaner's.

When we reached his door, he was sitting on the stairs as usual. But he held up empty hands. "Scholars," he said, "I'm temporarily out of stock. Would you like to come upstairs and listen to music?" It was the first time any of us had heard his voice. An older guy, a drug dealer in a bathrobe, invites some high-school juniors up to his apartment. To us, in 1985, it was the pinnacle of cool. Even Shackenberg was into it, and Joey and I only brought him with us because we needed his mom's car. We followed him upstairs. When we reached his apartment, the Captain asked us if we didn't mind taking our shoes off. There was a little rack outside his door.

The apartment itself was immaculate, two clean white couches, a coffee table with coffee-table books on it. There was art on the walls. A couple of large, well-stocked bookshelves. He had a cat.

We tried to hide our disappointment. The place was so dopey.

Joey made casual conversation. "So, who's your supplier?"

"A guy in Oconomowoc," the Captain said. "You know the place? Nice lake up there. Good swimming. Can I get you guys anything? Tea?"

We looked at our hands.

"We're good," Joey said.

"You guys into Keith Jarrett?"

He put on a record. We sat there listening while the Captain tapped his feet and grooved.

Drug dealers shouldn't let their guard down. They lose their mystique. It didn't bother us that this guy, by dressing up as a beloved children's TV character, preyed on suburban kids who'd pay double what city kids would pay for a dime bag. But a goofy-dad act? Joey shot me a look. *Give this a few minutes, see what happens.* When the music was over, the Captain went over to one of the bookshelves and pulled out a book.

"Listen to this," he said. "It'll blow your minds. 'One evening, I sat Beauty in my lap. —And I found her bitter—And I cursed her.' Rimbaud. Any of you young Turks been in love?"

Shackenberg asked if he could use the restroom.

The Captain shot his arm out straight. He made a clucking noise and jerked his thumb to the right. You know how some-times when people give directions, they overdo it? Normally, even back then, somebody quoted a little poetry—or whatever that was—and I'd get a little swoony. But I was beginning to feel sorry for him. The Captain was turning out to be one of those lonely people who just want you to stay. These people will do anything, including sit totally still, trying not to make one false move. Just so you won't leave. The whole time Shackenberg was taking a piss he sat like that, holding his book, as if he couldn't say a single word unless all three of us were present. He was just some guy in his early thirties. Totally presentable, aside from the fact that he was wearing nothing but a bathrobe. Without the Captain's wig, he had short black hair. Clean-shaven. A couple of droopy-looking tired eyes. He could have been anybody. Turned out he taught English at Loyola. We only wanted to get high.

This might have been a unique phenomenon of that era. Older guys befriending teenagers, not for sex (though I'm sure there was enough of that) but for a little company. Was it a time when certain people, for whatever reason, fell through some invisible social crack? There was this other guy we knew, Mel, who lived in a town house near the high school. We used to go to his place after school, drink warm beer, eat bag after bag of potato chips, and watch porn. But even this was oddly chaste. We'd sit there and stare numbly at the screen like we were scrutinizing plants.

We rode it out. We'd probably been there a couple of hours when the Captain, beat from keeping our little nonparty going, nodded off, slumped over on the couch with the cat in his lap. I've heard it said that it's impossible to hate a sleeping man. That a sleeping man's vulnerability is a kind of protection that wards off harm. We searched the place, pocketed a few pharmaceuticals. Shackenberg found a bottle of wine in a kitchen cabinet. After rummaging around in drawers to find a corkscrew, we took turns swigging it.

I find myself thinking about peripheral people in my life, people I hardly knew. Shouldn't I have forgotten about that forlorn clown by now? Why is the Captain—on the couch sleeping— more vivid to me than some of the people I see every day? We only paused in that apartment. It was a set of rooms we walked through. We knew that, whatever happened, we wouldn't be caught dead begging anybody's crumbs into our thirties. At least that much had been drummed into us. Our mothers had whispered we'd be kings. Of what it didn't matter. Joey took over his father's home-security business and turned it into an empire. He protects the entire North Shore from home invasion. Now he flies all over the world to run marathons. Shackenberg's a cosmetic orthodontist in the Loop. Even I'm regularly employed, in what you might call high-end hospitality. We went and got our shoes off the shoe rack, put them on, and went back into the apartment. On a signal from Joey, Shackenberg and I kicked him once each, hard, in the groin. I took a crack at the cat, missed. Cat yawned. We took off down the stairs into what's become the rest of our lives.

Solly

Not long ago, I came across a one-column obituary of Solly Hirschman. Solly Hirschman lived deep into the 2000s. How is it possible he'd been alive all this time? Solly was, for centuries, the owl-eyed editor of high-school sports for the *Chicago Sun-Times*. I'm sure he could've moved up to college or pro sports, but for Solly this wouldn't have been a promotion. Forget the Fightin' Illini, forget the Bears. Solly Hirschman breathed the infinite passion of secondary-school sports in Chicago. For a time, I was one of Solly's boys. Throughout my senior year in high school I'd drive my mother's car out to football games in Romeoville, Long Grove, Palatine, Bolingbrook, Mundelein. After the game, I'd call in the score from a pay phone. In the spring, I covered baseball, but this was only because football hadn't started again yet. Solly, like his readers, disdained baseball. Baseball was geometry and pansies. What he hungered for was full contact. The drill was that a stringer would attend a game and call in the score. Sounds simple, but it wasn't. Solly would pepper you with questions to satisfy himself that you'd actually been present at the game. Some of the more experienced stringers would often collude with stringers from smaller, local papers and call in a score without getting out of bed.

"Crowd?"

"Subdued. Wet."

"Weather?"

"Likewise, crap ass."

"Approximate temperature at halftime?"

"With the windchill or without?"

"Windchill's not a scientific fact, it's a cowardly state of mind."

And if the game was important in terms of the regional stand-ings, Solly would ask a few more questions, and you could hear him on the other end of the line, typing up a one-paragraph story.

"Any vicious tackles?"

"Second quarter linebacker Jablonski blitzed and knocked QB Thomason unconscious."

"Concussion?"

"Must have been multiple."

"Confirm with the coach or the team doctor?"

"Nope."

I was paid twenty-one dollars a game. The money was sent di-rectly to my house in the form of a check. Subtracting the gas I put in my mother's car to run all over Cook, Lake, Will, and DuPage Counties, I probably made more like ten bucks a pop. Didn't matter. And I've never cared less about sports, any sports. I was a reporter for the *Chicago Sun-Times*. I had a press pass that I had laminated at the fake-ID place on Dempster in Skokie. I used my credentials to gain access to the field at Deerfield High School when President Reagan landed there in a helicopter. I stood in a receiving line and shook Reagan's hand. It was huge and soft, more coddled foot than a hand.

And, once, I wrote a story for Solly Hirschman under my own name. It was about a guy who'd punted for Glenbard East and gone on, in the '70s, to appear as an extra on a few episodes of *Happy Days*. Now he'd come back to coach at his alma mater. Full circle, from Lombard, Illinois, to Hollywood and back to

Lombard. Amazing journey! It was the kind of human-interest sidebar that no genuine sports fan would have deigned to read.

My ex-punter was a dolt. All he wanted to talk about was how short Henry Winkler was. Like the man's a dwarf. "Did you have any idea?"

I told him I did have an idea.

"You knew!"

"That the Fonz is short? You can see it in the reruns. All you have to do is look at the heels of his boots."

But I got paid. Not for a score, for words. I've still got the clip somewhere. My mother had it framed. A few days after the story ran, Solly Hirschman called me at home.

"There's a man on the phone," my mother said.

"What man? Dad?"

"Your father's more of a mouse."

I took the receiver. One thing to call in a score and answer a few grunted questions; another for *Him,* unprompted, of his own volition, to pick up a phone and dial your number. Solly Hirschman had his little pixelated picture in the paper every day of every year. "Solly Hirschman on High-School Athletics."

"Come down and see me," Solly said.

"When?"

"Doesn't matter," he said, and hung up.

I took the train downtown early the next morning. On it, I ran into my father.

He lowered his *Tribune* and asked what I thought I was doing on the 7:08.

I told him I was fulfilling my destiny. He said fair enough, so long as it didn't cost him anything. The money he was sending my mother monthly was galling enough.

From Union Station, I walked to the old Sun-Times Building on North Wabash. More than a block long, it used to loom over the edge of the Chicago River. In Chicago, we build to destroy.

There's a grotesque hotel there now. I found Solly in his office on the fifth floor. No light on, no window, only the blue glow of his word processor. Before I poked my head in, I took a celebratory breath. I figured he'd praise me a little, rib me a little, and give me another assignment.

"Sit down," Solly said.

Behind his desk in the blue light he was all head and glasses, a life-size version of his picture in the paper. I never did get a look at the rest of his body, if he even had one. Everywhere, floor to ceiling, were stack upon stack of scores and notes on games. On his desk I was surprised to see, in the dim, a framed photograph of a little girl. The idea that Solly Hirschman had a child some-where was difficult to believe because it would have required him, at least once, to leave this habitat. There were no chairs or anything else to sit on.

"You don't have any talent," Solly said. "Your sentences are limp. You think it's too early to tell? It's not. Not that it matters. This building is crawling with limp sentences."

I waited for him to go on. He didn't. After a while he seemed to doze off but without taking his eyes off me. I was still standing there in front of his desk when a colleague, a columnist whose face I recognized, stuck his head in.

"He dead yet?"

"Can't tell."

"You a stringer?"

"Yeah."

"He say we're all hacks?"

"Yeah."

"He say you got nothing?"

"Yeah."

"Don't forget."

The columnist laughed his way out of earshot, down the bright fluorescent hall.

I didn't go home right away. I stood there in Solly's office. I'm a Jew, but I've always envied Catholics. They've got a designated place on earth to confess. The rest of us have to plead guilty to our silence, the sky, maybe a fogged-up bathroom mirror. Has there ever been a more genius invention than a wooden box you can enter, murmur a little, and, by the time you leave, you're in the clear? A visit with God's agent on earth and, voilà, you're free to steal and rob and fornicate anew. Who holds the patent on confessionals? We should put one up on every corner. Solly Hirschman was a Jew, too, somewhere in there, though he'd long ago put his faith in games, in scores, in young boys, in the way they bashed into one another every fall and into the winter, in the mud, in the cold, in the snow. He was right. I could fake my way through a story, but that's not the same as talent. I also knew it didn't matter, that it would never matter. I was young, the owl was old, and my limp sentences were in the *Chicago Sun-Times*. You were dead to me, Solly, before I even left your office.

IV

Castaways

Some persons are made more perfect by what befalls
them, as if whatever befalls them can never make them
less, can never bring them low, as it might others.

—Gina Berriault, "The Tea Ceremony"

Erwin and Pauline

They found Erwin floating facedown in the Chicago River, July, everything still in heavy bloom. He'd always been considered by the family to be a bit slow. Not very slow, just a bit slow. My grandmother always said Erwin was a very "pleasant" person. He worked, for years, as a custodian at Lane Tech High School on the North Side. He was much younger than my grandfather, who had always been more of an aloof father to him than a brother. The police decided there wasn't any foul play. It was hot the day they fished him out, over ninety. Maybe he just wanted to cool off, went one explanation. He was fully clothed, so this theory has never made much sense. Also, Erwin had never learned to swim.

Aside from how he died, the only other surprising thing Erwin did in his life was run off with a woman and get married. They drove to Reno and came back nine days later. She was a teacher. They'd met at Lane Tech. It wasn't that it was so shocking that she was black, though this wasn't unshocking, either. Didn't matter that it was the late '60s. Chicago is Chicago, and blacks and whites, then as now, lived in mostly separate universes. It was that Erwin had found a woman at all. Let alone a pretty one who wore high heels and taught French.

At the time they ran off together, Erwin was in his late thirties; Pauline was ten years younger. We called her Auntie Pauline because that's what she was. Still, I remember that when she was with us, we'd repeat her name multiple times, in the most ham-handed way. *Would Auntie Pauline like another drink? Auntie Pauline doesn't want to hear that story again. How many times do you think Auntie Pauline wants to hear about the time Erwin swallowed the half-dollar?* I say "we," though at the time I couldn't have been more than five or six. Even so, I, too, recognized the novelty of her being an official member of the family. Showing her my drawings, I'd say: *Auntie Pauline, Auntie Pauline, look, my dinosaur had babies.*

When we saw her, a few holidays out of the year, she was friendly and laughed a lot. Pauline also, we noticed, touched Erwin often. He'd be sitting there in his quiet way, and she'd be next to him on the couch, casually rubbing his forearm. The family was grateful. Grateful that Erwin didn't have to be alone anymore. We thought, What they say is true, there really is somebody for everybody. Beyond this, I don't think any of us thought all that much about them. Some relatives hardly seem to exist beyond the periphery of the family, or maybe the truth is they don't exist at all, on the periphery or otherwise, until they materialize on holidays, only to vanish again after a few hours.

Erwin and Pauline lived in a two-bedroom apartment on Spaulding, just off Irving Park Road. Maybe at night they put on a little classical music. WFMT. They were happy as far as anybody could tell.

Who knows where it went wrong, or even if it did. If we can't pinpoint such a moment in our own lives, why should we be able to in anybody else's? Maybe Pauline just got tired. Maybe, after a few years, it seemed like she was living with a child, because that's what Erwin always seemed to us: a big, friendly, somewhat-slow child. They split up in '74 or '75. For a while

Pauline continued to teach at Lane Tech. Then she moved away. On Thanksgiving of that year, Erwin uncharacteristically made an announcement at the table. He said that Pauline had accepted a job in Michigan, at the Interlochen School for the Arts.

"It's very prestigious," my grandmother said.

"Oh, it is," Erwin said.

Did he hear from her? Oh, yes, Erwin said. She calls every week. He smiled in the way he did, his eyes hiding, and went silent.

On holidays, those years after Pauline, he always let on how happy he was to see us. But you could tell he was going through the motions. Like he was indulging us, not the other way around. I think of him now, his stubble, his paunch, his sweaters with buttons, the stains on those sweaters, how he'd never look at you for more than a few seconds. He never recounted any memories himself. But when someone else told a story, he'd say, softly, *I do remember that, I do.* Then he'd go home and fade back into the life he lived, back to that apartment off Irving Park Road, back to his rounds at the high school. And the family remained grateful, grateful that he was still able to hold down a job, still able to care for himself. Erwin methodically moving from classroom to classroom, saying a quiet hello to a teacher working late. (Was this how he met Pauline in the first place?) A teacher who would say, Hello, Erwin. How are you? And back home again to the apartment, where he'd sit at the kitchen table and maybe read a magazine discarded by the school library. Because in the end we lacked imagination. We still lack imagination. His silence remains beyond us, the layers of it. The silence of Erwin breathing in the dark. What did we, who wouldn't have recognized the sound of our own beating hearts, know about silence, Erwin's or anybody's?

It was my grandfather who got the call. He said when he went to the Cook County morgue on Harrison Street to identify his brother, his body was swollen almost beyond recognition. "There wasn't a sheet over him," my grandfather said, "or anything. Isn't there supposed to be a goddamn sheet? City of Chicago can't afford a sheet to pull over my brother who was born here, died here?" But worse, he said, was that he immediately knew who it was. As if somewhere in the back of his mind he'd already pictured Erwin just like that, bloated, laid out on a table, prodded by strangers.

Everybody was waiting to see if Pauline would show up for the funeral, and she did, with a small boy in tow. She wore a brown business suit and flat shoes. But she couldn't hide that she was even more beautiful now, somehow. Maybe because I wasn't quite a kid anymore. When she took off her glasses, her hazel eyes were wet. She wasn't crying; it was as if she were storing up some tears for later. Wishful thinking (we pretended not to notice the ring), but we couldn't help but believe, if only for a moment, that the boy might be Erwin's son. A lost son we hadn't known was lost. The math didn't work out at all. The child was only four; she'd been gone at least a decade by then. Pauline hugged everyone—brief, efficient hugs—but they weren't without what we believed to be a genuine squeeze of affection. The little boy was polite and shy and shook hands with everybody. The two of them didn't come back to my grandparents' house for cold cuts.

Do You Have Enough Light?

By then Esther wasn't speaking to anyone, not my father, of course, the two hadn't exchanged words in years, and not her parents, my grandparents, either, though now she lived in their house again. Aunt Esther was in her late forties when she moved back home. The word was that she was "a little off." Nobody but my father went as far as to say she was crazy. He'd tell anybody who listened what a loon his sister was. That January she'd been picked up by the Chicago police in Lincoln Park whispering to trees, wearing nothing but a kimono. I've always remembered this, that my mother described what Esther had on that night as a kimono. I'm not sure I even knew what a kimono was, but I could see her. That gossamer dress, how it must have fluttered in the wind. The kimono incident almost had her put away. My father was certainly for it, but he lacked the authority to make it happen. Instead, my grandparents moved her into Olivia's old room in the basement. Olivia, my grandparents' live-in housekeeper for more than forty years, had finally retired a few years earlier and gone to live with her sister in Albany Park. Olivia's bed was still there, as was the tall bureau. Inside one of the drawers was a pile of Olivia's light blue uniforms. In the months after Olivia left, I remember going down there and stick-

ing my nose in those starchy uniforms as if that bleachy smell
alone could bring her back.

Having Esther in the house must have been a comfort to
my grandparents. At least now they'd be able to keep track
of her. In the morning my grandmother would make Esther
breakfast. She hadn't made a meal for anybody in years, Olivia
had always done the cooking, and my grandmother overdid it.
For Esther, she'd make French toast, piles of sausages, lox and
bagels, and a soft-boiled egg, which she'd put in one of those
funny eggcups and carefully saw off the top with a knife. And
she'd leave everything on the kitchen table covered by plates
to keep it all hot. Then my grandmother would flee the house,
not being able to bear it. A daughter who once had so much
going for her. What didn't Esther have going for her? Beauty,
brains, the whole package. Hadn't she graduated magna cum
laude from Champaign?

Esther never ate the breakfast. She'd leave for work without
taking a single bite. Esther worked the whole time she lived with
my grandparents. People forget this. My grandfather found her
a position in a dentist's office in Northbrook as a part-time re-
ceptionist. She could still face the world. It was her family she
couldn't stomach.

Those were mornings of the opening and closing of doors. My
grandfather would listen to the front door open and close (my
grandmother) and the basement door open and close, followed
by the front door once again opening and closing (Esther). Only
then would he emerge from his study, where he'd been sleeping
for years on the foldout couch. He was retired and occupied
his time organizing his letters and photographs from the war.
He'd creep into the kitchen in his socks and eat Esther's breakfast. In part because he was famished (he was on a special diet
for his heart) but also to make it look to my grandmother as
if Esther had eaten. I'm not sure he ever fooled her, eating, as

he did, everything in sight. My aunt, when she did eat, ate like a sparrow. And sometimes, after Esther came home from her shift at the dentist's, but before my grandmother came home—from shopping, a luncheon, or the exercise class she taught at the rec center—my grandfather would step heavily, slowly, down the basement stairs and knock on Esther's door and ask if she needed anything. "Another lamp, darling? Do you have enough light?" She never answered.

They'd always been close. On a shelf in the study, next to his golf trophies, he displayed the beer steins she used to give him every year on Father's Day. HAPPY FATHER'S DAY 1968, HAPPY FATHER'S DAY 1969, HAPPY FATHER'S DAY 1970, and so on.

My grandfather would stand outside the door to Olivia's old room and wait. His daughter wouldn't answer. He'd turn and climb up the basement stairs as if from the bottom of a well.

That year I hung out at my grandparents' house after school. My parents had recently split up. I saw my father on Wednesday nights and every other weekend. Most weekday afternoons I'd lie on the rug in my grandparents' living room and watch WGN on the big Zenith until my mother came and picked me up after work. On one of those afternoons, Esther rose out of the basement and asked me if I wanted to come downstairs.

"You can wait until after the Cubs," she said.

Though for years Esther always made a point of buying me stuffed animals, she hadn't acknowledged my existence since her return to my grandparents' house.

"I don't give a shit about the Cubs," I said.

"You don't care who wins?"

"No."

I was eleven. I had my own problems. Esther stood there in the kitchen archway still wearing the skirt and blouse she'd worn to work. It was always said that Esther was too beautiful for her own good. A prophecy that proved itself to be true. What did her looks ever do for her? Old friends of hers, to this day, recognizing my name, come up to me and breathlessly ask, What happened? What happened to Esther Popper?

Her glossy brunette hair piled chaotically high on her head, always a few strands dangling past her enormous, starlet eyes. About a year or so after she moved home, Esther was diagnosed with an advanced cancer and died eight months later.

I followed her down the stairs to Olivia's old room. I'd slept down there so many nights beside Olivia and her three cats, Henry, Harry, and Charles. The room looked the same, or as much the same as it could now that Esther was living in it. She hadn't changed anything or put up any pictures, and she hadn't seemed to have brought anything with her from the apartment in the city. Olivia's small crucifix remained above the bed. Had Olivia been trying to send us some message by leaving it behind? Only the good Lord can help these people.

Esther sat on the bed. She beckoned me to sit next to her, which I did. There was a book tented on the comforter. What I'd give now to know what book it was. My grandparents' house has long been torn down and all the contents sold or scattered.

Esther reached and picked up a bottle on the nightstand. "Excedrin?"

"No, thanks."

She popped a couple of pills in her mouth and swallowed without water. "Are you scared?" she said.

"Why would I be?" I said.

"Aren't I some kind of freak?"

"You work in a dentist's."

She stared at me directly, as if deciding whether to laugh. She seemed to decide in favor of it, but by then it was too late. She picked up her book and started reading again. Why did she summon me? Because I was a remnant? A token of a vanished time when even shopping for stuffed animals meant some kind of hold in the world?

The basement door opened. I listened to my grandfather's heavy, careful steps as he descended. He didn't have much time left himself. We were becoming a family of tatters. Three months after Esther's funeral, my grandmother came home and found him toppled over on the floor of the study. The paramedic said the attack was so massive he hardly could have felt anything at all. Like being blindsided by a bus, the paramedic said. Why is this always the measure? As if the absence of suffering in someone's final moments somehow cancels—

Happy Father's Day 1977, Happy Father's Day 1978.

When he knocked on the door, and even after he spoke, "But, darling, isn't there anything at all you need?" I didn't answer, either. And then Esther did laugh, not out loud, to herself. My grandfather didn't knock again. He stood outside the door for a couple of minutes before going back upstairs.

Uncle Norm Reads Spinoza as His Cookie Business Collapses Due to the Rise in Sugar Prices in the Dominican Republic

For a long time, from the early '50s to the middle '70s, it was a good business. He supplied cookies to 4-H Clubs nationwide. They weren't high-end cookies. They were basic cookies, simple vanilla wafers, nearly tasteless, but a cookie is a cookie, and even a bland one still has a certain joy in it. Alf Dolinsky sold floor coverings. Teddy Wolfson was in the plate-glass business. Sy Kuperchmid and his brothers exported umbrellas. Freddy Weissman made a fortune in hats. Irv Friedman, notebook rings. Notebook rings, in those days you could make a fine living selling notebook rings. Barry Gitlin sold zippers. Walt Kaplan, furniture and home appliances. Hal Hodash, sweaters, men's coats, and outerwear. Kermit Baumgartner, aluminum siding. They were Fall River men. They dealt in tangibles. Some businesses went bust; others lasted generations. Norm Litwak made cookies, and a man who produces cookies God smiles on, at least for a while.

All bodies are in motion or at rest.

A reader, Uncle Norm lamented, without ever saying it out loud, never having gone to college. College wasn't done. Not then. At twenty-one, he was already a married man with a daughter. Not that he had any illusions about what he might have learned had he gone. Norm prided himself on being a self-taught pointy-head. His office above the factory floor was stuffed with books. He'd often stay late, his feet on an open desk drawer, his glasses shoved up his forehead because he was both near- and farsighted and needed bifocals but had never bothered to buy a pair. Plus, he liked the smell of paper up close like that. He's up there now, having sent everyone home early. It's March of '76. The *Herald News* is on the floor. Enough with the news. Sugar's quadrupled. He's doomed. What else is there to know? He'll be lucky to make it through the month. He can't go home to Ida, not yet. She'll read the ruin on his face, and Ida's never been one to accept that ruin's the only constant there is and that unruin is snow in a Fall River August. So you can't call the end of a near miracle—twenty-odd years afloat in a fickle business—a catastrophe. Ruin, Ida, did you really think it wasn't out here waiting for us?

Bodies are individual things which are distinguished from one another in respect of motion and rest, and so each body must be determined to be in motion or at rest by another thing, namely, another body.

He knows he should be postulating upon practical considerations. Sugar and price and volume; credits, debits, and payroll. What Spinoza would call substances. All of which are part of an integrated system. Proving, by the way, in this particular case, that a little island in the Caribbean can reach out and plunk an inconsequential entrepreneur in southeastern Massachusetts right in the nose. Instead, he thinks of Ida sleeping, never at rest, always in motion. For Ida, sleeping is only a brief cessation of purposefulness, not anything resembling repose. Norm thinks of how some nights she sprawls across to his side of the bed, nearly touching him. Other nights she balls herself up so tight you'd think she was trying to vanish. And sometimes when he reaches for her it's as if she feels his touch ahead of his fingers, as if the slow movement of his hand creates wind and that wind breathes in her ear before even skin meets skin. Not a recoil— just a hardly perceptible edging away. But *other* other nights, it's as if she has a little room to spare, and she takes his reaching hand and pulls, yanks, him to her side and almost simultaneously into her, hurried but unhurried, now, and there is no time anymore so now could be yesterday, tomorrow, next week, and it's as Spinoza says, they merge, two unrelated things, substances, bodies in motion, together, yes, one, God and nature, everything and anything. And the rabbis said you didn't believe. Wasn't the problem that you believed too much? That our own standing as part of an integrated universe not only allows us but, by singular divine fiat, compels—induces—us to connect, to merge, to unify—

Am I even close, Baruch? That every bit *is* the whole, that every occurrence—

No, they weren't great cookies, but it was a living. The moment he walks in the door, she'll read his face. Out the grimy little window, he looks down on the shop floor. Lining the far wall are boxes waiting to be shipped. He'll break the news tomorrow or the day after.

They'll go idle in three weeks, maybe he can stretch it out to a month. Reduce to a skeleton crew. Friedman might take a few of his people. And he's already talked to Walt about Clarence, because he used to be a reupholsterer. Then, eventually, it will be just him and Sheila keeping vigil over the machines he might still be able to sell. The rest, scrap. He'll give up the lease, pay the penalty for early termination. (Talk to Plotkin, possible to write that off?) And then?

Well, nature and God don't cease over the early termination of a lease. And consider that all the ways in which a body is affected by another body follow from the nature of the affected body. As if it is the affected body itself that determines, invites—

Tonight, maybe, he'll reach for her. And maybe his hand will stop short before she can feel its wind and so remain, for the moment, an unaffected body, separate, contained, alone.

But another night—tomorrow night, or the night after—

Bernard: A Character Study

They found my mother's first cousin frozen in a rented cabin up in New Hampshire, not far from where he'd gone to prep school. A smart kid, Bernard enrolled at Harvard on a math scholarship in the fall of 1973. This was after his father, Uncle Horace, was busted for running a scam with his brother, Bernard's uncle, and their "investment firm" went belly-up. (The brother promptly shot himself.) But for the money the two brothers hadn't managed to con out of my grandfather, Horace might have gone to jail. My grandfather used his savings to pay the lawyers. Bernard was Uncle Horace and Aunt Josephine's only child. That he still made it to Harvard (Horace's alma mater), he was that much of a genius at math, was supposed to be the redemption of that side of the family. If Bernard made good, something might be said for disgrace. Harvard!

But LSD. It was the LSD Bernard took at Harvard, the family has always said, without evidence, that doomed him. Because wasn't the stuff everywhere? Wasn't Cambridge crawling with LSD in the '70s? They grew it in labs and doled it out to kindergartners. Bernard dropped out of Harvard, or was thrown out, midway through his second year and returned to Fall River, where he hung around for the next thirty years, clawing out a living selling ads for the *Herald News*.

I always had a soft spot for Bernard because he was kind to my grandmother. After my grandfather died, Bernard would drive her to the Peoples Drug or Almacs for groceries, or to a hair appointment. When I'd see him in person, it always cost me: a ten or a twenty, whatever I had in my wallet.

Bernard had a great talent for falling in love. There were at least two official marriages and one recognized by Massachusetts common law. There were (at least) three kids, one adopted son and two daughters of his own, and, as a result, multiple court orders mandating support he could never pay in full or on time. Even so, Bernard was a doting father, or at least tried to be, and he scuttled all over southeastern Massachusetts and Rhode Island trying to hold things together, which was impossible because there wasn't anything to hold together. There were only scattered families he'd had a hand in creating, but which had, as soon as he was out of the daily picture, naturally moved on without him.

If not for the job at the *Herald News* he wouldn't have had much of anything at all, and as it was he was constantly hard up. And yet: imagine young Bernard and his bevy of cousins, my mother included, prancing around Uncle Horace and Aunt Josephine's place in Mattapoisett back when not only wasn't the money tainted, it flowed, gentle, like the Mattapoisett River flowed into Buzzards Bay. The family frolicked in that cash for years. And think of Bernard, at fifteen, lanky in his suit and clip-on tie, leaving home for Phillips Exeter. And see him? In the fall of '73, in the aftermath of his uncle's suicide and all that subsequent public humiliation, Horace in the papers, and still Bernard marching, head held high and jammed with algebra so advanced it no longer had anything to do with numbers or even symbols that represent numbers, straight into Harvard

Yard, having made it there not because of but in spite of his father.

Bernard was a monumentally shitty driver, and when he drove my grandmother to the drugstore, she'd always clamp her eyes shut and pray to the God she'd never had much use for that they'd make it to the store in one piece, and Bernard would say, "Aunt Sarah, open your eyes and live a little," as the car careened down Robeson Street like they were escapees. Because Bernard always drove, walked, ran, as though he'd just scaled a wall or climbed a fence and might as well live it up on the lam while he still had the chance. Even if he was only on the run from his cubicle at the *Herald News* or his hardly furnished one-bedroom in Globe Corners, or on account of one of his exes sending the law to hound him over unpaid support—he was always in motion.

He used to call my mother, 3:00 a.m. Chicago time. *Just want to talk, Miriam. You can take your wallet out of your nightie. Though, in the morning, if you want to Western Union a contribution to save my ass, my ass would appreciate it.* But really, truly, at the end of the day, it wasn't money. What he wanted was to indulge in some mutual memory from their childhood, and he'd say: Remember when little cousin Jacob bled to death in the kitchen on Woodlawn Street? Who knew we had royal blood in the family? And my mother would say, Bern, you weren't even born when Jacob, there's no way you could have—

"You wouldn't think a kid so small could have so much blood. Niagara Falls. You think it's true about Molly and Max?"

And my mother would respond in a whisper as if her own dead mother could hear the betrayal from the grave: "Those two did have the same-shape heads."

Because even in the '80s it was still an illicit story, that dark old chestnut about my mother's (and Bernard's) grandparents being first cousins. The hemophilia being prima facie evidence.

The fact that I just let this out without being struck by lightning is a testament to how even the most closely held family taboos dissolve eventually into only words. Bernard especially liked the moral of the story—how the curse was visited on an innocent seven-year-old—because above all he considered himself the family truth teller. He took pride in always being willing to say what nobody else ever would. The man was a champion liar, but he could tell the truth like nobody's business. It was the only currency he ever had in abundance. Of his father, Horace, a man he dearly loved—Bernard was a man who loved generously, fiercely, all over the place—he used to say that by the time he was old enough to crawl into his old man's lap, he knew his father was a charlatan. "Beware of any man who walks around calling himself a philanthropist. Philanthropist isn't a job, it's a cover story."

I've no idea how Bernard survived after he finally got canned by the *Herald News*. He lived another seven or eight years. Eventually he was so broke he couldn't live in Fall River, which Bernard would have been the first to say is saying something. He loved his city as only a native could. He knew the streets, the potholes. He knew the hills, seven of them, just like in Rome. Bernard knew where the falls and the river that gave the city its name were hiding beneath the rubble of the now long-defunct mills. And if Fall River was getting shabbier, it was all right with Bernard. Unlike Providence, unlike Boston, Fall River no longer had an overpompous block on its map. Even the Highlands, where the mill owners built their mansions, weren't stuck-up anymore. Fall River made no effort to reconcile its present degradation with its once-glorious past. That's honest. And as a Jew in a Catholic city, Bernard would always be, no matter his knowledge, no matter his affection, a little at arm's length. But even this felt right. Fall River was home, but it never fully embraced you. That's honest, too. When Bernard returned from Harvard after a year and a half, only about an hour and change away, his city took him back, mostly. What's one more loser? Three more decades he lived there. Until even Fall River couldn't sustain him anymore.

The last time he called my mother, Bernard said he'd started a T-shirt and screen-printing business. No hard sell, he just wanted her to know, in case she wanted in on the ground floor. She'd see a return of something like 200 percent on her initial investment within just a few months because, Mirry, hear me out, I've already got more preorders than I can handle.

I don't know if it was the cold that killed him in the rented cabin or whether he froze only after whatever else got him first. I have no way of knowing. I'm sure there's a death certificate on file somewhere in New Hampshire, and I could probably go up there and cajole it out of a somnolent clerk on the grounds of being an interested cousin. Which wouldn't be true, though I am—was—a cousin. A second cousin once removed? Removed from where? A third cousin? But my point is, no, I don't want to make a point. I only want to repeat what you already know. That there isn't any limit to how far a person can fall in America.

How do you explain a life like Bernard's? Pretend that it was any single incident, or chain of incidents, that finally did him in? Go chronologically from the time his father and uncle were busted for a racket through each of Bernard's three or four wives? Why invent a timeline when every day the man managed to get out of bed and smile at the world—and he did smile, Bernard smiled all the time—was only another day closer to the day the landlord in New Hampshire found him in that unheated cabin after ten days because the rent was late? The smile must have been a mask, but there was, also, it's true, something frantically happy about Bernard. I think he woke up every day and thought, Today I'll catch a break. I can see him ginning himself up in the mirror: Got a few irons in the proverbial fire, something might pay off, I can feel it. And in the afternoon, I'll go and visit the girls, Kate in Brockton, Debbie in Seekonk. And tomorrow, Saturday, I'll take Jeff for French toast at HoJo's.

Because being broke, Bernard would be the first to tell you, is different from being poor. Broke signifies the possibility of becoming rich or, as in Bernard's case, rich again. Broke is temporary, subject to interpretation, fluid. Broke's always got a bright side.

He was the tallest member of the family on record. His parents were tiny human beings. Horace was squat and puckery. Josephine was wispy, doll-like, elegant. Bernard was a beanstalk who even in his teens towered over them. He was also the only one in the extended family with curly hair, a great mass of chaotic hair that rained dandruff. He'd be having lunch with my grandmother at the China Express in the strip mall by the industrial park and he'd say, "Holy shit, Aunt Sar, it's snowing in my wonton soup."

And there were the two large blue-black bowls under his exhausted eyes.

When Bernard returned to Fall River in 1975, Uncle Horace wouldn't speak to him. Since most people in town weren't speaking to Horace, he'd ripped that many people off, it must have made him feel better that there was someone left he could give the silent treatment. I think that for Horace, failure in business, even if that failure was caused by deliberately orchestrated financial crimes, was a whole different deal than what he would have considered "personal" failure. A man taking drugs when he wasn't sick? Wrecking a head for numbers that could have led God only knows where? Courting ruin from within when things were hard enough without? It would have made no sense to Horace. After Aunt Josephine's death, though, as he became increasingly frail, Horace had no choice but to allow his son to drive him to the pharmacy and to the doctors. And eventually it was Bernard who packed his father off to the Jewish Home for the Aged. It was Bernard who carried his father's few boxes of effects—all that was left—and stacked them neatly in a corner of Horace's final small room.

"It's a cell," Horace said.

"Looks like it," said Bernard, who'd known one or two.

He was forty-eight when they found him. The Fall River Philanthropic Burial Society, an organization that has been burying Fall Riverites for the last 140 years, buried Bernard next to his mother in 2004.

On the gate in front of Beth El Cemetery, there's a plaque with a Talmudic poem on it:

The world is like
A vestibule before
The world to come;
Prepare thyself in
The Vestibule that
Thou mayest enter
Into the hall.

I've stood at the cemetery gate and read this poem many times. Every time I visit my dead, I copy it down into whatever notebook I'm carrying. I'm drawn to this idea of the world as a vestibule, which I think of as a place to take off your boots: a mudroom. I doubt that Bernard made it into the hall, but it wasn't for lack of being busy in the vestibule. And who knows? Maybe this is what the rabbis mean by preparing thyself. Keep hustling. You'd see Bernard loping up South Main, that wild bramble of hair sticking out in every direction, from Columbia to Pocasset Street, heading for the *Herald News,* with great purpose and speed, as if, as I say, he wanted to put as much distance as possible between where he was going and where he was coming from. But the man couldn't go three feet without being hailed like a taxi. The deputy mayor, Lucille who worked at the Dunkin' Donuts, a cop, a junkie, some half-dead elder who knew his father from the chamber of commerce, the sexy librarian who drove in from Bristol, Rhode Island, the cashier at the savings and loan, Josiah Nadley who owned the comic-book/smutty-magazine store at 803 South Main.

Everybody demanded an audience with Bernard.

Nadley: "Hey Bern, how about that General Grant I lent you in February?"

Bernard: "February? It was April. Aren't I good for it, Josiah? Fifty? It was thirty-five. You charging interest? What, Shylock? My old friend? You can't be usurious!"

And Josiah Nadley, a titanic, sedentary man, roars a laugh and bellows to the entire street, to what's left of downtown Fall River, the old Borden Block, the vacated storefronts, the payday-loan outfits. "Do we love this guy or do we not love this guy?" Then he raises a shoe and wobbles a moment before ramming that worn-out brogan down hard on Bernard's foot, once, twice, three times. "How could anybody not love, love, *love* this guy?"

Fall River Wife

It's said that after Delmore Schwartz went bonkers, the aged wunderkind's poems began to sag like his once-lean body. Poetry no longer paid. I mention this because an uncle of mine had a brief connection to Schwartz during those final batty years. He wasn't my uncle. Uncle Monroe wasn't anybody's direct uncle. He was an uncle in the way that every man of a certain age is an uncle. Technically, he was an uncle's brother, Uncle Horace's. Monroe wasn't his real name, either. He'd been born Morton. Everyone in Fall River called him Mort. At some point, in the '50s, just as he and Horace were beginning to make it as investment bankers, Mort changed his name to Monroe. At first, people laughed. *Your father arrived cargo from Danzig in 1912. Now he captained the* Mayflower? Soon enough, the brothers were so rich, nobody thought Monroe's new name was so hilarious.

James Joyce says there's one tony relative in every family. In my mother's, there were two. The Sarkansky brothers made good. Made very good. Eventually: outlandishly good. Turned out they were only moving money around—first piles, then hills, then small mountains. The old con: rob Peter to pay Paul and around and around and around. A happy circle until Paul stops getting paid because Peter, for whatever reason, starts sniffing around and asks one too many questions. When that happened, in the mid-'60s, Uncle Monroe shot himself, leaving Uncle Horace holding an empty bag with a fat hole in it. By then, the Sarkansky brothers were in hock to the tune of millions. Only the major investors got anything back.

Family and friends ate the losses whole.

But for that good while, nearly two and a half decades, things were flush, and the two brothers were the highest of fliers. They called themselves industrialists. What exactly was meant by this, nobody knew, but a title like that seduces. And who wouldn't have been sweet-talked by Monroe Sarkansky? His Manhattan office address? An apartment on East Seventy-Seventh? The pied-à-terre in Nassau? (Before I was born, my parents once stayed in this pied-à-terre.) Uncle Monroe played a good tycoon. Flamboyance and conspicuous spending were part of his act. So were the fedora worn aslant and the fake English accent. My grandfather said he sounded less British than constipated. As if Mort had been stuffing all his dough up his you-know-what.

People should have known a dependable 8, 9, even sometimes 10 percent per quarter return on their investment was too good to be true. But whoever puts the kibosh on what's too good to be true? Start making money like that, people begin to think they deserve it.

Adding to his mystique was the fact that Monroe "maintained" a wife back home in Fall River. Monroe had, long ago, left domestic life behind, but he'd never, gallant that he was, divorce his Fall River wife. Occasionally, he'd breeze into town and visit the old homestead on Locust Street before screeching back to Manhattan in his limousine. On one of these conjugal visits, a child was conceived. The '50s were contradictory. Ike and picket fences. But if you had enough money and panache, you could get away with murder. Even Fall River couldn't help going a little nutty over a native with a chauffeur. He was always in the paper. A throwback to the heyday when Spindle City reigned supreme as the undisputed textile capital of the planet, when, it used to be said, Fall River produced enough cloth per year to wrap around the world fifty-seven times and still have enough left over to make a suit for William Howard Taft.

For years, I never even knew Monroe's wife's name. But I heard things. "Brilliant" was one. "Troubled" was another. My mother once let slip that she'd been "disturbed."

Uncle Horace was the more modest of the two brothers, less the conquering hero. He was quiet, diligent, bespectacled. And in his respectable way, Horace collected the life savings of family and friends, except, it is always noted, Irv Pincus. Irv, being a crook himself, knew a swindle when he saw one. But whoever listened to Irv Pincus? Sure, Uncle Horace had a palatial house up in the Highlands and a summer place at Mattapoisett known as the Shambles, but his role was to project sobriety and prudence. If any investor had doubts about the one brother, they could be reassured by the other, depending on their taste.

In '64, when a couple of shell companies went under unexpectedly, the brothers found themselves without enough cash flow to pay out that quarter's interest. The sudden announcement of losses tipped off some of the bigger fish that something stank. These investors called in their principals. The beauty of it had always been the utter simplicity. Money in, money out, easy as breathing. They didn't make anything, sell anything, or even, the amazing thing, invest in anything. When it collapsed, it all went poof, there being nothing there in the first place. (Aside, of course, from what they'd skimmed and spent.) The story goes that at a dinner party in Montauk attended by Sammy Davis Jr., Carol Channing, and a couple of sheikhs from Arabia, Monroe excused himself, saying, "Wouldn't it be jolly to have a look at the moon?"

He used a pearl-handled pistol.

Monroe's corny last line brings it back to Delmore Schwartz. At the apex of his wealth, Uncle Monroe began to pursue in earnest what was, apparently, his only true passion. He loved money, who doesn't, but more than anything else, Monroe Sarkansky longed to be a poet. A published poet. He found it no more difficult than hustling relatives. He hosted a few bohemian gatherings. He provided oceans of premium-grade hooch. The doors of the New York literary citadel flung open. One drunk writer led to another. It's said it was the critic Anatole Broyard, knowing his old friend was hard up and possibly losing his senses, who suggested that Monroe pay Delmore Schwartz for poetry lessons. "Pay him enough and he won't say no," Broyard told Monroe. Or, is said to have said. This is all third- and fourthhand. And Schwartz, though he may well have hated himself for it, agreed to give poetry lessons in his Greenwich Village apartment to a grotesquely wealthy man with airy dreams. Schwartz only demanded that Monroe order his driver to park the limo around the corner. He didn't want to see it when he looked out the window.

Now: there is no evidence, judging from the three volumes of poetry Monroe Sarkansky published in quick succession (one posthumous) with the Dial Press from 1965 through 1969, that he learned a single thing from Delmore Schwartz. At least not the Schwartz who wrote:

O Nicholas! Alas! Alas!
My grandfather coughed in your army,
Hid in a wine-stinking barrel,
For three days in Bucharest
Then left for America
To become a king himself.

Monroe would have understood the hunger to become a king of America. But no, zero, not a line of Monroe's poetry sings. I'm hard on the man out of loyalty to my people, especially my dead-broke dead grandfather who died before I had a chance to know him much, but even now I can't force myself to quote even one line, not even to make fun of it, which would be too easy—though I've got all three of Monroe Sarkansky's books right here with me. *Gardenias and Salamanders. The Golden Afternoon. A Mother's Love and Other Poems.* It is telling, isn't it, that after all their losses, my grandfather, and after his death my grandmother, held on to the books. The fake name on these spines is the only thing left of his fake fortune.

I can't help wondering about those poetry lessons. For six months, Monroe spent Thursday afternoons in Delmore Schwartz's apartment on Charles Street in the West Village. Most of Schwartz's friends had begun to distance themselves. (They'd wait until he was dead to write about him. Who from that time, from his set, didn't take a crack at Delmore Schwartz after they found him alone, crazy, and very dead in a Times Square hotel in 1966? His fall into madness was just too delicious.) So, it's possible that a dapper wannabe in an exquisitely tailored suit and a fedora was harmless-enough company for forty-five minutes. And at $150 per session, cash, it beat what most magazines paid for poems. Schwartz must have known the man was beyond hope. You might make a poet out of someone who's never written a poem. But give a fraud of an investment banker eyes to see? Even so, it stands to reason that the two of them, the poet and the eager student, must have settled into their afternoons together. Delmore Schwartz might have sat in a chair and recited a few lines as Monroe stood by hoping that mere proximity to poetry might do the trick.

Schwartz may have even told Monroe one of his darlings.

You know, don't you, that Wallace Stevens was a lousy lawyer?

They only kept him around the insurance company because he was such a magnificent poet!

When Schwartz laughed, he hooted.

And maybe after discoursing for a while, Schwartz would doze off, and Monroe would stand there and wait.

A half hour later, Schwartz opens his eyes and says, "You're still here? Did you pay me?"

"We still have eight minutes left on the lesson."

"By whose authority? The New York Stock Exchange?"

And I also wonder if there came a moment when Schwartz, more paranoid by the day but still, deep down, the street-smart kid from Brooklyn, let his obedient pupil know that he saw through it, the elegant suit, the fedora, the accent—

Schwartz makes a paper airplane out of one of Monroe's verses and launches it out the window. "What kind of kike uses the word 'bough' for 'branch'?"

"'Branch' doesn't rhyme with 'Frau,'" Monroe says.

Schwartz smiles. You can't argue with that. And it's been days (weeks?) since he's smiled. Not since he wrote a ditty commemorating the death of Robert Frost, that frosty-haired toad.

"Anatole tells me you've got a loony wife home in Holyoke," Schwartz says.

"Fall River."

"Ah, our dead mill towns are romantic, aren't they?"

"They are?" Monroe says. "I never—"

Schwartz probes a nostril with his finger. "So, this wife moldering away? Now there's a subject we can work with. How about a few lines about Miss Havisham? How many poems can one man write about mist?"

Maybe the pupil answered. Maybe he didn't. Probably he was just flattered that Schwartz took any interest in him at all. Still, he might have said, One man can write innumerable poems about mist, Professor Schwartz.

And it may have been Broyard (or Saul Bellow or Dwight Macdonald or Alfred Kazin) who recounts it, but eventually Schwartz tossed Monroe out on his ear. Farewell, my millionaire, I got vendettas to dream up, up, up.

If Monroe wasn't officially family, his wife was even less so. After all those losses, financial and otherwise—the amount of the loss always grew in the telling, year after year—who in the family wanted to be reminded of Mort Sarkansky or whatever the hell his name was? Or his wife? But even back in its brief peak, Jewish Fall River was still a postage stamp. A few blocks in the Flint. A few German Jews and upstarts scattered across the Highlands. In an ancient cabinet at the Temple Beth El office (a kind of card catalog of the dead) I found her name: Eleanor (Ellie). Maiden name: Weissman. Her father was a partner in a large Fall River hat factory, Marshall Hat, the company that made, among other headwear, Monroe's fedoras.

My mother and I were in the kitchen. This was about a decade ago now. My mother, keeper of our family secrets. All information is on a need-to-know basis, and the basis is you don't need to know.

"Why'd they sock her away?" I asked.

"Sock who?"

"Monroe's wife."

"Monroe?"

"Mort!"

"Oh, Mort. You know your father and I once stayed at his pied-à-terre in St. Thomas."

"Nassau."

"Was it in Nassau? Your father thought he died and went to

heaven. I should have left him there. The place came with a but-
ler. I wish I could remember his name. Marcel? I'd step out of
the pool, and this beautiful man would be standing there with a
robe, the softest—"

"But what about her?"

"Let the dead bury their dead, isn't that what people say?"

"Not Jews," I said.

My stepfather, Herb, called from the next room, where he was
watching the Blackhawks on mute. "He's right," Herb said. "Jews
don't say let the dead bury their dead. We say, 'Call Piser's and
let's get this over with as soon as possible.'"

"Why'd they put her away?" I said.

My mother took a sip of her martini and shrugged. Maybe she
was calculating the statute of limitations on material intelligence
concerning nonfamily members and figured what the hell. How
many people alive even remember these people existed?

"Mort had a stroke."

"What? What about the pearl-handled pistol? What about
Sammy Davis?"

"Sammy Davis was there, I think; so was Carol Channing.
Mort and Carol Channing may have had a thing. But it was a
stroke. My father made that up about the gun."

"Why?"

"Poetic justice?" my mother said, coughing and laughing at
the same time, remembering her father, a melancholic who
spent much of *his* life laughing because, as he said, what other
choice has a man got? Laugh or call it quits.

"Mom."

"You know my father never liked Mort. He'd have forgiven him
the money. What he couldn't stomach was anybody who thought
they were superior. And Mort always had to be the cock of the
walk. So my father did him in with a pearl-handled pistol, so what?
This is all water under a bridge that doesn't even exist anymore."

"I'm just asking—"

My mother sipped her martini. She ran her tongue across her teeth to make it go down slower.

"My God, it was so long ago. I remember she'd never quite look at you. Like she always found a spot on your ear to look at. Pretty, one of those oval faces. Always wore her hair short. And very bright. She spoke several languages, which for a Fall River girl was quite—"

"Mom."

"They must have sent her to a boarding school. For a while, Marshall Hat was one of the largest manufacturers of hats in the country."

"Mom."

"She and Mort had a few good years together. They'd come around to the family. Then the business began to take off, and Mort started to stay in New York for long stretches. After a while, he stopped coming home at all. With Mort gone most of the time, we stopped seeing her. She just sort of vanished, though she only lived over on Locust Street. We'd see her through the windows. And people started to say she was a little cuckoo, sure, but harmless. Then, almost out of nowhere, came the baby. And she refused any help. Any help at all. Of course, this alarmed all the aunties. Refuse help with the baby? Raise it herself? And then—darling, what's the score?"

"Predators up by one," Herb said.

"Predators?" she said.

"And then?" I said.

"Expansion team," Herb said. "Nashville."

My mother doodled on the telephone memo pad. "Nashville has a hockey team?"

"And then?" I said.

"She lit the crib on fire," my mother said.

"Huh?"

"It was the sixties," my mother said. "All kinds of wild things were happening. Setting a bed on fire was nothing. Anyway, the boy wasn't hurt. She dropped her cigarette by accident, that's what I've always believed. I never thought she was crazy."

"And then?"

"They sent her to Menninger's." My mother called to my stepfather. "Herb, where's Menninger's? Nebraska?"

"Kansas," Herb said. "Topeka."

"Kansas, that's right—"

"Why?" I said.

"Because she was crazy, she tried to burn the house—"

"But you just said she wasn't."

"Maybe she was, maybe she wasn't."

"And the boy?" I said. "What happened—"

"He went to Kansas, too. They had some sort of school for the children of patients. You know, Menninger's was *the* place when you lost your mind. They sent Gene Tierney there. There must have been some money left over from the hat factory. Either that or Mort had managed to squirrel some money away for her that the creditors couldn't attach. That's what my father always thought. Not that he begrudged it, he just assumed that Mort had outfoxed—outsquirreled? Can we talk about something else? How's your divorce going?"

"Who's Gene Tierney?" I said.

"He wants to know who's Gene Tierney?" Herb said.

"My God, Gene Tierney's cheekbones," my mother said.

"And then?" I said. "She couldn't have stayed in Kansas forever."

"Why not?" my mother said. "People don't live in Kansas forever? Listen, these people, they weren't family; Horace may have been a thief, but he was our thief, but Mort and Ellie—she's dead. Is that what you're asking? Of course, Ellie's dead by now."

"And the boy? Monroe's—Mort's—son?"

My mother. I have this picture of her and her father on a bike. I'm staring at it right now. It's on the wall above my desk. My grandfather has a cigarette hanging out of his mouth, and my mother is holding on to his waist, and her long blond hair is streaming in the wind behind her. My grandfather doesn't look like a rich guy or anybody who even wants to be a rich guy. He looks like a furniture salesman from Fall River, Mass, riding his kid on the back of his bike. My mother is right. These people with serious (stolen) money and private psychiatric hospitals. They weren't family.

"The boy?" my mother said. "The boy grew up. That's what boys do. But Mort didn't have a son. Coming into town every six months? That's not having a son. What is it about Mort? You've been snooping around him—"

"I guess I feel a kinship," I said. "Remember in college when I changed my name to Max to sound more Jewish?"

"You changed your name?"

"I lasted two weeks. Two weeks, I corrected people. 'The name is Max.' I admire a guy who can sustain that kind of bullshit for years, though I guess he wanted to sound less Jewish while for some reason I wanted to be—"

"You're Jewish enough."

"Not even that. I think I just wanted to be someone else."

"You're doing wonderfully, honey. Isn't he doing wonderfully, Herb? You're still sending your résumé around, right? Someone will call. And you had that interview with DePaul. Life takes turns, it—"

"The interview where I threw up?"

"Wonderfully," Herb said. "He's doing wonderfully. He dinged my car, Allstate wants to raise my rates he's doing so—"

"Also," I said, "I turned my back on a wife after she went nuts."

"That's not how anybody sees it. Your wife has mental health issues."

"I didn't help," I said. "I tried to force a kind of normalcy—"

"Oh, please! You tried, period. You tried harder than most people would have ever tried. Do you hear this, Herb? Now he turned his back—"

"I heard, I heard."

"Didn't he try, Herb? Didn't he try? For years—"

"Woo-hoo," Herb shouted. "Hawks just tied it up."

In the few pictures I found on microfilm at the Fall River Public Library, Monroe Sarkansky has dark, sleek, Sephardic features. Nothing at all like the saggy jowls of Horace. They don't look like brothers. And Monroe wears a mustache that somehow doesn't make him look ridiculous. And always that hat at an angle. Like an old-time private eye. I think the man was hiding out. He hid in Manhattan, on Long Island, in Nassau, but he also hid in the books that are sitting right here in a stack. And so, yeah, I feel a kinship. I'm only a poor relation who's not a relation, but I'm sure as hell hiding. I wonder if you reach a point when you don't even know who, or what, you're hiding from.

And though he may well have squirreled away some money for her, there's no evidence in any of the hundreds—Jesus, thousands—of lines of poetry he left behind that he ever thought much about the wife back home in Fall River. It was all clouds, and balloons, and his mother.

Ellie has never taken shape for me, either. Of her, I've never even found any photographs. I do know that at some point she returned to Fall River from Kansas because she died in the city. The death certificate on file at Government Center lists Eleanor Sarkansky's cause of death as drinking paregoric. My mother knew, of course. Why dredge it up out of the darkness, out of the years? For what? Still, imagination fails. A faker, a scam artist, sure, him I get, though I'll never reach Monroe's highs or lows. At best, I'm a midlevel operator.

Once, a few years ago, I peeped into a back window of the house on Locust Street. I must have thought I might be able to conjure a vision of Ellie's oval face by looking into what she had looked out of. All I saw was someone else's life. A pair of glasses on a kitchen table, some car keys.

V

Renters:
A Sequence

There were people who went to bed
with an open umbrella.

—Natalia Ginzburg, "Winter in the Abruzzi"

Rhinebeck

A t that point, they were still trying to solve it by talking, and so they went, together, to see a therapist who worked out of an office in her house. It was a charming place off a dirt road. There were always men working in the yard. It had a red roof. It was the sort of house that would always be unfinished. There were two of them, two therapists. The husband was retired, but he'd sit in on their sessions and listen. He never said anything, only sometimes he cracked his knuckles. Things were so bad that neither of them thought having this extra person in the room was strange. They were so desperate for the help they thought these people could give. And the therapist, the wife, the one they were supposed to be working with—ostensibly it was couple's counseling—was kind and understanding, and she nodded and asked kind, slightly probing questions. Whenever her husband cracked his knuckles, she'd give him a look. The house was so beautiful: wood floors, carpets, the workmen outside. Plock, plock, plock. How could these people not help them? And after the sessions, exhausted, they'd go to the little movie theater in town and sit there and hardly watch whatever movie played— but it was good to be there in the dark, slumped in those plush seats. They began to become the kind of people who sit all the way through the credits when there are no more names to thank and the whole deal stops.

"Remember when they used to end with that pop?" he said once. "Not that I remember—"

"Shhhhhh, I'm still watching."

Anything not to go home. Things were always worse at home. They were renting an old farmhouse that had been moved to town a 160 years earlier. He used to wonder how they moved it. Brick by brick? Door by door? The landlord used it as a summer retreat from the city. They were short-term renters. When she walked them through the place, the landlord called everything beloved. Here's the beloved kitchen, the beloved yard, the beloved scuffed wooden stairs.

One day the husband therapist, who still had never said anything, called him at work. "It's about your wife," he said.

"Yes?"

"You don't need couple's counseling. I mean, everyone could use couple's counseling, of course. Even Diane and I—" Chuckle, chuckle. "But you need to be aware that your wife is seriously ill and couple's therapy can only be truly efficacious if both partners are at least reasonably—"

He remembers looking out the window then, at the students charging by. It was the time between classes when everyone is on the move and purposeful. He was a visiting professor. This was in 2006. He didn't know anyone at the college. He was fleeting; people looked right through him. The psychologist talked on, offering the name of a psychiatrist in the city. He wrote the name and number down on the desk that wasn't his. Dug the pen right into the wood and carved the doctor's name and phone number for posterity. Your insurance should cover it, the husband therapist said, depending. Before he hung up, the man cleared his throat and, in a different, quieter voice, said, "Good luck to you."

He hung up and sat there in that office that was someone

else's, someone else's books, someone else's pictures of a smiling daughter, and he thought of her now in the rented house, trying to work, trying to read, trying to concentrate. She often said all she wanted was to be able to concentrate. *Why can't I concentrate? Why?* After they moved out, he got a letter from the landlord saying they'd trashed the house and that she was keeping the deposit. Then she sent more letters, threatening to sue him unless he sent more money. How could they possibly have trashed the place? They'd hardly lived in it. He sent her five hundred dollars he didn't have just to shut her up.

Historians

The well-known historian's wife was a historian also. Each of them, husband and wife, were on opposite sides of the room, at the center of small clusters of people. The well-known historian, to his cluster, boomed that his wife was by far the superior scholar and that she spoke four, no, five languages. "Compared with her, I'm only a lucky hack." He took an offhand swig of his drink. "Occitan's a language, not a dialect," he shouted across the room. "Am I right, darling?"

"That's enough, Kenneth," she said. "You can go back to talking about yourself now."

Nervous guests laughed. This was during cocktails. It was a welcome dinner for new faculty. He was only visiting for the year and had been invited last-minute merely to fill out the gathering on account of there being a few no-shows. His first novel had won a couple of minor prizes. At dinner, they put him catty-corner to the president of the college. His temporary status made him an easy sacrifice. The president, a despot, a famous renegade philosopher (his trilogy rattled the establishment in the late '60s), was renowned for not suffering fools. He forked a hunk of salmon into his mouth and, chewing, said, "Your novel. What's it about? Of course, I'll never read it." And he humiliated himself by attempting to answer. He told the president about his attraction to the quotidian, which isn't ordinary, no, not at all, not when you really—

The president leaned so far into his fish his nose almost touched his plate. Still earnestly discoursing on his affection for the commonplace, he examined that bald, shiny head so stuffed with virtuosity. He'd been warned. You had about forty seconds to make an impression on Himmelman. Blow it and you were dead to him forever. He drowned his own blather with a gulp of wine. Quotidian, did I really say—

Himmelman turned to the baby-faced sociologist to his left. "Justify your inane discipline, sir!"

The historian's wife, seated next to him, took pity. She spoke into his ear in a whispered shout. "You think I want to be here, either?" She told him her husband was invited each year to add a little star power and belittle the newbies. The husband had written a series of wildly popular bestsellers about ancient Rome.

"And your wife?" she asked.

"She's not feeling well," he said.

"Smart," she said. "I skipped it last year, and the almighty wasn't amused. He called me to his office the next day and said what was I thinking? Did I want to unleash my husband on some misty little assistant professor of film studies?"

He didn't know how to respond. He'd thought *Who's Afraid of Virginia Woolf?* was interminable the first time he'd seen it. He was exhausted, ashamed. All he wanted to do was go home, but home was an entirely different disaster.

"What's your field?" he asked the historian's wife.

"Let's not talk about work."

"Okay," he said.

"Nineteenth-century France."

"So, Napoléon?"

"The revolution. I focus on radicalism. How it spreads, infects, secretes—"

"My wife's losing her mind."

She laughed. "She's still got it to lose?"

"Truly. Off the rails. Either she is, or I am."

He turned to face her. There was no compassion in her eyes in the candlelight. When she looked the other way down the table to respond to somebody's question about the best restaurants ("Best? Around here? Are you kidding?"), he watched her left earring, a silver third eye. She was maybe ten years older. Maybe she was forty. Poised, confident, her long, long hair done up in a complicated twist. Her columned neck, he wanted to crash his face into it and die.

She'd turned back toward him and was tapping the edge of her glass lightly.

"What is your book about?"

"My what?"

They met in her office during office hours. He knocked. She immediately opened the door.

"Professor," he said.

"Professor," she said.

"I've only got my MFA," he said.

She pulled him into the room and closed the door.

"Your what?" she said.

"What if a student comes?"

"Students don't come."

"But what if one were to?"

"Office hours are like wagon trains. You see any wagons? Mormons?"

Books, everywhere books, on the desk, on the shelves, books piled on top of one another on the floor like cairns. He kissed her and pulled away. "Your husband. His office must—"

"The historian?"

"Jesus, yes, the historian."

"Three doors down on the right."

"Jesus."

"He's teaching. He's in Manhattan. He's at a conference in Beijing. He's in Reykjavík. He's in his office. No, Lima. He's in Lima. Anyway, he wouldn't deign."

"But what if he loses his keys, or one of the kids is sick or something?"

He was backed up against the desk, her body pressing against his. *Who's Afraid of Virginia Woolf?* Actually it wasn't that long; exhilarating theater, really, he'd seen a revival in Chicago.

"What kids?" she said.

"What about a janitor?" he said.

"Himmelman fired all the janitors. We're the janitors."

They slid downward to the cold floor, toppling books.

"No kids? Really?"

"Two. A boy and a girl. Beautiful little towheads. Shut up, will you?"

Frantic mutual unbuttoning. One bare shoulder, another. A few times he stopped and said something absurd like how grateful he was. For what? He couldn't explain exactly. That there weren't any complications? That she just opened a door? She told him the boyish thing came off better when he didn't talk. The blinds were down, but the window was open. Students chattered and laughed as they sauntered by on the walk outside. Even when he'd been a student—state school, he always said that proudly, I attended a state school—he'd always felt estranged from the chatter and the laughter. Why? Why had any sense of ease always felt so alien? And it would have been dramatic and maybe even cataclysmic had the sole student who went to office hours knocked and, without waiting, entered, or if the historian had, that one time, misplaced his keys, or one of the towheads really had taken sick at school, but nothing like that happened and the weeks passed, a month, and in early November he and Susan—that was her name—took a walk along the river. She slipped on a rock and fell on her elbow. There was a small cut, and he put his fingers over the wound to stop the bleeding, though there was hardly any blood, it was more of a scrape than a cut, but still he remembers the look of her blood on his fingers and how he convinced himself he was staunching a wound. Is it "staunch" or "stanch"? It was getting late, and colder. They sat down on their jackets in a small clearing near the water.

"What'd he do on Elba?" he asked. "Swim? Play cards?"

"Oh, fuck the pygmy. I told you, I study the way mass movements react, or don't react, with reference to the—"

"Right, right."

The Hudson churned by. Not a pretty river, a working river, a useful river. The reflection of the gray sky in the river, patches of white speckles. Above them a stand of leafless trees leaned out across the water as if trying to reach their brethren on the other side. She stood up and began calling the dog. She'd brought her dog. Her cover, not that she needed one, was that she was walking the dog. A half hour earlier the dog had run off to chase some birds and hadn't come back.

"Pompy," she called. "Pompy! Pompy! Pompeia! Come here, girl!"

Maybe tonight there would be calm.

And he thought of their bedroom in the little rented house. An upstairs room with space only for a bed, no night tables, no lamps, the sole light overhead.

How often in the night, in a new panic, his wife would leap up and tug the string of the overhead light and it was so bright and he'd beg her to turn it off. We should sleep, honey, last night we hardly—

And she'd say, I know, I know, and she'd turn it off, but a few minutes later she'd jump up and pull the string again.

You're not listening to me.

It's because I need to sleep.

You never.

Please, honey—

I'm just asking you to listen.

We both gotta sleep, that's what we—

For once—

Please, we have to—

The dog was nowhere. Susan sat back down. He began returning things to his pockets, his keys, his phone, his wallet.

"Maybe he swam on St. Helena," Susan said. "The water would have been warmer down there, no? And on Elba he was plotting his latest havoc. He wouldn't have had time to swim. But on St. Helena. Wait—so far out, there would have been sharks—"

"How come they didn't just shoot him to begin with? Why keep sending him on vacations?"

"It wouldn't have done to shoot Napoléon."

"But didn't they shoot everybody?"

"Yes, and they lopped off lots of heads, also. But he wasn't everybody. And maybe in the back of the minds of certain royalists he was more one of them than a citizen. Anyway, that's what Dunard argues, not unconvincingly, in the otherwise redundant book that got him tenure at Yale."

"I'd have stayed on the island. Any island." He stood and put his jacket on. He brushed grass off his pants.

"How long are you going to stick this out?" she said.

"I don't know," he said.

"Maybe you're a coward."

"Probably."

"No, you're very decent," she said. "But you do wallow in it. When I lose it, the historian will have me locked up in fifteen minutes. 'What a waste,' he'll say. 'She was so clever.'"

He brushed more grass off his pants.

"Stay," she said. "My dog's missing."

"I can't."

"Do you wallow for her? Or for yourself?"

He didn't answer. He lay back down on the grass and looked up at the trees. One day he'd learn their names. One day he'd walk along and point out—to somebody, anybody—the names of trees.

"I've got to get home," he said.

"I know you do."

"It's not like there's any chance of us—"

"Of course not," she said.

They stayed on the riverbank until it began to rain. The dog was waiting by her car.

Montreal

In the spring, he and his wife drove up to Montreal and stayed in a little pension. Their room was on the top floor; not a floor, really: the room was a glass box on top of the house and accessible only by a ladder. At the top of the ladder, you opened a hatch in the ceiling and pulled yourself up into the room. He wants to remember that the two days they spent up there were calm, that the little box on the roof, windows on all sides, was truly an oasis, that the psychosis, paranoia, mania—all the words that couldn't begin to describe whatever it was that was so particular to her (and what made him think he was so sane, either?)—abated and they were able to simply exist up there in that strange pod of a room. All they had to do was climb the ladder and open the hatch. *Hold it—You know it came and went, that it wasn't constant, that even amid what you call the worst times, there were long stretches, weeks, even months, when things were normal or some degree of normal, because what does "normal" even mean in this context? So to say there was something especially calm about your time up in that room—*

He remembers that in order to get up to Canada, they'd needed a decent car. The Honda was on its last legs. So they'd rented an old BMW sedan from a guy who worked at the local coffee shop and also rented cars. This guy had told them he'd come out to the Hudson Valley from the city intending to grow stuff—what, he wasn't exactly sure. He said he was thinking maybe pumpkins, but mostly he just wanted to watch stuff grow out of the ground. "You know? Like the cycle of nature?" When he realized he didn't have any idea how to make that happen—"A lot harder than it looks to grow pumpkins"—he had to do something else. He'd always had a thing for cars. So, yeah, why not an under-the-table car-rental business?

"Depending on how much time you two have, I could tell you two how I made the transition."

"How about show us the cars?" his wife said.

The coffee-shop guy led them out to a barn. Inside were a few cars covered in bird shit.

"Take your pick."

She pointed to a Beemer.

"Sixty for the weekend. An extra twenty-five if it's not back by Sunday at four. We good? I just got to find the keys."

And they drove up to Montreal and stayed in a glassed-in room on top of a house for two days, and they were happy, almost like they were floating up there—*It's just not accurate. It was no more happy or unhappy than usual, because even though the trouble came and went, it was always there, on the edge of any moment, and so, again, to say it was a happy couple of days*—

Yet the room exists in his mind as a kind of mirage that he can still conjure up, the two of them climbing the ladder and opening the hatch like you might in a submarine. Besides, he's got this need, doesn't everybody, to put certain things in a kind of rational order, and so that time in Montreal he files under: Things were good for a little while. For two days, things were—*Okay, let's say for the sake of argument it was happy. A little bit happy, but if things were already so wrecked, if there was already no possible way out, then what could two days possibly mean?*

And Montreal itself, the first time for both of them, was emerging from winter, and people were out on the streets, in the cafés, and the two of them wandered around and even laughed, tried out some high-school French, stuffed themselves with pastries, and went back to the pension and climbed the ladder. Up through the hatch and into the glass box. Over the rooftops, they had a glimpse of Mount Royal. One problem: there wasn't any bathroom up there. To go to the bathroom, you had to climb back down the ladder, but he remembers waking up in the just after dawn and climbing out one of the windows. He took a piss off the roof into the courtyard below. And as he turned back to the room, he looked at her sleeping through the windows. She always kicked away her covers. The way her bare legs looked, scissored across each other, as though she were in midrun.

The way her bare legs—

Two uneventful days, almost like a blessing, and they'd gone to an architectural museum where they'd seen Giacometti sculptures, thin women walking. And she'd talked about how making the same thing over and over was a kind of genius. Because it's never truly the same thing, right, by definition? So long, she said, as you create each woman from scratch, one woman walking can never be another woman walking. You see what I mean?

And again climbing up the ladder, holding a bag of takeout because even the takeout in Montreal was—

And then the border post on the way home.

Why rush it? Can't we—

It was almost nothing, a weekend trip. It's over and you've got to head back south and cross a border that's hardly even a border and—

Right, he thinks, and the border post should have been funny. How the border guard ran the plate and the car came up stolen. They were detained. Detained! It should have been funny. It was funny. They were only in Canada. They weren't car thieves. He was a visiting professor. She was an artist. The two of them, they had graduate degrees. It was a misunderstanding; they were in Canada, not Turkey—*But she wouldn't stop screaming.* "*You're arresting us?*" *she kept yelling.* "*Arresting us?*" *They'd had to restrain her. You forgot? The original guard and then a woman cop, and they cuffed her*—and he couldn't convince her, This is funny, we're in Canada, don't you see how hilarious this is? Can't you see, please, I love you, please see

Other Nights

Other nights were so bad he didn't even put on his shoes. He'd grab a pair on his way out and shove them on outside. A small town. There wasn't any place to go. There were a couple of bars, but he was afraid he'd run into students or, worse, other faculty. He wandered up and down sidewalks. If it was cold and he hadn't thought to grab a jacket, he'd go to the convenience store at the gas station to warm up a little. If he'd remembered his wallet, he'd buy something. A bag of Doritos. Once he ate one of those hot dogs that roll all day and night. Delicious, hot and salty. Standing there by the gas pumps wolfing. If he didn't have his wallet, he'd browse the store shelves for a few minutes, as if he were looking for something they didn't carry, and then leave before he seemed creepy, especially if there was a female clerk. He'd flash the ring on his finger but wasn't sure if this made it worse. It was better on the sidewalks. All the small dark houses. The sleepers in their bedrooms. So easy. You said good night. You turned out the light. You fell asleep. Maybe someone was in your arms or maybe someone wasn't. Another time, in May, he didn't even have time to grab his shoes. She'd stood in front of the door screaming, and he'd had to knock her over in order to leave. He'd slopped across bogged grass and mud barefoot, the way he used to when he was a kid. The mud slick and cold under his feet. A couple hours later, he went back. He always went back. She never locked him out. He'd crash on the couch downstairs. In the morning, she'd be kneeling beside him. "What time do you have class? Don't you want to get some real sleep?" And she'd apologize for what she remembered and forget what she forgot. A lot depended on what they both forgot.

The TV Room

It wasn't visiting hours. They let him in anyway. She was on the fifth floor. He needed a special code to work the elevator. After he buzzed, he was led through two locked doors and down a corridor to the TV room. She was sitting on a bench, holding a book. He joined her and handed her a small paper bag.

"I brought you a brownie," he said. "You're too thin."

"The food's not terrible," she said.

"Maybe you should eat more of it."

"I look thin?"

"Yeah."

"Good."

"You're going to be all right."

"You know, I've been thinking," she said. "Maybe it doesn't really matter."

"You will. Soon. It's just going to take—"

"No pep talks, all right?"

He looked around the room. There was no TV. In one corner was a pile of tattered board games. Life, Sorry, Clue, Connect Four.

"Have some brownie," she said.

"I brought it for you," he said.

They used to say they lived in the country of us. Years of mornings, years of nights. He used to read her his stories. The minute he'd finish one he'd beg her to listen, and she'd sit on the couch with her feet tucked under her legs and her chin in her hands, and if a line rang wrong, she'd dip her head slightly, only slightly, but enough so he'd notice, and he'd make a mark by that sentence because he knew right there he'd blown it.

"They let us wear our own clothes, thank God," she said. "How's the baby?"

"Let's not—"

"I'm asking. How's your kid?"

"She's fine. Not sleeping much, but that's how it—"

"Right. That's how it goes. You forget I basically raised two little brothers?"

"I didn't forget."

"Eat some brownie," she said.

"Where's the TV?" he asked.

"They roll it in."

He reached over and took the brownie from her hand. His fingers grazed hers.

A half hour later, the man who'd let him in, a kind, shriveled man with a vaguely Eastern European accent—Polish? Czech?—came and told him that he was sorry but that it was time to leave. Mandatory rest period. The TV room would be locked. She stayed on the bench and looked at her hands. The old Pole or Czech walked him out to the corridor, unlocked the two more doors, and let him out.

Evergreen Garden,
San Francisco, 2012

There were times when she was alone and confused, at times delusional, at times not (other times it was almost impossible, for her, anyway, to tell the difference), and she'd go to Evergreen Garden, a Vietnamese place on Eighteenth and Harrison. At a corner table in the back she'd wait out whatever there was to wait out, it was different every time, but it always had to do with thoughts, rampant thoughts that wouldn't let up. Eating out sometimes helped a little. It was as if being in public kicked in a kind of muscle memory. She'd study the menu like a customer was supposed to, even though she always knew what she wanted. At the Evergreen Garden, the price of each dish was crossed through meticulously with a pen. Next to the old price was the handwritten new price, fifty cents more for each dish. She appreciated the thrift. Why make new menus? It was also a lesson in inflation. She'd stare at the brown and white floor tiles, at the peculiar modish chandelier that looked like it belonged in a different restaurant, at the old man behind the counter sleeping on his feet. When anybody spoke to him, his son or his son's wife, he'd open his eyes slowly. Then he'd answer whatever was asked and go back to sleep.

There was also, in the center of the dining room, a cylindrical fish tank, crowded with goldfish, surprised looks on their faces, fleeing round and round. She often wondered why they didn't get dizzy, or maybe if you were dizzy all the time you had no idea what not being dizzy felt like. Made her think of the pills. When the pills didn't seem to work. Or when she forgot to take them. Or when she'd run out of them and it was after seven on Sunday and Walgreens was open, and you could buy a refrigerator's worth of food, socks, a clock radio, a beach ball, but the pharmacy was closed—

The waiter, the son, approached her table. He never recognized her, though of course he did. But acknowledging her might have caused trouble with his wife, since everything else under the sun seemed to. She ordered a beef noodle soup (now $7.75) and a beer and sat there without a book, wondering how she could have forgotten one again, and waited not for calm, which would have been too much to ask, but only that her body allow her to breathe without feeling like she was panting. Though she wasn't panting, at least not out loud. The thing about being delusional, or at least her version of delusional, since everybody's had to be different, was that even while it was going on, she could always see past it. She knew that whatever she happened to believe at the moment was fantastical, or at least partly fantastical. There was always half the delusion that was true— as black-and-white true as the prices of these dishes crossed out and rewritten in pen. Didn't Jean Rhys say if you're paranoid, you've got a reason to be?

So she had this ability, this talent, for being able to half watch herself as if from a distance, believing whatever it was she was believing—today that her landlady had it in for her, was blaming her alone for all the plumbing trouble in the whole building, saying it was her hair and her coffee grounds causing it all, and she was going to start eviction proceedings soon, that was for fucking certain—and at the same time not believing it (the landlady wasn't singling her out, the woman was a fucking bitch to everybody, who wasn't she a fucking bitch to?), and this not believing made her feel at least a little—what?—removed during the very worst of it. No matter how much anarchy in her thoughts, or in the things she'd say, or when she'd sometimes flail around on her bed and scream out the apartment window, or even those few times out on the street when the cops came and said, We're here to give you a hand (at the same time radioing: *We've got a 5150, female in her thirties, corner of Twenty-Ninth and*—), there was always this island in her brain that held something back, and even when it didn't hold anything back, even when she let the panic take over completely—or couldn't stop it—still, even then, she knew the island was there and she'd be able to swim to it later, and in this she knew she was lucky; she'd met more than enough people on the ward who had no islands at all.

The old man at the counter stood with his eyes closed, his face crunched together like a fist. Was it comfortable there in his cocoon? His son and his son's wife were squabbling again in the kitchen. She'd had a husband once, too. He'd been her TA in college. He was gone now. Not far away, but gone. There'd been a time they were never out of each other's sight. Maybe the little old man was sleeping, maybe he wasn't. She watched the fish in their cylindrical tank. Around and around they fled. Her soup was cold, her beer warm. But here she could sit for hours.

Strand

He found a strand of her hair in a book. A long dark brown piece of her hair that made a curlicue on the page. The book was Frank Kermode's *The Sense of an Ending: Studies in the Theory of Fiction*. Why he happened to take it off the shelf that morning, he wasn't sure. He'd never had any interest in theory. And a theory of fiction? A theory that explains waking up in the dark of a familiar room and forgetting where you are and how you got there? Some books sit on the shelf for so long they become part of the landscape. One day, a spine catches your eye, and you slide a book from between two others, open it, read a little.

On the page where he'd found her hair, she'd underlined a sentence: "In the Bible the world is made out of nothing." In the margin, she'd written, *Nothing? What about silence???* He spent the rest of the afternoon reading, careful that the strand didn't drop out. He fell asleep reading, woke up to someone, nobody, calling his name.

VI

Walt Kaplan Is Broke: A Novella

The bed's oak
and clumsy, pitching
with its crew,
a man and a wife—

—Rita Dove, *Thomas and Beulah*

Perhaps it was worth being poor for a long time
to be so rich for just a little while.

—John Kenneth Galbraith, *The Great Crash of 1929*

1

Truesdale Hospital:
Fall River, Massachusetts,
July 21, 1977

The first time Walt Kaplan died, Irv Pincus was at his bedside crying crocodile tears and murmuring in pidgin Hebrew. Walt opened his eyes and thought, Heaven or hell, I'll take either, just get me the hell away from Irv Pincus. Only Walt wasn't dead, and only Irv's Hebrew was fake. The crocodile tears were the genuine article. Irv's wife, Dottie, had finally cajoled Sarah, her sister, into going home and getting some sleep. Irv had been assigned the night watch. Ah, the graveyard shift, Irv had said, and Dottie told him to can the comedy. Just sit there, don't sleep. And if he wakes up, for Christ's sake don't tell him anything. Call a doctor, call the nurse. Just don't open your trap. And so there was Irv weeping and praying and gripping Walt's arm in the half dark, and if Walt had had the strength to scream bloody murder, he would have.

"Irv?"

"Easy, Walt. You've had a helluva."

"What are you doing in my bedroom?"

"You're at Truesdale, old buddy. Good news is that you've got a view of the Narragansett."

The room is dim but for the hallway light leaking in through the slightly open door. Truesdale? Even when he's not smiling, Irv Pincus is smiling. That puny bush of a mustache, looks like he cut off the tail end of a cat's tail and stuck it under his nose. Alf Dolinsky calls it a pussy tickler. His wet, beady eyes in the darkness, unnerving. Must be his secret. That smile like he knows your number. Nothing's free, even what you think you've already got. Irv could sell you your own shoes on layaway.

With a long, slow, theatrical swipe of his forearm across his face, Irv wipes away tears. "Hate to be the one to break it to you, old soul. Your heart stopped. Sidewalk. Up the hill on President Avenue. If not for some nosy out on her porch, you'd be a door-nail. Ambulance came in a few minutes. Lucky they weren't on a slowdown. Damn the unions. Pumped you so full of drugs you could open a pharmacy. They thought you might need a bypass. Turned out, no. You're some kind of medical miracle. They're saying your heart righted itself. Still, Sarah's half out of her wits. Dottie took her home a couple hours ago. Where were you walking?"

"What time is it, Irv?"

"After four in the morning. You've been out eleven hours."

"Where I was walking where?"

"That's what I'm asking. President Avenue at two thirty in the afternoon on a Wednesday. Not that I'm lording. Never once have I ever lorded. Have I, Walt? But you of all people know that a small-business owner has the right to expect an employee, even an employee as eminent as yourself, to understand that a payroll's a payroll, and a man has to put in the time if that man expects—"

"Irv?"

"Yeah, Walt?"

"I got a view?"

"Fifth floor. The Braga Bridge will be clear as a bell in the morning. Power plant in Swansea, too."

"What day is it?"

"Told you. Wednesday. No. Used to be Wednesday. Now it's—"

"Do me a favor, Irv? Will you?"

"Anything, Walt. You say the word and I'll—"

"Beat it! Will you do that for me, boss? Will you beat it?"

"Walty, I'm your brother-in-law and I love you like a brother-in-law and if you think these tears aren't real you can fuck yourself."

"Nurse!" What kind of hospital there's no nurse? "Nurse!"

And it's strange. The room begins to float a little, and Walt's head, he's never had a heavier head, sinks to the pillows, and again he's pretty sure this is the end of the line, the last station, and it's almost lovely, even if Irv Pincus is the conductor punching tickets. And yet at the same time, Irv, if he's still in the room at all, is nothing more than a disembodied voice calling him from far away and, along with the floating, there's an opposite feeling, a kind of tingling fallingness in his legs, his feet, his toes, like when he drinks too much coffee, a falling that doesn't seem to land anywhere. Such delight, such ecstasy, in this falling, maybe worth your whole life, every tired morning, this moment of simultaneous floating and falling.

The Braga Bridge will be clear as a bell in the morning.

"Lazy!"

A large-headed little man in a dove-gray suit and red tie rises from the abyss at the foot of the bed. Looks like an oversize puppet. Dark eyes, large pouches underneath. You could pack a bag in those pouches. Looks like he hasn't slept in a decade, maybe longer, but this man's not sleepy, not at all. The man sniffs as if laziness is a smell he's picking up on the wind.

"Poppa?" Walt says.

"Lying in bed how long? Who's manning the store? Didn't I tell you that when the cat's away the mouse will rob us to the tune of three hundred ducats a month?"

"There is no store anymore, Poppa."

"What? No store? My store—"

"It's good to see you, Poppa."

"I turn my back five minutes and—"

"They built the new highway right through Kaplan's—"

"Highway? Highway to where?"

"To the Cape. You know, so people from Providence and New York can—"

"Through the store? At Fourth and Pleasant?"

"There is no Fourth and Pleasant, Poppa. Only on the old maps."

The old man begins to wail, in the ancient beseeching way, Job-like, his head facing the ceiling, his arms outstretched. He stops, has a thought.

"But you fought them, Son, oh, did you fight them. You fought them tooth and nail. They hardly knew what hit them. Am I right?"

Even now, in spite of his oversize head, the old man is still compact, well-built, and when he speaks he thrusts his whole body into each word, every word a punch. But it's as though his father's lips and tongue can't keep up with what he's saying. The man's out of sync. Reminds Walt of when Milt and Pearl Feldman make him and Sarah sit through their interminable home movies. People talking like their mouths are filled with syrup.

"Well, Poppa, I sat through hearings. Think of the jobs, they said, think of the boon I-195 will bring to downtown renewal. Think of the shopping, people will come from Connecticut, New York, New Jersey, to shop in Fall River! I stood up and said, 'Drive a stake through a city's heart, people are going to drive right past the body.' And nobody, not the city, not the DPW—"

"Brick by brick, I built that store. One square block, two streets off South Main. Location like that, they must have paid us a fortune—"

"Eminent domain, Poppa. The state paid what they considered the land alone was—"

His father brings his hands to his head and pushes his ears together.

"For the good of the community," Walt says.

"But the money they did pay, at least that—"

"Most of it I invested with the Sarkansky brothers."

"The curtain makers?"

"Turned investment bankers. Opened up shop in the Academy Building not long after you—"

"Hoaxes!"

"You got that right."

Somebody should have made a bust of his father's head. He'd have put it on his desk in a building that no longer exists.

"Listen, Poppa. That was oceans ago. Irv Pincus says I had a heart attack."

"He's a doctor now, Irv Pincus? Sarkanskys are bankers and that dumbkampf is—"

"Irv's got his own store. I work for him. On the floor, I—"

"A Kaplan for a Pincus? It's a nightmare is what this is, me a visitation, a phantasm, and I'm the one having a night—"

"I feel woozy, Poppa."

"Sloth!"

"My feet, I can't feel my feet."

His father tugs a chain out of his vest pocket and looks at his watch.

"You have to leave, Poppa?"

"Eight minutes past doomsday. But they've been saying that for years. How old are you now, boy?"

"I'm fifty-eight, Poppa."

"How much do you need?" His father fishes around in his trouser pockets. "Will a ten-spot do you?"

"I'm so broke, Poppa, I don't need money anymore."

"Fifty-eight! When I was fifty-eight I had three whores a week, plus your mother. That kind of stamina."

"Jewish whores? I always used to wonder if there were any Jewish whores."

"You think there aren't any Jewish whores?"

Hell, maybe I am in heaven.

"House full of them on Spring Street—eight thirty-two Spring Street—down in the Flint in the twenties. What a man can buy with money you can't imagine. See-through pink dresses like they used to wear back in Poland. Pink on pink! I'll cash some stock, I've still got shares in Bethlehem—"

"And Mother, Poppa?"

The little man's cheeks grow big as balloons. "You're calling your dear mother a whore?"

"I'm asking did you love her, Poppa."

His father's monumental head begins to wobble. And it's like someone has punctured his cheeks with a needle, because they go flat. And his whole body, too, goes slack and folds inward on itself, and the little man begins to droop, slowly, slowly, out of sight below the precipice at the end of the bed. And Irv Pincus snores boisterous, wet, sloppy snores. Walt shifts on the mattress. If he doesn't relieve himself this minute, he'll spring a leak. Can't move. Legs like two slabs of beef.

"Nurse!" Walt shrieks. "Toilet, Nurse!"

"Easy, Walt," Irv says. "You got a thingamajig in there with you."

Walt feels around. "Ah. Aha."

And in the late-morning light: Sarah. Sarah, Sarah, Sarah. Sarah, handbag in the crook of her arm, like a shopper at attention waiting for the morning doors of McWhirr's to fling open. And beyond her, out the window, yes, the Braga Bridge and, beyond it, rising up out of the trees on the other side of the bay, as also foretold by Irv Pincus, the bulbous white cone, the power plant at Swansea. On the table beside the bed, flowers. On the one chair beside the bed, flowers. On the floor by the door, flowers. Sarah has on a new straw hat. Black band around it. Walt closes his eyes. Eyes hurt. Funeral hat. Funereal hat. One noun doubles as an adjective; the other, what? An adjective inspired by a noun? He'll have to check his *Oxford Concise* when he gets home. *Home?* If he makes it home. My God. Wife. His. He thinks of the first time he laid eyes on her. Nineteen thirty-seven. Sarah Gottlieb, the hatcheck girl at the Hotel Mellen. In her hatcheck-girl hat. Smaller hat than today's. A bellhop-looking hat, a muffin top on her head, and he'd stood there in a line of men waiting to check their hats and reached up—a hatless head. And he'd run out into South Main, bought a three-dollar hat off a guy for five dollars. Got back in line, and when it was his turn, he said, "Walter Kaplan of Kaplan's Furniture. You're familiar? All the name brands, 139 Pleasant Street. Osborne 6-8571. Open eight to seven, weekdays; nine to four on Saturday."

"You want to check your hat? Or don't you?"

"What hat? Oh, yes. This—"

A month later they eloped to Rhode Island.

"Irv said you were out of your wits," Walt says.

Motionless, she stands there with her handbag. "You're going to leave me an empty house? Who's going to fill it with brooding? Who's going to water the plants?"

"What plants?" Walt says. "Aren't they rubber?"

Sarah steps forward and leans, reaches for him, cups Walt's chin, draws his unshaven face close to hers as if she needs to feel it in order to know the man's still alive. Backs away again to access him from another angle. "Jews don't do last rites," she says. "You never see a rabbi with a Torah in his briefcase, running red lights."

"You're using my material," Walt says. Who knew she listened? "New hat?"

"Why not?" With both hands she doffs her hat one way, then another, as people do to accentuate a hat. "Why not a new hat?"

"The merry widow. Look at Sarah Kaplan, née Gottlieb, jaunting around in her new hat. Come closer with all of you. My head, my everything, my feet. I feel clobbered. My eyeballs ache."

And Sarah comes closer, again, and she collapses her newly hatted head on his chest and grabs his neck with both hands as if to strangle him. She'd sure as hell like to. Both are silent. They listen to each other breathe. Walt thinks, When was the last time we were so still we heard each other breathe? *Don't think, Walt, just—impossible—simply impossible to experience anything without commentary—shut up, Walt, shut up*—her plump squeezable plumpness. Like an overripe eggplant. The British call them aubergines. French word must be. Less fun. Fondle an aubergine? An eternity without this body? What kind of vile god. Sarah's handbag is still in the crook of her arm. At home he often tries to lift it. What does she carry around in there, a block of Fall River granite? God of the Five Books of Moses, that's who, nasty murderous son of a bitch. All punishment, no mercy, no sense of humor. Maybe the Jews need Jesus after all. Died for us sinners, got himself tortured. New Testament says he's Jewish, doesn't look it, flowing golden locks. Guess they all were, or most. Not Ishmael, as he was Hagar's—but didn't Jesus laugh once in a while? Not Adonai, this ogre never—Jews for—didn't Oliver Gevelber's granddaughter run off with Jews for Jesus?— oh, Sar, I'll miss you, there's no calculating—remember how we used to roll around like happy hippos. Used to? If today's Thursday, then Monday, Monday we copulated—

"This gown's got no backside," Walt says.

"Makes it easier to do your business," Sarah says.

"Moon nurses, anyway. Are there nurses here?"

"Gittleman says it was relatively minor, all things considered, and that your ticker's running normal again."

Her head rose and fell with Walt's breathing.

"A heart episode he called it. A farken-something."

"Sounds German. All things considered? What does that even mean? How much of all things must we consider?"

"You're fat, Walt. Not overweight. Fat. Obese, Gittleman says—"

"Gittleman's not so undernourished himself."

Which is good. Nobody wants a doctor who looks too healthy.

"He says you should get one of those bicycles you ride in the living room."

"An Exercycle?"

Sarah raises her head to look at him. "What were you doing walking? Something wrong with the Lincoln? I thought we just replaced the carburetor."

"I was getting some exercise."

"Walt."

"No joke, they got nurses at Truesdale? White scratchy dress, pointy white hat, squeaky, squishy shoes? Look like walking bandages. Angels of healing. What happens when a man—a patient, for instance—needs a glass of water? I use a divining rod?"

Sarah stands. Obscured by the flowers, on the table beside the bed, is a glass and a pitcher of water. She pours him one, and Walt hoists himself up on his pillow and drinks the water so fast it gets clogged in his throat and he gags.

"Walt? What? You got a honey on the side? A Little Miss Muffet stashed away on Eastern Avenue?"

"Pour me another, will you?"

Couple of gulps and he drinks that water down, too.

"I'd be impressed," she says.

"It's like I've been in the desert," Walt says.

"Doesn't Alf Dolinsky have an Exercycle?" Sarah says.

"Irv's got me punching the clock like a stock boy, and you want to know if I've got a honey on Eastern Avenue?"

"So where were you walking?"

"You're right, Alf does have an Exer—"

"Walt."

"And you can tell Irv Pincus to kiss my ass, my gelatinous moon of an—"

"Don't start," Sarah says. "He was kind to help us out."

"Help us out? I took one look at his smug last night and died."

"You didn't die, hon, you're—"

"Wouldn't know it by all the flowers. It's a funeral in here."

"Arthur called."

"Which Arthur?"

"Your brother."

"Oh, that Arthur."

Sarah, worn out from being up most of the night (at home she didn't sleep, she cleaned), takes a bouquet off the chair, puts it on the floor. Sinks into the chair. Sighs. "People love you, Walt, you don't even know how much people—"

"You know what Alf calls Irv's little Hitler mustache?"

"A thousand times, you've—"

"Pussy tickler!"

As if on cue, a nurse enters holding a tray. Squishy shoes, no white hat. Holy Christ, this is a hospital.

"I won't ask what that is," the nurse says.

"Don't," Sarah says.

"Breakfast, Mr. Kaplan?"

Nurse sets the tray down on Walt's chest. Nice design, the tray has little baskets on either end that prop it on the bed. In one basket is silverware, in the other a napkin and a package with a moist towelette. Nurse is pretty, tall. Tall women, less need for a hat. Maybe early forties. Or still in her thirties and working here has aged her into her forties. Slightly upturned nose, Walt always likes a slightly upturned nose. Not too much or it's haughty, but a little turn upward, that's—

"Wait, I know you. You're Josephine—"

"Downey. Was. I'm back to Borger now."

"Do you live on Eastern Avenue?" Sarah says.

"I live in Somerset."

"Across the bridge," Walt says.

"But I used to shop at Kaplan's. We bought our wedding furniture from you. A dinette, a refrigerator, a bedroom set."

"Satisfied?"

"The bed was sturdier than the husband."

Sarah laughs out loud, first time in two days.

"And the fridge?"

"It gurgles at night like it's alive."

"A Westinghouse?"

"How should I know?"

"Your Westinghouses will do that. But it works? Things are built like tanks. You could cross the Rhine in one of those fridges."

Josephine, with a deft movement, lifts the sheets to retrieve the bedpan. "Well done. Sleep good? You missed some excitement."

"Like the dead."

"You should see the difference," Josephine says. "I walk in on a corpse, I know it right away."

"Peaceful?" Walt asks.

"More like exhausted. Your friend was here all night. He's very devoted."

"He's a circling turkey vulture."

"His brother-in-law," Sarah says. "Loves him like a—"

"Need anything else? I'll be back in a bit to check your vitals, and Dr. Gittleman will be here to see you this afternoon."

"Egg rolls," Walt says. "Couple few egg rolls?"

Squeaky shoes out the door without an answer.

"Sold that nurse a Westinghouse!"

Sarah starts rooting around in her purse for a tissue.

"No, come on, Sar, don't—"

"Drop dead and I swear, Walt, I'll wipe the floor with you."

Sarah honks her nose. A container ship marking territory on the Narragansett. And out the window Mount Hope Bay and the Braga Bridge. The Braga used to be green. Due for a new paint job. Crazy thing is before the bridge linked up with I-195, he'd loved it. A beauty of an unfinished bridge reaching across the water from Somerset. Each day, it inched a little closer. They named it after Charlie Braga, a Fall Riverite sacrificed at Pearl Harbor. Poor kid. Never found whatever was left of his body. They could have named London Bridge after him, wouldn't have mattered to Charlie Braga.

"Listen, Sarah."

"It doesn't matter. What could it possibly matter? I want you to get that bicycle. Do you think Alf—"

And silence, the kind of silence where they talk with their eyes because if they said what they were thinking it would get so maudlin it would disgust them, which would only make it more maudlin. Strange conundrum that after all these years they can still sweat over each other at the drop of a hat. Even here amid the smell of disinfectant and flowers. People down the hall breathing their last. Drop of a hatcheck girl's hat and the two of them, Walt and Sarah, Sarah and Walt—

"You think I could afford a honey on the side?" Walt says.

"Walt. Eat a little, will you?"

"Listen, I spoke to my father last night."

"That man didn't make you miserable enough when he was alive?"

"You wouldn't believe what used to go on in Spring Street in the twenties. Right under our noses. Just when you think the world's exhausted its possibilities—"

"What, the whorehouse?"

"You knew?"

"Eat some breakfast, Walt."

2

August, Bedroom

Walt and Sarah, the heat, the swelter, they lie, panting, separate beds.

The air-conditioning's been out since Tuesday.

"You want to push the beds together?" Sarah says.

Snowy thighs in the dark and Walt thinks, What an offer. What did I ever do to deserve anybody's thighs, much less thighs like these thighs? When two twin beds merge! And yet, later, after, glorious after, he knows that he'll wake up in the darkest hour with the heartburn he's always convinced is another heart attack. Now that he's had a real one, you'd think he'd be able to tell the difference, but the heart is a fraudster, a greedy muscle—

"Walt?"

"Yeah?"

"I said do you wanna push the beds?"

"God, yes."

"But you're just laying there."

"I'm indulging in anticipation, one of the most unsung of life's great pleasures. Studies have shown that anticipation is actually chemically more potent than—"

"Walt."

Their little bedroom in the dark. Nice how the two words

cling together so natural. Bedroom. Rolls off the tongue, *bed-room*. Miriam used to pitter in here more than half asleep from her room across the hall and climb into bed with her mother and immediately conk out completely. And he thinks of those nights, how he'd bridge his arm across the beds and nudge her, and Sarah would murmur, Walt, the kid, and he'd say into the darkness, *This kid wouldn't even be here in the first place without a little wadda wadda.* They'd leave the sleeping kid in their room and creep across the hall to the kid's. First time, Sarah worried they'd break the bed. What will we tell her in the morning?

We'll tell her it was Mama Bear.

Wouldn't it be Goldilocks? Isn't she the one? Slow down, partner, slow down—

Walt ripping her nightdress apart like a hero.

Let's see you, Goldilocks!

Funny, all those nights and they'd only had the one. He'd always thought they'd end up with a house full of squealers. Run a little piggery.

Marriage as nightly romp. Who'd believe it? Who the hell would want to know? And now, deep into their fifties? *You wanna push the beds?*

"So hot," Sarah says, "I feel like a baked Alaska."

"Baked Alaska's cold on the inside," Walt says.

"Did you talk to Angelo again about fixing the window unit?"

"Said he'd be here tomorrow."

"Didn't he say that yesterday?"

"Says his wife's been sick again. He says this time the doctors—"

"Oh, Carmela. She can't catch a break. I'll go see her. Walt?"

"Uh-huh."

"What are you doing?"

"What am I doing?"

"I'm asking."

"Ruminating, taking stock, mulling—"

"Listen, I've got Renda Grayboys coming to pick me up at seven thirty for Frieda's luncheon. And you know she'll be in the driveway at ten after seven. So if you—"

"Who eats lunch at seven o'clock in the morning?"

"We've got to lay the table, put out the flowers, count the chairs, do the seating, the place cards, make sure the soup— Walt, Gittleman says you can use all the exercise you can get, including—"

"You talked to Gittleman about carnal relations?"

"You haven't got a bimbo somewhere?"

"I can't take myself out to lunch. Alf's been picking up the tab at Gus's. I mention it to him and he says if I don't like it, he'll go and eat alone at the Chinaman's. Bimbo? Listen, Sar—"

"Don't start confessing, Walt. You've got a confessing voice."

"Pringle?"

"Tonight, yes."

Walt reaches for the can he keeps under the bed, takes two perfect potato chips—how do they do it?—and hands one across the space between the beds.

Together, they crunch in the dark.

"All right," Sarah says. "You want to get this show on the road or not?"

The dip in the ceiling where the dormer cuts into the roof where he always knocks his head whether he remembers to duck or not, history of a room, this room. The single window where the three of them watched Hurricane Carol lift the roof of Vicente Alves's house next door like a big housewife in the sky lifting a lid off a pot. And Sarah said, The basement, Walt, we've got to get to the basement. And Walt said, You think I didn't buy you a sturdy house? And Miriam begging to go out in the yard because she wanted to fly. Cars and houses were flying, why couldn't she? Sarah's closet, the room's only one (Walt keeps his clothes in his study), how there's always at least one shoe poking out. Other castaways, his shirt, his belt, his pants, lying on the room's only chair in the corner. Has ever a pair of buttocks sat on that chair? No, that chair's only for the stray clothes Walt's just taken off, nothing more, nothing less. Is buttocks singular or plural? The chest of blankets at the foot of the bed. How some nights, in the '40s, before Angelo installed the central heating, they'd pile their beds high with blankets, and he thinks of the time before the cold went away. That was the best, when you were still so cold but you knew that soon the warmth being birthed in the blankets would engulf you, smother you. The gap between the beds, that alley, that trench, that chasm, that abyss made for breaching. Always got to have a border to smuggle across. Why else maintain the fiction of the sovereignty of the flesh? But people do. Alf says he hasn't been laid since last Thanksgiving. Who'd want to hear that Walt and Sarah had found a way to still believe they were reinventing it even if they did it pretty much the same way every time? Sarah on top until she got tired, and then she'd flop on her back or stomach, depending, and say, All right, Walt, finish the job. I got Renda Grayboys coming here... But even amid the sameness there was always the hint of something novel because of some shift in position, or a thrust at a slightly different angle, or, yes, a finger exploring (again) regions heretofore said to be unexplored. That they could still think there were forbidden territories was itself...

Our exotic smells, our coughing, our strained muscles.

And now, again, Sarah's snowy thighs. My God, who'd believe it? And after, still, even these days, we pant like a couple of sweat-greasy horses. Slowed down a little, of course—who wouldn't?

Oh, but back in our day! Sarah used to fret. You think Mirry heard?

What if she did? Hurt the kid to hear us happy?

And think of the '60s, when the whole country got a little wilder and we joined in and did it twice a night? You remember, Sar? Now twice would be like rising from the dead, but history is history, and if not set down on paper it should at least be ruminated upon. Sarah and Walt Kaplan, one night, more than once, two entirely separate fornications. You got to acknowledge it, all of it, otherwise...

Otherwise what? What, Walt, what?

To ensure we don't merely exist in the dead present? Is that it? What do I even mean? That the oblivion of the now as opposed to the ecstasy of looking back—but wait, wait, if the present *is* the past, you fool, dissolving this very moment—then it is incumbent upon us now, now, to create the past because—so obvious! so rudimentary!—it's the uncreated past that is dead, not—yes! Push the beds, I wanna push the—

"Sar?"

No answer.

"Sar? Sarah?"

And Sarah's puttery snores in the dark and Walt lying spent in that same dark and Renda Grayboys (Renda? short for Brenda? must be) will be here at seven thirty—no, ten after—and why not just call it lunch. Why the extra *eon*?

3

Gus's Highland Spa

Walt and Alf Dolinsky lodged in their booth, the third one on the left if you're facing away from the door, slurping cold coffee, Gus's at Highland Avenue and Robeson Street. Only Gus calls the place the Highland Spa. The place is empty, but for them. Eleven a.m. on a Monday. Walt's having a salad. In unhappy solidarity, Alf's having one also. When Noreen got done howling, she went into the kitchen, and Gus howled for a while. Five minutes later, Noreen brought them both a bowl of iceberg lettuce and a half a slice of a blue-looking tomato, topped by a thick crown of bumpy Thousand Island. Neither man has taken more than a few bites.

"So how do you feel?" Alf says.

"You'll laugh."

"I'm asking."

Walt stabs a piece of lettuce and with determination and grit brings it to his mouth and masticates it for the roughage and essential vitamins.

"I feel reborn," Walt says.

Alf laughs.

"Took one look at Irv Pincus," Walt says. "Thought I was a goner."

"I heard. Sarah told Ruthie."

"Completely rejuvenated."

"Great."

"I don't wake up tired anymore."

"All right already."

For a while the two of them listen to the low babble of the television that hangs on precarious chains over the lunch counter. One day it's going to flatten somebody. A weatherman presides over a map of Massachusetts, an otherwise uneventfully shaped state. But for the flexing bicep of the Cape, we'd be as square as Nebraska. The weatherman predicts high humidity throughout the rest of the week.

"Now, there's a job right there," Alf says. "How much you think this jackass rakes in to tell us in August we've got high humidity?"

"But there's something," Walt says. He picks up a sugar packet and shakes it one way, shakes it the other way. Always the right amount of wiggle room. That's good packaging. You don't want too tight a fit.

Alf's watching a commercial. "What is it?" he says. "You're reborn. But what?"

Gus's. The Formica tabletops, the babbling TV. The little booth made for a couple of shrunken biddies. Walt and Alf hardly fit and are forever trying to prevent their knees from touching. There's the fly Walt murdered last week, still on the wall beside the steel napkin dispenser. A little bloodied asterisk. Hello, old friend, and my apologies. Only a lucky slap with an open palm.

"Sarah doesn't know," Walt says.

Alf pushes his salad away in disgust. "Sarah doesn't know what?"

"You know Sarah."

"Sure, I know Sarah. What doesn't she know?"

"I'm saying. She knows and she doesn't know."

Alf takes a long sniff at nothing. "Maybe you ought to see a shrink? They say it eases the mind. You've been through the wringer last couple of years. All you have to do is sit there and talk in circles. You'll love it for thirty-five dollars an hour."

"I talk to you free."

Alf's sleepy. He's always sleepy. With some people he actually falls asleep in the middle of the conversation. Ask Ruthie. But not with Walt. With Walt he's sleepy, but Walt has a way of keeping him just this side of conscious. Because with Walt, you never knew what was on his mind. It was always possible he could say something you couldn't see coming from here to Boston.

"Ruthie's got a nephew," Alf says. "Young kid but a little Einstein. Went to Brown Medical, the whole shebang. Doctor of psychiatry. I could give the kid a call and—"

"Alf, listen to me."

"So you got secrets. Big deal. You think I don't have a couple of secrets from Ruthie? And, listen, I, for one, don't give a damn where you were walking up President Avenue—"

Walt talks to what remains of his fly. "I'm telling you. Not a secret, just a thing she doesn't know."

"That's a fucking secret."

Noreen swings by with the coffeepot. "Hotten your sludges?" She pours, struts off.

"I'll say it again," Alf says. "That's one friendly set of buttocks, friendlier than her mouth, I'll tell—"

"It's all the walking," Walt says.

"Something to be said for it."

"Listen, Alf—"

"Christ almighty, Walt, I'm listening."

"I love my wife."

"I got to get back to work. I got linoleum to—"

"You don't understand."

"I understand you're nuts is what I understand."

Walt eats more salad. Alf takes a long swallow of scalding coffee and examines his friend, his oldest friend, the brother he never had. But how often do you look straight at a friend's face? All these years? You ever notice the changes? A friend's face never changes until one day you look straight at it and you find it's aged. It droops. It's tired. Wrinkles don't radiate out from his eyes only when he squints. Upper face crowded with tributaries. Because this whole time you've been seeing it—not seeing it— you've been seeing someone who's not there anymore, someone younger, a lot younger. You thought you were younger, too.

"I'm listening, Walt."

"You won't laugh?"

"I want to laugh, I'll laugh."

Walt shakes the sugar packet one way; he shakes it the other. "I'm afraid of dying because I love my wife. Before, and you know this, I welcomed dying almost like a hobby. More than that, often I craved it. And now—"

"Kid's name is Rothstein. Dr. Edward Rothstein. I'm telling you, he's smart. Maybe he can give you some pills."

The two hold their eyes on each other. First time, truly, in how many years? Walt Kaplan, Alf Dolinsky, such good buddies they bought family plots side by side at Beth El Cemetery.

Alf calls over Noreen.

"Yeah, Tubby?"

"Two turkey clubs. Hold Walt's mayo."

Noreen shouts, "You hear that, Gus, now they want turkey clubs. Tubby says hold Walt's mayo."

From the kitchen, Gus shouts, "Don't tell the chef what to do. If it goes good with mayo, I'll put on some mayo."

Noreen returns to her post by her coffeepot, under the TV.

"I'm telling you, that ass," Alf says.

"The walking."

Alf can hardly repel an urge to reach across the table and stroke Walt's face. Wan, stubbly, no matter how much Walt shaves, his face is always stubbly.

"Sarah says you want my Exercycle."

"I never said—"

"Take it. You think I ride the thing? Every time, I fall off. It's a hazard. You were going to do yourself in?"

"I had a notion. I had more than a notion."

"By walking up President Avenue? It's steep, but not that—"

"I wanted to be dead. That's all I know. I left the store and started walking. I wasn't thinking of anything else. I hardly even thought of Sarah. I was going to take High Street west and circle back down to the bridge. I don't know, Alf. I can't explain it. I must have wanted to see the city one last time. Love this city."

"Somebody's got to. Irv that bad?"

"You think I'd do it because of him?"

"So why?"

"You'd think I'd be able to explain it. Only this tiredness that wasn't even making me tired anymore. A tiredness that wasn't tiring. Because I was past all that. Which is why it felt over. All I had to do was finish the job. Does this make any sense?"

"No, but Rothstein—"

"Forget Rothstein."

"So you start walking."

"Yeah."

"And God said, You want to say goodbye? I'll show you good-bye, you fat bastard."

"Exactly. One ungrateful atheist Jew down. How many more to convince?"

"Walt, you think I wouldn't have had a heart attack if I'd tried to march up President Avenue in July?"

Walt just looks at him, his tongue poking out his left cheek, like a kid.

"And now?" Alf says.

Walt shrugs. "You know who President Avenue is named after?"

"No."

"Taft, when he visited in 1918."

"He'd need a crane to get up that hill," Alf says.

Beneath the table, Alf slides off one of his brogans, and with socked toes he tries to scratch his left ankle. Yeah, I love Walt Kaplan like the brother I never had. We were kids together in Fall River and we got old without noticing and we bought burial plots side by side on a lark, as if—what?—we thought we'd never need them?

"And now?" Alf says.

"Now I want both."

"To live and to die?"

"Right."

"Join the fucking club," Alf says.

"No, I mean it."

"You think I don't?"

Noreen clatters two plates before them. "Held the mayo," she says.

4

Gang Plank (at the Cove)

Walt wonders, as he always does when he and Sarah get together with Milt and Pearl Feldman, what the four of
them could possibly have to say to one another that hasn't been
said. The truth is there's comfort in the repetition of the same
stories, jokes, complaints, and petty jealousies, the same sneak
attacks on absent mutual friends. *You hear Goodyear's gonna fly
Alf Dolinsky over Fenway?* Sure, the ailments are becoming nas-
tier: cataracts, back trouble (though the new arch supports help),
hemorrhoids (ever-present open wounds), and, yes, people in
their circle have begun to die. But hadn't they always? Burl
Wanger, who'd been one of them for years, dropped dead in his
driveway at what? Thirty-nine? And before him, others. What
about his nephew Jacob, eight years old and nobody knew he
was a hemophiliac until he stepped on a piece of glass in—
what?—1937? 1938? Did Jacob bleed to death in the kitchen of
the house on Woodlawn the same year as the hurricane of '38?
Why can't he remember? Here they are again, Sarah and Walt,
Milt and Pearl, and amid the breathless rush of talk, the drinking, the food, the chewing, isn't it easy to lose yourself in the
uproar? Sarah and Walt planted together, squeezed, at the head
of the table, sporting plastic bibs with happy cartoon lobsters,

presiding over the dismemberment of real (a lot less happy) lobsters.

Milt, after who knows how many scotch and sodas, rises from his chair, glass raised, and Walt says, "What are you, the Statue of Liberty? Siddown, Milton."

But Pearl shouts, "No, no, you gotta hear this. He's been working on it, practicing in the mirror and everything."

And Milt raises his glass even higher, as if he's standing on his tiptoes, and begins to intone, "To Sarah and Walt Kaplan on the occasion of their thirty-fifth anniversary, I do humbly—"

"Oh, knock it off, Milt, siddown!"

But Sarah, swallowing lobster, says, "Let him say it, Walt, he's been practicing."

"As I say," Milt continues, "humbly wish to go back into the not-so-distant past to say that if my dearly deceased father could see me now in the company I keep—"

"Oh, for Christ with the humbly—"

"My father who fled the czar's conscription in 1888 wearing nothing but a jockstrap—"

"Siddown, Milt!"

"—was to imagine in his wildest dreams that his only begotten son would be sitting in a four-star establishment eating shellfish of all forbidden fruits barred to the chosen—"

"For the love of God—"

"Wait," Pearl says, "the Gang Plank only has three stars, if that. It's not like it's the Venus de Milo in Swansea. And isn't this supposed to be about Sarah and Walt?"

"Would you shaddup, Pearl? Would you? I'm getting there, I'm getting there, I'm getting there, I believe that my father would be less shocked by his son's material wealth"—the only thing Milt loves more than the sound of his own voice, Walt thinks, is the silence of other people while they're listening to that voice—"than by the quality of his comrades around the table, the flaunting of archaic dietary laws notwithstanding. Indeed, yes! What would have amazed my little pushcart-pushing father the most? you ask. Friendship! I propose that America's greatest gift to the Jews was not merely the opportunity to make a killing, noble pursuit that it is (I sell cardboard boxes, and I'm a merchant prince?), but time! Time itself! Leisure time, if you will, to pursue, in peace, without fear, friendship, in this case with two of the finest, noblest, kindest, generousest, er, generousistic—"

"All right," Walt says, "all right already, please, all right."

And to Walt's surprise, Milt, red faced and exhausted, sits.

Pearl applauds. "You may now kiss the bride," she says.

But it's Sarah who leans over and slops a buttery kiss on Walt's cheek. Walt pops another fried clam in his mouth. Then Sarah's all elbows again as she wields her clacker and squeezes a claw like she's crushing a skull. A crack, a spurt. With her fingers she tears away a bit of shell and pulls out a lump of pink-and-white-speckled meat. Walt finishes off another fried clam and dips the last of a tail into the little paper cup of butter, lobster being only an excuse to imbibe guiltless quantities of melted butter, elixir of the goddesses. He calculates what all this is going to cost Milt. Friendship is friendship, but at twenty-five dollars a pop? And Walt never more by himself than when he's surrounded by wife and friends. His cocoon of loneliness. Inside the noise, a shroud of silence. The rising din, the mayhem of the Gang Plank on a Saturday night. He's always able to do some good thinking in a crowd.

And before them on the table: carnage. The bright, unnatural-looking red-orange shards, little hills of the green stuff, the entrails Sarah insists you can eat, that they're full of nutrients. Demonstrates by gobbling. (Pearl said, "But isn't that babies?") Only human beings could make a party out of boiling a few fellow creatures alive and then cracking their backs open.

Now Pearl's saying they're saying saccharin causes cancer and the government's going to ban it. "Did you all read that? Walt must have read it. Walt reads everything."

"What doesn't cause cancer?" Milt shouts. "Tomorrow it will be twiddling our thumbs. Day after that, no blow jobs."

"You'll be safe!" Pearl claps.

Milt pleads to Sarah and Walt. "It's true, I haven't had head since Eisenhower."

"Ford, dear. Ford," Pearl says. "Just after Nixon's resignation. To celebrate. But if you think you're getting a blow job during Carter, forget about it."

"I voted for Nixon twice," Milt says. "I'd do it again tomorrow."

"Walt, on the other hand," Sarah elbows. "Walt enjoys his fair share—Walt? You here, Walt?"

"I voted for Hubert," Walt says.

"Think about it," Pearl says. "All the skinny women in the entire country are going to be hoarding the stuff like gold."

"A black market," Milt says. "Good business opportunity right there, Walt. Then you wouldn't have to 'aye aye, sir' Irv Pincus anymore—"

"Shush," Pearl says.

Sarah elbows Walt again. "There's a lot of meat in the feelers."

"In the what?"

Sarah holds up a thin, hairy lobster leg. "The feelers!"

"That's a leg, Sarah."

"Fish need legs like I need fins. You suck the meat out like this."

"Enough with all the sucking," Milt says. "You want to torture a guy?"

"Crustaceans," Walt says. "Lobsters are crustaceans."

"That doesn't mean they're not fish," Sarah says.

"I don't get it," Pearl says.

"Walt's educating us," Milt says. "Walt's a scholar of life. He thinks us philistines don't know lobsters are crustaceans."

"I just don't like the taste," Pearl says. "I want to eat chemicals, I'll drink Drano."

"What chemicals?"

"Saccharin!"

"She's back to saccharin!" Milt says. "So don't eat it, hoard it."

If I'm anything, Walt thinks, I'm a scholar of death. "The old rabbis," he says, "thought shellfish were bottom-feeders, the pigs of the ocean, which shows what they understand about the cyclical nature—"

"See what I mean? The man's a professor. You missed your calling, Walt. Could have spent your life stuffing wisdom into unwitting ears like your brother, Arthur. Think of the pension—"

"Didn't Itchy Burman drink Drano?" Sarah says.

"Honey Burman's brother?" Walt says. "Sold insurance? Moved to New Bedford? Used to come into the store and scoff at the prices? That Itchy? He drank Drano? The guy seemed so sure of how much everything should cost. He must have taken a Ward's catalog and calculated—"

"Honey and Itchy, are those real names?" Pearl says.

"How many Itchys do you know?" Sarah says. "Calculated what?"

"Wasn't there an Itchy Rosenberg at Brown Elementary?" Milt says.

"There was," Walt says. "What happened to Itchy Rosenberg?"

"No idea," Milt says. "Didn't go to Durfee High. We'd know it if he went to Durfee, wouldn't we?"

"At least there's a point to Drano," Pearl says. "Trying to scald your insides or whatever. I just don't see the point of saccharin. It's fake for the sake of fake."

"Except that it causes cancer."

"Good point."

Itchy Rosenberg. Walt remembers the kid used to walk on his

hands. He'd wave at everyone with his feet and walk from school all the way to Robeson Street on his hands. The people we knew once as kids, where do they disappear? Two Itchys. Isn't it amazing, in a single lifetime, one man can know two Itchys? One was a skinflint who drank Drano, the other waltzed on his hands and then vanished? If God were ever called upon to explain himself, what the hell would he say? *Behold, I am the creator of uncountable forgettable souls. Nonetheless! Some of them will carry immortal nicknames into oblivion.*

Walt looks out the big plate-glass windows of the Gang Plank, or tries to. Because of all the light, he can't get past his own reflection and the reflections of the other diners. But they don't call it the Gang Plank for nothing. The restaurant stretches narrow out into Mount Hope Bay. Sooner or later a hurricane will carry the place away. For the moment, there's money to be made. He thinks of the cold, dark water of the bay. How he'd craved it, or convinced himself that he craved it. To be or not to be isn't the question. Did he want it, or did he only want to want it? How can you tell the difference? Ay, there's the rub. His mother used to say, Walt, you don't know yourself coming or going. Always chasing your tail. One question asks another and another and another. But some questions have answers. You hear me, Walter? Some questions don't need another question.

"'Crustacean' is, of course, the proper term," Milt says. "'Shellfish' is a colloquialism, but Walt always feels the need to light the way. You see, Walt's a ponderer, he thinks deeply about deep things, he's like that statue we saw in Paris, the naked guy who pondered himself into a pretzel—"

"Milt," Pearl says quietly. "Wait." And there's something different about her voice, something out of the flow of talk, less hyena, less stupid. Her real voice, the voice she must use in the bedroom, in the morning, before they shove the curtains open.

"What is it?" Milt says.

"Your face," she says even more quietly. "Blood. Blood's pouring—"

And it is, and Milt puts his hand up to his nose. "Nosebleed," he says. "You know I sometimes get—"

"Not in public," Pearl says. "Here." She tries to hand Milt her soiled napkin. And it's hard to say exactly, but there's something off-kilter. Maybe they've all had too much to drink, especially Milt. He refuses to take the napkin and looks at his wife with his bloody face. The blood looks almost blackish in the light, and it's draining out of his nostrils, down his lips, off his chin.

"Milt, please."

Sarah's pressing her heel down into Walt's shoe.

Do something about it.

What do you want me to do about it? He doesn't want a napkin, he doesn't want to cover it up, he wants—

Something between Milt and Pearl. Who knows what? Something buried rising? If we're mysteries to ourselves, how can we possibly know other people? As if he wants her to look at him now, here, in public. Sometimes the blood just has to flow? This won't, Walt knows, be one of those stories they tell. *Remember that time Milt's nose bled at the Gang Plank? Pearl tried to give him a napkin, but he wouldn't take it.* No. They'll remember it, but they won't tell it. Why not? The color of an old friend's blood is that shocking?

Yeah.

"Milt, your face."

"Itchy Rosenberg walked on his hands," Walt says. "Do you remember?"

"He did!" Milt shouts, his nose still pouring forth, a little geyser, the tablecloth like a crime scene. "I do remember. Amazing, that kid could walk for blocks!"

5

Garbage Day

Oh sweet smell of Monday in a Fall River August, after the garbage crews have torn through like marauders, dumped their hauls, and heaved the corrugated-steel trash cans back into the street so that they roll to the edge of the curb, where they lie like scattered souls. That smell, putrid, syrupy rot, fermenting in the bottom of the cans, how greedy Walt is to inhale it. He stops the Lincoln in the middle of the street and gets out and huffs it up, the odor of his city, like smelling your own armpits, there's pride there, a private pride, but pride...

6

The Jaffe Girl

Earlier that night, as they were leaving the service, Walt had watched Sarah say a few words to the mother, Lorraine Jaffe. This was in September. It seemed to Walt that as each month went by, every year, worse and worse things happened. Stupid. Where to start? How far back? How long ago was the Inquisition? Bad few years right there. Impossible to say that, even in its most terrible moments, this abominable century has been a worse time to be a human being than any other. And yet maybe there was something to be said for the notion that the horror was creeping ever closer to his own street, his own doorstep, his own wilted geraniums in their sun-bleached orange pots. A sixteen-year-old girl he and Sarah both knew found strangled in the woods behind Kennedy Park? Nero, Attila the Hun, Isabella and Ferdinand (were those the bad ones or the couple that was chummy with Columbus?), Hitler, this loony tune Pol Pot who'd pluck your eyes out for wearing sunglasses—with these characters you knew where things stood. But rape and murder and pillage under the reign of Jimmy Carter? It just didn't add up.

Every once in a while, if they'd seen all the movies that were on at the mall in Seekonk, Sarah and Walt would attend Friday-night services as a social occasion. Sarah wasn't especially de-

246 • PETER ORNER

vout, but she appreciated the ritual of gathering among people she'd always known, even if half of them she no longer spoke to. Walt complained coming and going. It's smoke and mirrors without the smoke and mirrors. But he, too, felt at ease at Beth El. They were Jews like they wore shoes or overate at lunch. They stood whenever everybody else stood and sat down when everybody else sat down. Walt couldn't deny that there was a certain military mindlessness to it that wasn't entirely unpleasurable. He'd sit and gaze up at the tall stained-glass windows that depicted the twelve tribes of Israel. Let's see, we've got the Levis, nice folks, aren't they in the carpet business? And oh yes, the Dan clan. Husband's all right, it's the wife you got to watch out for. Woman sold me a camel lame in the foreleg, had to leave him to die in Smyrna. And Walt also couldn't deny, either, that the sanctuary itself was stately, if now too grand a scale for a vanishing congregation. The only Jews who stayed in Fall River were the ones who'd died and the ones waiting for the opportunity. And this particular Friday night, Rabbi Ruderman had spent forty-five minutes hectoring the few people who'd shown up about those who hadn't. *Those of our members who choose shallow entertainments over the perpetuation of their own culture...* Walt had cupped his hand over Sarah's ear, and said, "See? Told you we should have seen *Silver Streak* a third time."

Now home, in their room, Walt wants to know what Sarah had said to Lorraine Jaffe. Sarah's sitting on the edge of the bed, hunched over, pulling off a heel. She stays like that for a moment, frozen in the act of pulling, and looks at him. Walt's standing beside the bed loosening his belt.

"What did I say?" Sarah says. "What could anybody? I said I'm sorry."

"You said more than that," Walt says. "I saw your lips move more than sorry. How long's it been?"

"About three weeks."

"Her face looked like it just happened."

"I would think," Sarah says. "Wouldn't you think? That over and over, it would just keep happening. That first moment you heard?"

Sarah returns to the battle with her shoe, wins, and tosses the heel through the open closet door and out of her life forever. Never again will those shoes meet these feet. She stands, yanks her dress over her head, and examines her girdle-clad self in the mirror screwed to the back of the closet door.

"I can hardly be contained," she says.

"I'll contain you," Walt says. "Come here."

"I said, 'I can't imagine.' I said, 'Lorraine, I can't even begin to imagine.'"

Walt lets fall his pants and tosses his belt toward the corner chair, misses. Once again, the two of them in their little bedroom. The AC's been fixed, but they turn the unit on only just before they go to sleep. Save a few bucks. And anyway at this point in early September the humidity's so thick their sweat is another layer of skin. They hardly notice it anymore. They could undress in separate rooms now that Miriam's in Chicago and has been for nearly twenty years, hard to believe, but they've never spread out to her room. Here they huddle, night after night. The overhead light's off. Only the lamp beside Sarah's bed is on. The familiar yellow-brown burlap light. As if they're in a cave. There's not enough room on the walls for their shadows. Hardly recognizable blobular shapes hulk down from the ceiling.

"But you can," Walt says. "You can imagine."

"It was something to say."

"You think Miriam never went in the woods with a boy she hardly knew?"

"More than once with that Fradkin."

"That's what I'm saying."

"What?" Sarah says. "What are you saying?"

"That we're always dodging bullets."

"How many times can we have this conversation, Walt? Wake up in the morning, you're dodging bullets. Go to sleep, dodging bullets. Walk down the street—" She stops, unfastens her clasps. "I almost look better without all the armor."

"Why didn't he just—?" Walt says. "Why'd he have to—?"

Sarah turns to face him, and Walt, in spite of himself, can't help but think, Breasts, what strange, exquisite gifts bestowed to a wholly unworthy malekind.

"You mean why spoil a good time by choking her to death?"

Sarah grabs a nightdress off a hook in the closet, pulls it over her head, and once again faces the mirror. Walt unbuttons his shirt. We put on, we take off. We button, we unbutton. On, un, on, un.

"Now I look like a curtain."

"I guess I do mean that," Walt says. "Yes. Exactly, why spoil—"

"It must have gone hand in hand," Sarah says. "He must not have wanted the one without the other. Also—"

"A body can't talk." Walt's standing there in shorts and shirt-tails. He's still got his tie on, his Friday-night noose.

"Right," Sarah says. "A body can't talk."

Walt watches Sarah in the mirror. Which is different from looking directly at someone. She's looking back at him. It's like they're spying on each other. They'd both known the girl, seen her grow up. Walt had been noticing her downtown in recent years. Pale, almost translucent skin. Something furtive about her. But lately so many of them had that look. The dope, the boredom, too young to leave here, too old to have anything to do with their parents. Wandering in place. Miriam had taken the first boat out in the form of a young lawyer from Chicago. Used to bother him, and certainly it could be going better for her. Philip's angry, all the time angry, Miriam says. What's he got to be so angry about? God knows. As Sarah says, What hurts you, hurts you. A man's angry, he's going to be angry, whatever happens. Still, he couldn't imagine Miriam having stayed in town, even if she hadn't left so fast.

Sarah goes across the hall to the bathroom. Walt listens to her run the faucet as she relieves herself, as is her custom. Does she do this for his benefit or because she doesn't want to listen to it herself? How many thousands of nights and he doesn't know the answer to this basic question, either. But shouldn't there be some things they'll never know about each other, not out of shame, but simply because? Because because because.

A guy out walking his dog found the girl in the morning. There'd been a rock concert in Kennedy Park the night before. He's heard people blame the music. Irv Pincus, for instance, that great thinker, ranting around the store about jungle music, as if an electric guitar had seized her by the throat. Three days later they arrested the kid in New Hampshire. Two years out of Durfee High School, lived with his mother in Mechanicsville, unemployed. Not Jewish, everybody so relieved.

Sarah's still in the can. Walt knocks.

"Have you seen my slippers?"

"No."

"What are you doing?"

"I'm doing what I'm doing."

"So you think he just wanted to screw her and then decided to kill her after? Or he wanted both from the beginning?"

No answer. He waits.

Five minutes, he stands there. All's quiet. The door opens. She's wearing a robe. Her face is caked with the white goo again. The goo makes her eyes look different, heightens their intensity, big mummy eyes that stare out at him from a great distance. White goo means separate beds separately. Unusual for a Friday night. Walt steps aside to let her pass. You can't touch the stuff, apparently ruins its effect. But when he returns to the bedroom, she's lying on his bed, unrobed.

"The light?" Walt says.

"Leave it on," Sarah says.

"Yeah?"

7

Gus's Highland Spa

Y ou want to know something?"

"Today," Alf says. "Today, I just want to eat. Cheeseburger, Noreen. Extra cheese."

Noreen on a stool beneath the TV. She's watching a game show where one partner tries to get the other partner to say a word without saying the word. Like charades, with words, which defeats the purpose. *It's like when there's water coming down on your head. Like it's raining except it's not. Raining out of the spout, you know, and you've got soap, a bar of soap—*

A bath!

Right, right, but you're standing up—

Shower!

"Did I say I was prepared to take your order?" Noreen says.

"And screw the salad," Alf says. "Salad can go to hell."

"How did you know?" Walt says.

"Know what?" Alf says.

"That I've been reading Dante."

"Dante Palandri?"

"Dante Dante."

"A writer. I've heard of him. You think I'm undereducated. An Italian poet of the Renaissance."

Noreen says, "What kind of cheese?"

"Gorgonzola."

"Late Middle Ages," Walt says.

"Gorgonzola?" Noreen says. "On a cheeseburger?"

"Just before they're about to enter the hellfire," Walt says, "you know what Virgil says to Dante?"

"Don't know, don't care."

"You two scholars need a little more time?"

"Okay, cheddar," Alf says.

"Walt? What are you having?"

"Roast beef," Walt says. "Please. Your cheeks are very rosy today, Norry. They are always rosy, but today the rosiness is more pronounced—"

"Hold the mayo?" Noreen says.

"Hell, no."

"Alf, what kind of cheese on the burger?"

"I told you cheddar. No, make it Swiss now that you forgot the cheddar already."

"Why can't you be polite and gracious and have a sense of joie de vivre like Walt?"

"I didn't almost die," Alf says. "See, he almost died, or thinks he almost died, and now he's Jesus's little helper all of a sudden."

Noreen saunters. First, she saunters in place, which is a nice trick. Then she saunters away. They could measure their lives in how many times Noreen's done that little strut without moving before swinging around and walking away from their table, slow, that swingy walk—back to her post beneath the TV. Couldn't they? It's something she does with her knees as she walks, a slight bend followed by a tiny upward spring.

"What does Virgil say?" Alf says.

"He doesn't say anything," Walt says.

"What?"

"The old man smiles."

"Why?" Alf says.

"Why?" Walt says.

"I just asked you why," Alf says. "You always have to why my why?"

Walt reaches across the table and grips his old friend's head and pulls it toward him across the table. When was the last time he touched Alf's head? Has he ever?

"You going to kiss me?" Alf says.

Walt shouts: "Because other people's suffering is a hoot!"

"Fat men," Noreen says, "keep it down. The other patrons."

"What other patrons?" Alf says.

"Okay," Noreen says. "Business is a little slow. But there's potentiality."

From the kitchen, Gus says, "Business has been slow since 1953."

"Hope springs eternal," Noreen says.

On the TV, one player is shouting, "It's like this thing, you know, that a woman puts on, you know, to hold up her—"

"Bra!" Alf shouts.

"You want to know something else?" Walt says.

"No," Alf says.

"I'm on canto eight," Walt says. "And already I've committed every sin there is to commit. Can you believe it? A monogamous, generally by choice, furniture salesman in a forgotten midsize American city, wife, daughter, two grandkids, no criminal record, a few smutty thoughts here and there, and I've committed them all? Gluttony, check. Greed, double-check. Sullen? Sullen's a sin. When am I not sullen? Despair! That too. It's a sin to despair. But the kicker, you know what the first one is? Guess what the first sin in the whole book is. Go ahead, guess."

Alf sticks his tongue out. Little pink button of tongue. Doesn't want to, who would willfully want to, but Walt thinks of the penis of a small dog they used to have. Porgie. Ran into Robeson

Street one day when Miriam was seven, and that was the end of Porgie. Flattened by a Dodge. And yet somewhere in a murky corner of his brain, little Porgie's dick lives. And now: it's poking at him out of Alf's mouth.

"Mediocrity," Walt says. "First sin's mediocrity."

8

A Single Chair

The thing was, the more unsuccessful he became, the harder he worked at it. Everybody loved him, and this of course was the problem. Walt Kaplan was simply too likable. His father had warned him. *Don't get too chummy with people, they'll fleece you blind.* And it's not, old Max used to say, about selling any one thing. Don't think of a chair as a chair. A chair is forty chairs. Get sentimental about selling a single chair, and you're doomed. But for Walt that was exactly it. One chair *was* one chair. He couldn't, for the life of him, look at a single chair and see forty's worth. Because Walt Kaplan, unlike his blessed father, understood the poetry of furniture. A chair *is* a chair, and you sell one chair, you're selling a harbor for one's body, a chair that will, day after day, accept the exhaustion of loins, welcoming them back home, call it a kind of stand-in for a mother's womb...

You still don't see this, Poppa? I trade in small harbors.

And you wonder why you're broke?

9

TLAW Packaging

In 1972 Fall River elected an undertaker mayor. Walt voted for him. Why not? He figured a guy who knew his way around embalming fluid was the guy their beloved city needed. Enough already declaring Fall River dead only to resurrect it a few years later in order to declare it dead again. Let it be dead and stay dead. Now dress it up and make it look pretty. Driscoll turned out to be just another pol in a dark suit, empty promises growing like the hair out of his earholes. Four years later, this past January 1976, Driscoll presided over the opening of the new city hall as the cars and trucks zoomed by underneath, past Fall River, as Walt Kaplan hadn't needed to be a clairvoyant to predict fifteen years earlier. You build a highway through a city, people aren't going to pull over and shop in your stores. The only city hall in America constructed over an interstate. To build it they had to obtain special air rights from the federal government. Out of some cramped sense of nostalgia, the city fathers had insisted that this new city hall rise, more or less, where the old one had stood unmolested for 117 years. Even the Great Fire of 1928 couldn't bring down the old granite city hall, and to this day whenever he stands on South Main looking northeast, Walt can't help but see it still, sooty, ugly, gloomy, churchlike. The place always made him think of burning witches. They blasted it to bits in '62. People now say it was elegant and stately. It wasn't. It looked like a Transylvanian prison. But it was Fall River. It was us. What's this new one? Floating over a highway? Already falling apart?

Not fair to blame this albatross on Mayor Driscoll. The thing was in the works long before he took office. But back in '72, Walt was willing to put more than a little faith in the mortician, believing he'd put his experience to use. Walt had stood there in the crowd in front of the Hotel Mellen, the temporary city hall, where so many years earlier he'd fallen for a hatcheck girl, and listened to Wilfred C. Driscoll deliver, from the hotel steps, his inaugural address in a voice he must have used to console the family of the deceased. Even, measured, practical. The intonation of a man with capable hands and a touch of the poet. *My fellow Fall Riverites, we find ourselves at a time in our history that is critical to our future. In my lifetime, Fall River has declined from a prosperous industrial center... I think it is apparent to all that our city cannot change its course without additional monies. That is not to say that with the acquisition of money all our problems will be solved, but I would suggest that without additional revenues we will be severely limited in what we can do. Money begets money. Investment begets investment. And progress begets progress... But there is no reason to accept these conditions if we have imagination, stamina, and resolve to look boldly into the future rather than regrettably into the past! Let us begin to dream broadly and guilelessly, if only to balance those who never dream at all.*

Guilelessly? After the address, Walt had walked back to his small storefront office at 290 Columbia Street thinking over the undertaker's choice of words. He'd recently opened his own packaging business, one of several businesses he'd founded since Kaplan's Furniture closed for good in 1965. There'd been a short-lived candy store on Ferry Street. He tried to start a mail-order catalog business out of the house. He'd been a silent partner in a now-defunct sweater factory.

Walt called this new venture: Tlaw Packaging.

"Like it, Sar? Get it? 'Tlaw'?"

"Is it supposed to mean something?"

"Think about it."

"I'm thinking and there's nothing—"

"Tlaw! Tlaw!"

"Walt, I don't—"

"Right there. You're close. You're warm. Tlaw. *T—L—A—W.*"

"Coleslaw?"

"Forget it."

"It just doesn't have a ring."

"Too late. I already printed up the stationery, the business cards, commissioned the sign. Bernard's going to run an ad in the *Herald* on Tuesday."

Business wasn't booming. Friends tried to steer accounts his way. He called in a few chits from way back. Layaway plans he never collected on after the store shut down. "Keep the couch, Vic, but look, could you steer some orders my way? I'm sinking here…" But he needed to work the phones, expand his territory. Drum up some new clients, connect with some of the younger sales managers who lived out in Freetown, Swansea, Dighton. But the phone itself, the very sight of it sitting there cradled, waiting for his hot air to give it some life, exhausted him. And this was before he even dialed anybody. A pre-exhaustion, an anticipation of exhaustion. The thought of speaking into the mouthpiece for the express purpose of cajoling a stranger into parting with his money, to give it to Walt Kaplan as opposed to someone else offering roughly the same service for roughly the same price, had become intolerable. Face-to-face on the floor, you could look someone in the eye, tell a joke, complain about the wet snow, exchange a laugh. Something personal about furniture. You sold people an idea of who they thought they were, or who they wanted to turn into. Did they aspire to a classical look, to an idea of refinement? *You strike me as Ethan Allen types.* Or maybe they wanted to be more modern, up-to-date? *Just received a shipment of Scandinavian-style recliners. They're saying they're ergonomic, whatever the hell this means. Sit and you tell me.* Always better to play the rube than the know-it-all. Now he sold plastic wrap. Sarah said, "Hard to start a business in your fifties, Walt, just give it time." He did give it time. He gave it nothing if not time. He'd sit there in that little office, visible from the street, and try to talk his fingers into a cold call. Unlike at the store, he had no employees, no salesmen, no upholsterers, no secretaries, no cashiers. He didn't even do the packaging. He subcontracted to a company in Pawtucket. A solo middleman. Calls, not many. Now he talked so much in his head even he no longer paid attention.

Dream guilelessly? Sure, that I can do, Mr. Mayor. And so all that afternoon in 1972, he did; in honor of the newly minted funeral director, Walt dreamed guilelessly. Gross profits? Net profits? Investment begets investment? No, as the mayor so profoundly noted, money will not solve all our problems, oh no, he dreamed, daydreamed, guilelessly, as he often did, about the Great Fire of 1928 and how his father took him downtown the morning after. (Apologies, Mayor Driscoll, but I only dream of the past, regrettably and otherwise.) As he stared at the stillborn phone, Walt thought of how his mother woke him up before dawn. He was around ten. His mother dressed him up in three coats. It was that cold. And you could smell the smoke all the way up the hill, even inside their house on Dudley Street with all their windows closed. He walked with his father straight down icy President Avenue. And there it was. Or rather there it wasn't. Where's downtown? From Bank Street to Pocasset, annihilated. A descent into a frozen hell. Charred ruins of all that had been so familiar were caked with white crust. The night before had been so frigid that the water froze moments after it left the firemen's hoses. Where buildings had once stood were tall, hanging pillars, stalactites, of ice. When the sun comes out, if the sun comes out, stand beneath one of those and it will melt and stab you to death, his father said. The Rialto Theater, the Hotel Mohican, Granite Block (where his father got his hair cut and visited his accountant *and* saw his doctor and his dentist), the Buffington Building—gone. Temple Beth El—gone. The banks: the Metacomet, the Union (where his father kept his money), the Mattapoissett-Pocasset—all gone.

Fire companies had come from as far away as Newport, Boston, Hartford. And in the morning, there they stood, the firemen, in their black coats and pointy hats. They looked like giant leprechauns. Of special interest to his father and the other businessmen who'd come to survey the ruins were the safes that survived. He remembered their distinguished names. One was an Underwriters; another was a Herring-Hall-Marvin. You'd think it would have been a mournful morning, but the fact was the men were so giddy they could hardly contain themselves. Extraordinary! The safes are hardly scorched! And in the spirit of Underwriters and Herring-Hall-Marvin, Fall River, they proclaimed, will rise up once again, strong out of the ashes. Better than before! Two little girls, the Sullivan sisters, the fire chief's daughters, handed out pink carnations. The men all put them in the lapels of their long coats. The Sullivan sisters, one was Mary, and the other—

The phone rang.

"Tlaw Packaging. You make it, we seal the deal."

"Mr. Tlaw, please."

"Speaking."

"What sort of packaging do you do, Mr. Tlaw?"

"Industrial."

"Industrial. It sounds—how shall I put it?—quite a manly undertaking."

"You don't know the half of it. And you are?"

"Oh, me? It's Mrs. Nalpak."

"Mrs. Nalpak! Now there's a name for a packaging company. Why didn't I—do you have any widgets I might package for you, Mrs. Nalpak? Say in the two-to-three-hundred range."

"Aren't you the one with the widget, Mr. Tlaw?"

"I'm not even sure of that anymore."

"Now, that's just not true. I can testify—you forgot your lunch."

"I know."

"You want me to—"

"It's all right."

"Any better today?"

"Nope, not that I've—people walk by, they peer in, they say, Isn't that Walt Kap—I got to get some blinds."

"What about Irv?"

"Over my corpse full of maggots."

"He says he needs someone of your depth of experience."

"The minute Kaplan's shuts down, he opens—"

"It was three years after you closed and he—"

"Popular Furniture? What kind of man calls his own store popular?"

"They're coming for dinner, Irv and Dottie—"

"I just feel banged up, Sar."

"I know, sweet."

"Nothing's even banged me up and I feel—"

"I know, I know," Sarah says.

"I got to go."

"Where?"

"Calls, I gotta—"

What was the other Sullivan sister's name? Mary and—who?

10

Massachusetts v. Rhode Island

On a map Fall River looks like a tolling bell. Walt used to sit weekend days in his shoebox study, hardly insulated from the bedlam of his little family (extraordinary, what a racket two females can unleash on a house, such hollering, such pattering up and down the stairs, up and down, up and down the—), smooth flat a map with both palms, and behold: *Fall River*. A bell in motion, swinging left. A map is not a closed system. Look at a map long enough, and it always yields something that wasn't there the last time you looked. Today, the discovery of a little street in the Flint called Merino. Merino? Wool? When did Merino Street come to be? Has it always been there, hiding off Alden? Maybe, maybe not. An impossibly detailed view of a city, one you couldn't even get up in a plane because there's no way, even from up there, you could take in every contour, every rumpled edge. No, believers, a map isn't a precise render; it's a beautiful guess. A lonely surveyor's exquisite shot in the dark. A map's a fantasy. Spill some water on a piece of paper and wait for it to dry. Doesn't take long for a shoreline to form along the edge. That's a map of somewhere. Oh, imperfect ejaculation! And here lies Fall River spread open before me, a lovely city, still. He runs his finger from Steep Brook to Brayton Avenue, a length of maybe fifty inches of paper. All that pavement, all that sweat, longing, striving, house after house, triple-decker after triple-decker. Before him a symbol that can hardly contain what it's supposed to be a symbol of. Silently it seethes. And yet this very map, flimsy and rippable as it is (How about the time they were driving to Maine and Walt shouted, "Which way, Sarah? What does the map say, Sarah?" And she ripped the map into shreds and said, "That. That's what the map says"), remains the only viable instrument that can provide us, with any reasonable degree of certainty, the answer to the elemental question: Where does Fall River begin and where does Fall River end?

(Related but not, of course, essential: Where does the irrelevance known as Tiverton, Rhode Island, otherwise known as some trees, begin?)

And yet, again, and yet. In this instance, the map failed, failed utterly. Take note: the great boundary tumult between Fall River and Rhode Island, formally known as 37 U.S. 657. Yes, the question of Fall River's southern boundary reached the august chambers of the United States Supreme Court in 1838! The roots of this maddeningly overcomplicated wrangle had to do with the original purchase of colossal swaths of Pocasset territory in exchange for some muskets, a few bushels of grain, and twenty pairs of leather shoes. To the Indians, who had no concept of private ownership of land (how could land possibly be divisible from sky?), it seemed like a good deal, at the time. Occupy land? In perpetuity? Impossible. When the impossible became a lot less impossible, King Philip and the brave squaw, Fall River's own Weetamoe, saw the writing on the wall and rose up. Eventually both: crushed. Philip ambushed. Weetamoe drowned in the Taunton. They stuck her pretty head on a pole. Call King Philip's War a bloody footnote. Haven't we always? Named our banks, our streets after them. We kill, we honor. We rented on Weetamoe for seven years when Mirry was little. After Plymouth and the Massachusetts Bay merged in 1691, George II, fifty years later, was of the opinion that Massachusetts was getting too big for its britches and so lopped off a piece of it. Roger Williams was a nut, but Rhode Island kissed better royal ass. Besides, what was the harm in giving away a piece of the pie that to an English king was an abstraction anyway? George II didn't know Rhode Island from Punjab. Henceafter, Fall River's southern border was demarked as the old buttonwood tree on the east side of South Main, just south of Columbia Street. South Main and Columbia? You got to be kidding me. That meant everything south of Corky Row was Rhode Island? At that time fifteen hundred taxable souls and property, but even then it was foreseeable that here Fall River would soon be spreading. It must have felt to the Bordens, the Bluffoms, the Higginbothams, the Moneypennys, the Wombats, like they'd had a leg amputated. Took a revolution and a few more decades to right this wrong, and even then the Supreme Court stopped short. According to Orin Fowler's history, the court "granted full claim to neither state." But the majority of urban blocks were returned to Fall River, and the line is now at State Avenue, at Townsend Hill. Thank the God I wish I could believe in.

Mirry's eyeball at the keyhole. "What are you doing?" she says.

"I'm overseeing the restoration."

"What?"

"Righting monarchical wrongs."

"The crimes of Rhode Island again?" Mirry says.

Where's the key that belongs in that keyhole? It's been lost since—what?—1941? You'd think somebody would have stumbled on it. Fell in a vent? Mouse took it?

"The repercussions reverberate to this day. Globe Corners still suffers from lack of economic integration and adequate transit routes."

"Anything else new?" Mirry asks. "Any discoveries today?"

"Actually, just now, this second," Walt says. "I did notice there's a little neck north of Bluffom's Beach I've never—"

"What are you going to call it?"

"Don't know."

"We're out of dead Indians?"

"We might be."

"That's because we only know a few of their names."

"Holy smokes, you *are* my daughter! Funny, just today I was wondering about your mother, contemplating a paternity test—"

"A what?"

Walt gets up and sinks, heavy, to his knees, peeks into the keyhole. It's shining. A daughter's eyeball. Map that, ye cartographers.

And Sarah, downstairs, shouts: "Miriam! Grilled cheese!"

11

Rachel Plotkin

The evening *Herald News* reported that Plotkin's wife drowned in North Watuppa Pond. What wasn't in the paper was that the following morning, a Tuesday, Plotkin, a stockbroker, went to work as usual. On his lunch hour he left his office and walked two blocks to Beth El on High Street to make the arrangements.

Immediately, he waved away the rabbi's condolences. When the rabbi tried to close the office door, Plotkin said, "Please, leave it be."

The rabbi, actually a substitute rabbi filling in for Rabbi Ruderman, who was convalescing after a hernia operation, wasn't going to rock any boats. And wasn't he well versed in the angry confusions of grief? The quieter ones, the substitute rabbi thought, suffer more. It bottles up.

The rabbi, on the advice of Fred Solinsky, president of the congregation, permitted Rachel Plotkin to be interned in a consecrated section of the cemetery in the Plotkin family plot, as opposed to across the service road. Besides, the substitute rabbi, who'd come to Fall River from Albany and couldn't wait to get home, justified, to himself, since nobody else had questioned it, that it could have been an accident. From what he'd read in the paper, she'd left no note, and there were no rocks in her pockets. That she'd gone for a swim in the Fall River water supply in October was far-fetched, but hadn't stranger things happened under the eyes of God? And: Jewish law is nothing if not flexible.

The rabbi and Plotkin agreed to a brief graveside service, to take place Thursday morning in order to give relatives time to be present.

"There will be no shiva," Plotkin said.

"That's your choice," the rabbi said. "But you can't stop other immediate relations."

"I know."

"If you want to talk, as you can see," the rabbi said with a laugh, "my door's always—"

"I don't want to talk, Rabbi."

The two shook hands. The temple secretary, Connie Blum, listened to all this while pretending to file documents in the front office. Connie told Renda Grayboys, who told Ruthie Dolinsky, who told Sarah, etc., etc.

Rachel was Sarah's optometrist. She'd tested Sarah's eyes and fitted her out for new glasses not a month earlier. Jerry Plotkin had gone to school with Walt and had been, for years, Walt's broker.

Sarah and Walt attended the service on Thursday morning. There were five or six rows of chairs, all filled. The rest of the mourners stood. One of those sunny days in October when the light had that gentle yellow hue. Plotkin sat in the front with one chair separating him from Rachel's two grown children. Their mother's chair, Walt thought. The substitute rabbi spoke lovingly and briefly about Rachel's love of family, as well as her commitment to her work.

One of the children, the daughter, stood up and spoke about how her mother enjoyed walking at Horseneck Beach after a storm. "She was at home out there in wind." Then she sat down.

Plotkin himself didn't speak. He didn't take off his dark glasses. Nor did he willingly receive any consolation from those who wanted to offer it. A few people refused to recognize this unwillingness and hugged him anyway, Plotkin's arms stiff at his sides. He didn't join the line of mourners who emptied small, tentative shovelfuls of dirt upon Rachel's casket.

That night, they did sit shiva at Rachel's brother's house in Providence. Sarah and Walt drove up with a casserole.

"After my last exam, I probably spent an hour dithering over frames," Sarah said. "I'd choose one frame and then another and go back to not liking the first one. She only laughed at me."

"While Rome burns," Walt said.

"What?"

"I said while Rome burns."

"Turn off at West River," Sarah said.

"Where?"

"West River."

"How will I know it? The smell? Would it kill Rhode Island to put up a street sign?"

No, there hadn't been a social friendship, but there had always been warmth. When Sarah cheated on her exam, Rachel would swat her elbow. "Close your left eye, Mrs. Kaplan. I'm not the Mass RMV."

A second marriage for both Plotkin and Rachel. The first Mrs. Plotkin (née Borowitz) had left after three or four years and moved to Connecticut. Whether it was Plotkin, or Fall River, no-body knew, but it was said the ex-wife remarried richer. Rachel was originally from Warwick and, before she married Plotkin, had only worked in Fall River, and so nobody knew what her née was. (Plotkin, too, met her while he was having his eyes examined.) She'd once told Sarah she'd lost her first husband young. "I was just a kid and we had two more kids. He was there, and then he wasn't there." At the brother's house, Rachel's two children stood at the door and dutifully accepted the casseroles and condolences of a stream of a Fall Riverites who'd come to tell them how much their mother had meant to them. Maybe it had something to do with the fact that she'd cared for so many pairs of eyes. People were rattled by her death as if somehow it might affect their vision.

Plotkin didn't show up.

There was side talk that Rachel might have been ill for some time, and that as a consequence she'd decided to take things into her own hands. It was possible, but Sarah thought back to the last time she'd seen her, how buoyant she'd seemed, more so than usual. But hadn't she heard that for someone who's made up their mind, everything becomes so much lighter? It made sense, in a way. Like suddenly nothing costs you anything anymore?

In the absence of any actual facts—Plotkin wasn't talking and who would be crass enough to ask her children?—the murmuring, at the shiva and around town, naturally gravitated toward blaming Plotkin, who'd always been gruff, stubborn, and standoffish. All these qualities magnified now.

The Plotkins were one of those couples you didn't see together. You saw Plotkin at his office on Rock Street. You saw Rachel in the shop on South Main. But the fact that they weren't seen together in public didn't necessarily mean their marriage wasn't happy. On the contrary, in Sarah's experience, the more attached at the hip, the more sniping, the more potential for knocking each other around. Nora Kupernick bopping Teddy so hard on the head with a hair dryer he had to go to the hospital only a recent case in point. The Plotkins lived up in the Highlands on Ray Street in a house set back from the street. There was a little garden in the side yard, and once or twice Walt, out walking his streets, had actually seen the two of them puttering around there. An Adam-and-Eve sort of image. The front walk was always clear of leaves and snow, though probably Plotkin hired somebody, since it was hard to imagine him out there with a rake or a shovel. Neither Walt nor Sarah had ever been inside the Plotkin house.

The funeral, the shiva, and that would have been it. The sadness would have, as it must, given way to another piece of news. But it turned out that Walt had a previously scheduled appointment with Plotkin for the following Tuesday. Sarah and Walt debated whether he should cancel, but they decided this wouldn't look right. Sarah said, "Just show up, and if he's there, he's there." So 10:00 a.m. Tuesday, Walt parks the Lincoln in the small parking lot adjacent to Plotkin's building. The place used to be home to some of the city's best lawyers, accountants, stockbrokers, and investment bankers, but now Plotkin shares space with a baseball-card dealer, a hair salon, a frequently drunk chiropractor, and most recently a clairvoyant named Madam Fontaine.

Plotkin worked alone. He'd once been in business with his father, but the older Plotkin had died in the early '60s. Back when Plotkin and Walt had gone to school together, Plotkin was considered a whiz kid bound for Wall Street. He'd gone to Wharton on the Jewish quota, but after only a couple of years in Manhattan he returned to Fall River to work for his father. Plotkin, it was often said, was one of those who "failed to live up to his potential." Vindictive word, potential. You lug it around like a third foot. It's always going to trip you. Walt didn't want much to do with anybody who'd lived up to their potential. And though Walt no longer had any money to invest, he always made a point of going to see Plotkin every few months to check up on his pennies.

Walt knocks softly on the door.

"It's open."

Plotkin sits behind his desk, his coat off, wearing a crisp-looking white shirt and red suspenders. The room is stuffy. A radiator hisses in the corner. For a few moments, neither man says anything. Against the glass of the office's single window, a branch screaks. On anyone else, the red suspenders might look festive. Plotkin, who'd once run track for Durfee, had, like them all, filled out considerably over the years. But he didn't seem to have bought any new clothes. The suspenders aren't holding any-thing up. He sits there pinched.

"Walt."

"Jerry."

"You good, Walt? I heard you had a scare."

"I'm good, Jerry."

"Sarah? Miriam?"

"Good, they're both doing fine."

"Good, good."

"Listen, Jerry, lemme just say—"

Plotkin leans forward, elbows on his desk, hands splayed to-gether, all ten fingers touching. "What can I do for you, Walt? I looked over your numbers. Not bad, considering how much we're talking about. You got IBM down a few quarter points. Kraft's up three and a half. Bristol-Myers up one and a quarter."

He doesn't look down at any paper. Plotkin hasn't taken his eyes off Walt since he's come through the door. Walt feels like a shoplifter. Not the first time. In a store, whenever he feels eyes on him, he always has to resist stuffing something in his pants. *You want a thief, I'll give you a thief.*

"People like cheese," Walt says. "Cheese always—"

"And Midlothian Oil's down four points."

Plotkin's face has gone in the opposite direction from his body. Gaunt, it's as though his cheeks have turned inside out. Lit-tle hollows. Walt thinks of the frilly soap dishes Sarah is always buying. They've always got more soap dishes than soap. That's because soap doesn't last as long as plastic, Sarah says.

"But even so," Plotkin says, "we could buy more oil. With this so-called energy crisis, we could pick up some bargains."

"If that's what you advise, Jerry."

Plotkin's small green eyes watch him. Walt looks away. Nothing on the walls besides smudges, as if somebody or something has rubbed itself in a few places. No pictures, no certificates, no diplomas. Talk is that Plotkin doesn't even have an updated license anymore, but if he can do this in his sleep, what does he need with the state of Massachusetts telling him he knows how?

"So," Plotkin says. "You want to sell a little cheese and buy a little oil?"

"I do like the idea of cheese, I feel like people are always going to—"

"Walt, this is why you have no money."

"I have no money as a result of a number of factors."

"Aside from all that."

"Aren't you supposed to make me some?"

"I can't turn water into wine, Walt, I can't just crack my knuckles—"

The radiator adds knocking to the hissing. The place is grubby, hasn't been cleaned in years, and yet Plotkin still talks big. Still the kid that went off to Wharton to do his parents and Fall River proud. Plotkin begins to tell Walt what he always tells him, that only money breeds money. Nothing else, no substitutes. Yeah, people talk, they'll always talk. Because talk, Walt, is money's great opposite. Talk's always a net loss.

Plotkin and Walt aren't friends, but when somebody knows—pretty much exactly—how much money you don't have, there's a certain unspoken intimacy.

"Look, Jerry, I just about did it myself."

"What?"

"Not the Watuppa, the Braga Bridge. The day I had my heart attack, I was fully intending to walk up the Braga—"

"There's no way to walk up the Braga Bridge, Walt, and you know it," Plotkin says. "There's hardly a breakdown lane."

"What did I care? A car hits me, a car hits me."

Plotkin stares. They could still have been talking about stocks. In a way, maybe they still were. Stocks being all about might or might not.

"A fog, Jerry. Felt like there was no end to it. Hardly thought about Sarah. It was like she didn't exist. I'd just made a sale. Dinette set. Nice couple, new in town, if you can believe it. Bought a little house in Steep Brook. Moved here from Worcester. Maybe Fall River's got something on Worcester? Irv gives me a wink, like *Attaboy,* I still got the touch. That's when I walk out. Been thinking about it months, I don't know, years. Don't know why that day. Irv shouts, 'Hey, where you goin'?' but I'm walking, I'm floating, really. It was like I already felt myself falling, you know what I mean? Like I was on my way to do something that I'd already done?"

"You want to buy and sell a little, Walt?" Plotkin says. "Otherwise, I got work."

They sit for a bit. Walt shifting and reshifting in his chair. Plotkin, his hands now fisted, waiting for this visit to be over.

"Sometimes I think of all the money I'd make," Walt says, "if I really put my mind to it."

Plotkin lets go his fists, laughs, laughs with his whole body. Him jiggling in his chair, and Walt thinks, We know as much about what goes on in other people's heads as we do in other people's houses. Closed blinds, front walks, faces, eyes, all tools of the hiding trade. You think because you grew up with a guy you know him from Adam? Walk in here and try to—what?— *relate* (isn't that the word?) to another man?

They pulled her out of the North Watuppa. A cop and a couple of guys from the water department. She was floating, hadn't sunk. Sad operation. Plotkin was back to talking about not a here-and-there investment but a long-term strategy, enough with this futzing around—"I'd need at least five or six thousand to do a thing for you, Walt, but the only thing you've got that even comes close is your life insurance"—except that today even his set speech, even his joke about life insurance, sounds as though he's reciting it from memory, like a prayer he's refused to forget but no longer believes in.

We attempt consolation at our peril. Because what if it's accepted? Then what? What would it look like? Jerry Plotkin in tears? Walt would run out of this office so fast—

Still, Walt wants to say to him, Jerry, you belong to no clubs, we never see you at Magoni's or the Gang Plank or the Chinaman's or even at Gus's. You never make an appearance in temple, even for the sake of business, even on high holidays when people are busting down the doors of the place to be seen. You think I'm such a believer, Jerry? I turn up at Beth El out of loyalty to my dead. You see? It's once removed. I sit there. I don't listen to a word of it. I watch myself being loyal to my mother, to my father. A far cry from belief, whatever that is, but it's something. Not for them, not for the sake of the talk, for you, for Rachel. At the very least, Jerry, you can look at your loyalty, which is not nothing—

"—but like I say, I'm not a magician. You scrounge up a little cash out of some forgotten savings account or out from under the mattress or some old bird aunt leaves you a few dollars, I'll—"

The branch screaks against the window.

"You ever talk to the fortune-teller?" Walt asks.

"Only when she needs the bathroom key."

12

Notes on Practical Salesmanship

The summer Walt graduated Durfee High, Max sent him to do a three-week course in practical salesmanship at the National Sales Training Association in Chicago. He took the train west from Boston. It would be the longest stretch of time he'd ever spend away from Fall River in his life. He slept in a Loop hotel rented out by the association. His roommate was a seemingly mute older man from Arkansas who sold farm equipment and slept in his clothes. At night, in his dreams, this man screamed. Night after night, the salesman from Arkansas screamed. Walt got into the habit of getting dressed and walking the streets until dawn. Then he'd return to his room because the man would by then have finally descended into a deep-enough sleep. Whatever he was so afraid of could no longer reach him. Aside from the man from Arkansas, Walt retained only one memory from the course in practical salesmanship, something deliciously unpractical. It was an anecdote that the instructor, a cigar-chewing typewriter salesman (he'd chew the cigar during class, leave a little trail of moist bits as he wandered around the room) told on the very first day about Thomas Carlyle and John Stuart Mill. The typewriter salesman read it out of a textbook. I got a little story for you chickadees to start us off. Don't know who wrote it, but it's some good stuff. Lesson one, narrative is the key to selling!

Let's say you are selling Thomas Carlyle's book on the French Revolution. You will greatly interest your prospect by telling him that after Carlyle wrote his masterwork, he sent his only copy of the manuscript to the great English philosopher John Stuart Mill. One night Mill laid down the manuscript in a careless manner and in the morning, the maid, thinking it a lot of useless paper, put it into the fire. What you get for sending a book to the competition! The most painstaking scholarly work, years of hard labor, up in smoke. Carlyle was prostrated by the loss and couldn't bring himself to the task of returning to it, but later on, while pondering the matter, he watched a workman laying the foundation of a building and mused, "That wall will one day hold up the happy house of someone and that worker will have made it possible." Abandoning his moodiness, Carlyle set back to work. Now who wouldn't want to buy Carlyle's History of the French of the Revolution? *Narrative* is the key to selling!

Not a day in his life, presiding over Kaplan's Furniture, his feet up on the desk on the mezzanine level—Walt loved the mezzanine, a sort of in-between place, not quite here, not quite there, the perfect perch from which to think—did Walt fail to think of Thomas Carlyle. Carlyle looking out the window and seeing a man actually working. I am inspired! Walt felt the same way watching Ukey, his upholsterer, at work in the shop. It almost made him want to—what?—work? And whenever he thought of Carlyle, he also thought of the farm-equipment salesman from Arkansas. For Walt, the two would always be a pair. Carlyle returns to work, in a fever. The man from Arkansas, silent all day, but at night he, too, in his way, went to work. His screams must have kept the entire hotel awake. A few times Walt reached out and touched him, tried to comfort him a little. But the man from Arkansas didn't want comfort. He wanted to scream. And so Walt, rather than try to sleep, wandered the streets of Chicago, a city that didn't so much overwhelm him as stifle him. The geography of the place made no sense. It was a city with no vantage point from which to experience it. One of the old boosters said of Fall River, *As one approaches the city from Providence, Fall River appears to be like Rome, built on seven hills as it rises majestically from the waterfront.* Chicago did not rise. It spread, like an infection, block after block, like a caricature of oblivion. Later, when every couple of years he'd return to Chicago to visit (two days maximum) his daughter and two grandsons, he'd again wander the city and wonder what happened to the man from Arkansas.

A few times when she was small, Miriam cried out in her sleep. Walt would run into the room from across the hall like the house was on fire. But how could he protect her from what only she could see? Our history is not a continuous line; it's a circle we draw over and over on a desk blotter. Chicago, Fall River, Chicago. Thomas Carlyle, the man from Arkansas, my own daughter, Thomas Carlyle. Work, not work. The terrors of the sleeper and the helplessness of those awake.

13

Gus's Highland Spa

S omething else," Walt says.

"Can't there be a day of nothing else?" Alf says. "A single day when nothing whatsoever occurs to you?"

"I've got this idea."

"Yeah?"

"Kaplan's History of Fall River."

"A book? You're writing a book? Now, there's something that will occupy your idle hours and keep you so busy maybe you'll work through lunch—"

"Not a book."

"Noreen?" Alf says. "Where's Noreen?"

Gus from the kitchen: "Out back. Smoke break. Union mandate."

"Noreen's unionized?" Walt says.

"I was kidding, Jimmy Hoffa," Gus says.

"Can we order direct from the bountiful source?" Alf says.

"You know the system," Gus says. "I make the slop. You order from Noreen."

Alf's added another chin since Monday. It's like a colony. One chin hears it's good down there below the end of his face, and all his friends keep coming and coming.

"A history sounds like a book."

"That's the beauty of it," Walt says. "I'm taking Carlyle one step further."

"Carlyle's a toity hotel," Alf says. "Ruthie's cousin got—"

"Thomas Carlyle."

"You're losing me. You always lose me—"

"I'm not trying to rewrite the history," Walt says. "I'm thinking it. Get it? It disappears as soon as I think about it, but that doesn't mean it didn't exist. I'm composing something as ethereal as history itself. I can still make a house, only it's in my—"

"Tomorrow, I'm going to Wong's, and I'm going to listen to the music of my own lack of thoughts."

"Go," Gus says. "Nobody's stopping you."

"You don't see the beauty?" Walt says.

"Beauty of what? History of what?" Alf says.

"Everything. Shoelaces, farts, love, death, cantaloupes—all I have to do is remember."

"Noreen!"

"You've got Fowler's *History of Fall River.* And, of course, Philip's three-volume history. More recently there's Alberto Caeiro's pamphlets. Wonderful stuff. Terrific chronicle of the fire of '28. Excellent work on the highway and the removals. But what happens? Any history will sit on the shelf and eventually molder with the other relics. Why? Alf, you ask me why."

" 'Cause books get moldy in our humid climate."

"Because they aspire to completeness! They've got a first page and a last page. That's the killer right there. The beauty, I won't say brilliance, of Kaplan's history is that its essence is the essential fact of its incompleteness, that's what makes it so—"

"No Jews," Alf says.

"No Jews what?" Walt says.

"No Jew ever wrote a history of Fall River. Written or unwritten."

"That's true."

"But why would they?" Alf says. "Not our town. Never has been, never will be."

Noreen comes up with her notepad.

"Do you two ever work?" she says.

"We're independently wealthy," Alf says.

"Two clubs?" Noreen says, and without waiting for an answer, saunters away.

"I'm born here, I'll die here," Walt says. "It's not my town?"

"No."

"What's my town?" Walt says. "Some feudal village in the Carpathians I see only in my nightmares? That's my town?"

"Yeah," Alf says. "That's your town.

"The Irish, the Canucks, the Italians," Alf says. "Even the Portuguese. It's their town, Walt. Jews here, we're—what?—ephemeral, that's it, we're—"

"The Irish aren't ephemeral?"

"Nope."

14

Agudas Achim

I dreamed you buried me in the old cemetery out on Fish Road."

"Fish Road?" Sarah says. "Where all the ancient Jews are?"

"You think we're immune from becoming ancient Jews?"

"Last time we were out there was for my aunt Winona. Abe's wife? Remember Winona and Abe? Ran a little store in the Flint."

"Sold hats?"

"Right! And also sundries."

"Always loved sundries," Walt says. "Buy myself a comb, maybe a box of toothpicks. Sundries both."

"Walt?"

"Yeah?"

"What about our plot at Beth El? We're not paid up?"

Talking in the dark again. Consider the flow of talk, the river of words, and yet it's as though the darkness acts as a kind of op-positional sun—a black hole?—and the words, millions of them, evaporate, vanish, fall. Dante's Virgil says that hell is hollow. I can see it already, an old, rotten, hollowed-out log, and we talk our way down, down—

"Walt? We're not paid up?"

"What? No, we've got perpetual care, whatever that means. May thine lawn always be mowed and windblown garbage disposed—I wrote Ruderman a fat check years ago."

"So why Fish Road?"

"You tell me. I'm in the back of the hearse and instead of taking Highland Ave north, the driver swings right on Walnut and makes another right on Robeson. I'm confused. South? He's heading south? I try and tap the driver on the shoulder—Hey, pal, wrong way—but my hands don't work and anyway, right, I'm stuck in a box. I can see out of the box, which makes no sense. South on Robeson? Then I think maybe I get it, there's only one place they bury Jews south of the temple, and that's at Agudas Achim. You know? Fish Road Cemetery? Except there's no Fish Road on any map, never has been. It was only because the Jews used to peddle fish, and that's why they used to call—I figured you were planning on remarrying. Dump me at Agudas Achim. Out of sight, out of mind. And why not? Don't I want you to be happy?"

"You got anybody in mind?"

"What about Kermit Baumgartner? Widower, family money, aluminum. Nice house on Albany, white trim, red shingles."

"Kermit's gimpy," Sarah says.

"It's an old war injury," Walt says. "Kermit got shot on D-Day. The man's an authenticated hero. The shrapnel's still—"

"Walt?"

"Yeah?"

"I want to tell you something."

Never a good sign, this announcement. "How can I run for cover when I'm already under the covers?"

"Alf told Ruthie about the bridge, and Ruthie, of course—"

"Brutus! Brutessa!"

"Fuck you."

"Sar—"

"You think I've never thought about it. What? I'm not intellectual enough? That there aren't days I'm exhausted, long past exhausted? Shut the windows and stick my head in the oven like a poet. You think I'm incapable?"

"Sarah."

"Listen, I'm talking. Remember when we first moved into this house? The lady died, what was her name—"

"Lucy Harrison."

"And her son wanted to sell as soon as possible because he was going off to the army, what year—"

"Forty-two," Walt says. "It was 1942 when the son, Alan—"

"Right, but I'm talking," Sarah says. "I'm—so there was an urgency about it and not just on the son's side but on ours, too, because we wanted the place right away, as soon as we saw it we wanted it, the little place on Weetamoe was too cramped with Mirry getting bigger, but it was beyond all this—it was like the place was already ours. Like we already lived in it before we paid a cent, and I remember thinking, We're going to wear it out, the carpets, the linoleum, the plumbing, and, yes, the beds, we were even going to wear out the beds of this little—"

"We got new Sealy Posturepedics five years ago. These new beds don't even creak—"

"And you said to the son out on the sidewalk, We'll take it, we'll take it as is, no inspection, we didn't even have Angelo come and check out the boiler, remember? And the kid said, Don't you want me to move out the stuff, and you said, Take what you want, and he did, and that was that, and for years, no, still, still we live with that old lady's cups and saucers, her bowls. My sisters used to laugh, but what did I ever care about crockery? I never gave a damn about crockery in my entire life. Have I? Have I ever?"

Walt climbs over to Sarah's bed, and the two of them lie side by side.

"You think I wasn't serious," Walt says.

"I know you weren't. But that doesn't mean you wouldn't have done it. Plenty of people who weren't serious have jumped, if only to prove they were. Is the idea that I'll always play the widow? What if I don't want to? What if I refuse? Walt? What if I'd rather not?"

"Sarah."

"No, I'm talking."

Except she doesn't, and they remain side by side, each leaking a little over their respective edge, okay, more than a little, but side by side.

15

Kaplans

Max Kaplan, founder of Kaplan's Furniture, once told his son Walt this, or something like it: "No. We didn't work in the mills. We didn't build this city. But we weren't the mill owners, either. From a pushcart to a store on Fourth and Pleasant is an eternity, an honorable eternity, an eternity of progress. We were never going to work in the mills. Back when I was starting out, you know what they called us? Parasites! But where are the mill owners now? We're still here—Jews are still in Fall River—where'd the mill owners go? Their heirs are holed up in their Newport mansions. Fall River? Where's that? We ought to get a little credit for sticking it out, no?"

"Jews have been fleeing this city for years, Poppa. Like we fled Shershov."

"Chased from Shershov, we were chased—"

"Chased, fled, same difference."

"Never us! And not from here. Not these Jews. Kaplans stay in Fall River."

16

Dumb Luck, Brief Treatise

The headline on the left side of the front page of the *Fall River Herald News* on the day it also published Max Kaplan's obituary, April 7, 1958, was as follows:

GIGOLO NOT UNWELCOME SUITOR, LANA ADMITS

The paper's been in the top drawer of the desk in his study for nearly two decades. Every once in a while, Walt unfolds the yellowed paper and rereads his father's obituary, as well as the details of Lana Turner's affair with a B-level mobster named Johnny Stompanato. Never mind that he was stabbed by Lana's daughter for beating up Lana. Which goes to show you, he thinks. Goes to show you what exactly? he asks.

It goes to show you. Period.

What do you mean?

Why do I got to spell everything out even to myself?

Funeral services were held this morning for Maxwell Kaplan of 81 Dudley Street, this city, at Temple Beth El, 385 High Street, with Rabbi Samuel R. Ruderman eulogizing, assisted by cantors Marcus Gerlich and Moses Schwimmer. Bearers were attorney Everett Dashoff, Luis T. Ravosky, Simon Gourse, Dr. Daniel Weinstein, and Walter H. Kaplan. Internment was at Beth El Cemetery, North Main Street. For many years Mr. Kaplan was the proprietor of a furniture store bearing the family name, Kaplan's Furniture at Pleasant and Fourth Street, Fall River.

Take your last breath, you might as well enjoy it, because somewhere some small-time, undeserving hood is making it with Lana Turner. Happy now? There it is.

Thank you, Walt.

You're welcome, Walt.

17

The Woman at the Alhambra

It's not as though it was foreordained. There was a time when he could have left. Why didn't he, even if only for a few years? Why didn't he run from Fall River when he had the chance after his father died? Sell the store and go while he still had stamina enough to get a little distance between him and here? At least he could have made it to Boston. Now only fifty-five minutes away with no traffic at sixty miles an hour on the fucking new highway. Back then it might have taken an hour and a half on Route 6. Think of the libraries, the bookstores, the brains! A man with a wife and daughter running away? But a man can have a wife and daughter anywhere. And Sarah would've left; she'd have come with him. She'd have missed her sisters, her friends, but she'd have left; she'd have packed up the house and...but hadn't he realized long ago that you could run away without running? That you could stay put in a place you loved and still be gone? And yet. How was it possible he'd die before seeing China? Or Egypt? But wait, he had seen Egypt. They'd gone to Cairo in '63 with Milt and Pearl. They saw the pyramids. Interesting architecture, amazing what you can do with slave labor. And Spain. They'd gone to Spain, too. In the '60s, when they had some money, they went all over Europe one summer. Was that trip before or after

Egypt? All he remembers of the Alhambra is that a Russian countess accidentally stepped on his foot. He was walking up a staircase—beautiful, the railing was also a waterfall—and this woman with a great kremlin of gleaming hair was walking down it. She'd stomped a high heel so hard on his left foot he'd let out a yowl. She apologized so elegantly in Russian-inflected English that Sarah said she must have been exiled aristocracy. They had been places, though that still left China. And what about India? Brazil? When are we going to have enough dough to fly down to Brazil, Sarah? Home. Run away, you end up carrying it with you, right? Stay put and your load's lighter? Banishment without the banishment?

18

His Mother

Mother, mother, mother! Walt could no longer conjure her face or her body. He could no longer hear her voice, and he told himself (lied) that this was because she was too much a part of him to be remembered as a distinct person separate from himself, body and soul. The fact was in all those years he'd rarely looked at her. And if he'd listened, his ears would have told him she was saying something he already knew. So why tune in? She'd hovered on the edge of his life like a hummingbird, in the background of every scene, darting in and out of rooms, handing him a tart, an umbrella, mittens. He remembers her buttoning his loden coat, her fingers pulling the little horns through the buttonholes. His mother's short, bony fingers like the little half pencils you get at the library. How is it possible that he knows not a thing about her? What was Molly Kaplan's favorite color? Did she believe in God? She had, didn't she, a narrow face? Like somebody had pushed her ears together a bit too much? A face people called dignified. Nobody ever called his mother pretty. She wore her hair pulled back so tightly on her head that it must have felt like someone or something was forever tugging on her scalp. She was afraid of flies. They didn't annoy her, they terrified her. When one landed on a table, she didn't scream. She stared at it, bug-eyed. She called him Walter, and she'd say it with two distinct syllables: Wal. Ter. As if she were still practicing her English. She was the only person who ever called him by his given name, which added to the sense that, for her, he was someone he never was. Walter? Who's Walter?

19

Beth El Temple Notes,
October 8, 1939
(copy saved in Walt's desk drawer)

Miss Frieda Posniak is recovering from an appendectomy
at Union Hospital. Sumner Levine, son of Mr. and Mrs.
Lewis Levine, again distinguished himself by winning second prize in the state finals of the American Legion Or-
atorical contest held in Concord last week… *The Shining
Hour* will be presented by the Women's Players on Thursday
evening, November 16, in the women's club. Mr. Lester
Ravosky is the director and the cast includes Miss Anita
Chaveson, Mrs. Alfred Dolinsky, and Mrs. Toby Fin-
klestein. Wardrobe and set design by Mrs. Walter Kaplan.
We are proud of the selection, by the Fall River Council of
the Boy Scouts of America, of Alfred Sherwin, for the Silver Beaver Award, one of the highest awards in the field
of scouting… One of our own YPC members, Miss Jeanne
Lifrak, had the distinction of meeting Mrs. Franklin D.
Roosevelt while she was in Fall River last Sunday. Mrs. Roosevelt visited with Mrs. R. Howe, who resides next door
to our temple… Many items of clothing have been left in
the temple by the children from time to time. These items
should be claimed at once or they will be given away… Next

Friday evening Rabbi Ruderman will present the lecture "Moral Leprosy: What's wrong with American Marriage"... Remember Friday night is temple night!!! But please do remain until the close of the service and discourage others from promenading about.

20

Miriam's Egg Experiment

In 1942—was it spring? was the light coming into the kitchen through the northeast window?—Miriam dropped an egg on the kitchen floor and it didn't break. This was curious, so she did it again, dropping said egg on purpose this time from roughly the same altitude above the counter. Impossible for Walt to explain why it broke the second time and not the first.

Still, he tried: "Things break only when you don't mean them to?"

21

His Scar

Running into the house on Delcar one day in '51 ('52? '53?), Walt Kaplan tripped on one of his own front steps. Gash in the dent between his lip and his chin required stitches. For years he could still feel the scar. But what was the hurry? What was it he wanted to tell Sarah?

22

To the Dark

You give me a quiet house, a sleeping daughter, a sleeping wife, and I'll show you what it is to be alive. I, Walt Kaplan, thought this not once but throughout my life, and often narrated it—buttery sentimentality be damned—to the dark, to the walls, to the carpet on the stairs that already needed to be replaced, to the sink in the bathroom when I got up to take yet another leak, to the glass of water that smelled of sulfur, to the throat that accepted the water, to the urinary tract that would soon expel said water. You give me a quiet house, a sleeping daughter, a sleeping wife, and I'll—

23

Kaplan's Furniture, Fourth and Pleasant Street, March 1961

Was that the afternoon Walt Kaplan sat at his desk on the mezzanine level of the store and contemplated his hands? They were the hands of a man who talked for a living. Soft, stumpy hands, unburdened hands, that in the night would often bridge that so-easily-conquerable divide between two separate beds, that come-on-over, that Maginot Line of love—a voice, either his or hers, *You wanna?* Two beds as an abstraction, a horizon, two beds as Jerusalem, Shangri-la, Oz. Atlantic City.

Now, a philosophical as well as a practical question: Why didn't we just push the beds together and leave them there? Ah, because that would be a lie, no? The nature of the reaching, the nature of the whispered entreaties, a thousand variations on the same invitation, is that both the reaching of the hands and the question in question invariably lead to moments of complete incompleteness. Because the upshot of coupling is uncoupling. The essence of association is disassociation. Because you can fuck till you're blue, but at a certain point the inevitable nightly drawing apart happens for good, am I right or am I right? Spell it out again: the retreat once again to separate beds attains a cementation that precludes any further *you wannas*. After a certain point *you wanna?* is no longer an invitation for rumpus; it's a cry from oblivion. And who's going to warn you? Who's going to say, This, Walt, this is the last time you'll touch Sarah Kaplan, née Gottlieb?

24

Moonlight

Biltmore Hotel, Providence, Rhode Island, June 18, 1934, Sarah conked out, mouth open, breathing heavy, nearly a pant but measured, followed closely by a slow, watery snore. Walt Kaplan watches her in the moonlight. There is no moonlight. It's the light from the hall. It doesn't reach her face. But in memory, it's moonlight, and it's on Sarah's face.

25

Walt's Spending Diary, March 15, 1978

Two toothbrushes for Sarah at Peoples (no rubber tips). $3.00 + 7 cents sales tax. Total: $3.07.

26

The Life Jacket

When Walt Kaplan was six, Max took him to see a traveling display of a life jacket salvaged from the *Lusitania*. His first memory. Whether remembered or instilled in him by repetition of the story, he'll never know. Nobody alive any longer to ask. The life jacket, pale and torn, was housed in a glass box in the library at the Quequechan Club. Not every day they let Jews in the door of the Quequechan. This was a special occasion. Though the war was over, his father, enraged, shook his little fist at the relic in the glass box. Walt only wondered out loud what it would be like to float out there in that jacket, horizon in every direction.

27

Statistics

THE COMMONWEALTH OF MASSACHUSETTS
Division of Vital Statistics
Medical Examiner's
Certificate of Death

1. Place of Death:
   County
   Bristol
   City or Town
   Fall River
   Precise Location
   Truesdale Hospital
2. Legal name, address, and other particulars:
   (a) Full name (no nicknames): Walter Hyman Kaplan
   (b) Birth date: Feb 2, 1919
   (c) Place of birth: Fall River, Mass.
   (d) Permanent residence: 100 Delcar Street, Fall River, Mass.
   (e) Was deceased a U.S. war veteran? If yes, specify what war:
       No
   (f) Sex: Male

(g) Color: <u>White</u>

(h) Age (be exact): <u>59 years 1 month 16 days</u>

(i) Single, Married, Divorced, Unknown? (write the word):
<u>Married</u>

(j) If married, state wife's or husband's name (give maiden
name of wife): <u>Sarah Gottlieb</u>

(k) Usual occupation (kind of work done during most of life):
<u>Sales</u>

(l) If applicable, state the name of current employer: <u>I. Pincus
and Co./Popular Furniture</u>

(m) Name and birthplace of father: <u>Max Kaplan, Russia</u>

(n) Maiden name and birthplace of mother: <u>Molly Winograd,
Russia</u>

3. Date of Death: <u>March 16, 1978</u>

4. I hereby certify that I have investigated the death of the person
above-named and that the CAUSE and MANNER thereof are as
follows (If an injury was involved, state fully):
<u>Acute myocardial infarction/dead on arrival</u>
Date: <u>March 18, 1978</u>

28

Beth El

Milt Feldman ambles over and rests a small, hairy paw on Alf Dolinsky's shoulder. One man's demise brings a little swing to another's step. For a moment Alf looks at Milt's hand and considers taking a bite out of it.

"Not a striver," Milt says. "No, he wasn't a striver. But as good a man as ever wore a suit. Look at this horde. You'd think the rabbi was handing out cash. I just saw Hildegard, you know the meter maid? The one with the crooked face? Crash your car into a phone pole, your head bleeding, she'd give you a ticket for blocking the intersection? She's decked out in black. Wet eyes on that crone. I'm not kidding."

"The meter maid's name is Hildegard?"

"Call the bitch whatever you want. I parked all the way on Robeson. Had I known she'd...But I guess we shouldn't be too surprised, I mean if ever a man—"

"*Et tu?*"

"What?"

"You also, Milt? I mean, you also."

"You parked on Robeson, too?"

"The beautification. The man's been dead six minutes and even Broom-Hilda, the meter maid—"

Milt releases Alf's shoulder and leans in close. "I gotta get a seat. Place is mobbed."

Mid-March and there's a slow, cold rain. There are a few early leaves on the trees. To Alf, the rain hitting the leaves, blam, blam, sounds like pistol shots. He stands on the sidewalk and watches a straggler, a man he doesn't recognize, holding a newspaper over his head as he hurries inside before Alf, too, ascends the temple steps. People do love a dead guy. It's living people everybody's got such trouble with. In death, even with the biggest jackass in town, it's all about *rest his generous soul in peace.* But with Walt, it's no bullshit. They're not hamming it up. People aren't taking a day off work out of obligation. They're here because they want to do something with how they feel, and nobody's ever been able to come up with anything better than this phony holiday we call a funeral.

Alf stands in the back of the sanctuary, his back to the open door and the rain. Latecomers are still nudging past knees to get to the empty seats in the middle of the rows. Why do people who come on time always sit on the edges? To rub it in? Alf looks at the tall glass windows, huddled figures in robes. Why does everybody in the Bible always wear robes? Doesn't seem that pragmatic. Think of the sand up your crotch. The windows are supposed to represent the twelve tribes of Israel. Why tribes? Didn't Walt have some bit about the twelve tribes? Alf's never been able to concentrate in this building. But what are people supposed to concentrate on? Faith? Alf never had any. Immortality? Not interested. Sell that to somebody else. My feet hurt. Were Jews ever promised immortality, or did Christ bring that to the table? Cheat the grave? Walt would know. The first of how many things I don't need to know he'll never tell me.

Rabbi Ruderman intones, drones, moans. *Thou art God. Thou turnest man to destruction; and sayest, Return, ye children of men. For a thousand years in thy sight are but as yesterday...* A woman rises, half stands in one of the rows closest to the casket. It's Ruthie. Soundlessly she mouths, *Saved you a seat.* Alf shakes his head. He's okay where he is. Next to him is Fischer, the real master of ceremonies here. But Fischer is gracious. He cedes a little time for the rabbi to recite his mumbo jumbo and then a few too many words about what a great all-around guy—

But this is Fischer's death, Fischer's body up there at the front housed in wood. Alf sneaks a look at the funeral director. He's gaunt. Skin hangs down his face like melted cheese. Probably starves himself to look the part. Because if ever a man was in the growth business. As the rabbi forges on with the preliminaries, this death merchant calmly rubs together the hands that protrude from a suit jacket with too-short sleeves.

Mortality for profit? Every corpse lines the pocket? Should be a public utility, like the phone company, like the library. Walt would get a kick out of the suggest—

For a thousand years in thy sight are but as yesterday.

At breakfast when he'd complained about having to attend this farce, Ruthie said, "It's a ritual, you're supposed to suffer through it. That's why rituals got invented. You think if they were fun we'd do them over and over?"

They should make Ruthie the rabbi.

Thou carriest them away as with a flood; they are as a sleep.

Alf can't take it anymore and retreats back into the rain. A big man, he walks daintily, on weakened knees, down the wet granite steps. Fall River granite, Walt would say, quarried from our own rock-hard soil by the sweat of hearty, singing Irishmen. Two of Fischer's men stand in the street by the open door of the hearse. Guy drives Connies his whole life, they're going to stuff him in a Cadillac for his last ride? Insults upon insults.

Alf stands by the fire hydrant at the corner of High Street and Locust and waits in the Waltless rain.

One of Fischer's two minions, bored of standing there in the rain in his gray suit and white gloves, begins walking toward Alf. The kid hands Alf a mimeographed piece of paper with directions to Beth El Cemetery.

Alf says to the kid, "What? You think I don't know how to get there?"

"Sometimes people come from out of town."

A pimply kid in such exquisite calfskin gloves. How does he keep them so clean? Does Fischer issue a new pair for every burial? Come get your gloves, boys, we got another croaker. No, that'd get pricey. Undertakers, even their assistants, shouldn't come young. Fischer is a good reaper, but this Cub Scout?

"How do you get your gloves so clean?"

"Pardon, sir?"

"Your gloves. How do you keep them so clean?"

The doors flying open. Fischer pokes his head out one way, and then the other, as if he's looking to make sure there isn't a train.

"Bleach," the kid says before he hurries back to his post by the open door of the hearse.

And out the doors, conducted by Fischer—Watch your step, gentlemen, watch your step, it's wet, quite slippery, gentlemen— the pallbearers carry Walt Kaplan. Alf's known each of these men his entire life, but there's something regal about the way they fulfill their office. For the first couple of moments he hardly recognizes them, as if they truly aren't the individual men he's lived among since boyhood but solemn, even majestic representatives of the human race gently carrying a fellow sojourner across the threshold. Wait. Wait. Irv Pincus? How in the hell did Irv Pincus get to be a bearer? Oh Christ. Oh Christ…

The rain begins to pound harder.

Alf watches the men thrust the casket into the back of the hearse. Fischer's men secure it and slam the door. Like a barn door. The mourners pour out of the sanctuary. Slowly, but the

truth is they can't get out of there fast enough. Who isn't thinking of their own day in the casket? Will I fill the seats? Umbrellas
thoop open, one after another. Muted conversations commence
right and left, and Alf, cursed with the hearing of a basset hound,
takes in the jabber from his spot by the hydrant.

Took it as it came. The good, the bad. No enemies, not a single one.
What that says about a man.
    True, true. Notta one, not a single one.

I heard Sarah's penniless, absolutely destitute, truly.
    No.
    You didn't hear? Walt was broke as a clock. Word is First Meta-
comet is foreclosing on the house.

Miriam! You're even more lovely than you were as a child! And
look at your adorable boys! Your father must have been so…

Don't forget, you've got the dentist at two thirty.
    Shhhhh, Doris, we're at a man's funeral.
    You're not allowed to go to the dentist? Someone dies and you're
not allowed to go to the dentist? It's a holiday from dental appoint-
ments?
    Please, Doris, just—hiya, Angelo, Carmela. Sad, sad day, huh,
Angelo? Carmela, you know my wife, Doris, don't you?

His own brother-in-law took him for what, thirty grand? And still
the man—

Which brother-in-law? Pincus?

Not Pincus, Sarkansky—but you think Walt held a grudge? Had a smile for everybody, always took a moment. You know what I mean?

That wasn't smiling. That was thirty grand of biting his tongue, I'll tell you that—

But it was really I-195 really did a number on him, store was in the wrong place at the wrong—

Right, right, that fuckin' jackass highway—

Darling Sarah, what can I say? You were the luckiest. And you know why. Because he was kind. How many of these fat nothings forget to be kind?

You should have seen him boot the Alveses' cat across the lawn. Oh, Sarah.

Alf looks down at the rain-soaked piece of paper in his hand.

DIRECTIONS TO BETH EL CEMETERY
   North on High Street, LEFT on Pearce
   RIGHT on North Davol Street
   Follow ramp to 79 North (Taunton/Middleboro)
   Turn off on Exit 8
   LEFT at top of the ramp
   At rotary, follow North Main Street
   Cemetery is across from the Cumberland Farms

Left on Pearce? And 79 North? You take High Street to Highland Ave and hang a left. Highland all the way, past Royal Crest, up to 24. Take Airport Road to North Main. City streets! You take city streets to the cemetery. But Walt always did get a kick out of the Cumberland Farms being spitting distance. How bad could eternity be if he could get a *Herald News* and some cheese? Milt rejoins Alf by the hydrant.

"Where's Pearl?" Alf says.

"Still inside. She wanted a couple of minutes alone. And for Pearl to want a couple of minutes alone—"

"Ruthie, too. Cried half the night. Was he heavy?"

"Of course he was heavy," Milt says. "Listen, Alf, the rabbi's looking for you."

"He doesn't have anything better to do? Comfort the widows and orphans? Feed the poor? Plant some grapefruit in Israel?"

"You were listed as a bearer in the program."

"You all did fine without me."

"You want to hear how much Irv enjoyed saving the day?"

"No."

"You're asking me was he heavy?" Milt says. "Yeah, he was heavy."

"I just thought of something," Alf says.

"Yeah?"

"You know, the last few years he kept track of every dollar, every penny. Had a spending diary. Kept it in his briefcase. I mean every penny. It all went into the diary. He'd give a forty-cent tip, he'd write it down."

"I do that. He got that from me."

"Maybe, but you're loaded."

"It's why I'm loaded," Milt says.

"Right, but what I'm saying is that Walt could see it all draining away, dime by dime—"

"Poor guy. I knew and I didn't know, you know what I mean? Who wants to know how broke—"

"No, Milt, see? Don't you get it? It's beautiful. The exact opposite of poor because every dime he spent meant something, you know what I'm trying—"

"What are you, a Communist?"

Rabbi Ruderman materializes. Mourners part before him like the waters. Milt backs away. "I'll see you later, Alf, I gotta find my wife."

"Rabbi," Alf says.

"Rabbi," Milt says. "Pearl, I gotta go find—"

Rabbi Ruderman's head has seemed out of proportion to his body, so stuffed is it with knowledge, wisdom, criticism, wrath. "Never," the rabbi says, "in twenty-eight years on the bimah have I ever known a pallbearer to shirk their holy responsibility. His closest friend, hooky!"

"Had trouble parking, Rabbi. Quite a crowd. One way to get people to temple. Anyhow, Walt wouldn't have begrudged—"

"Now Alfred Dolinsky speaks for the dead?"

Sorrow loosens you up as easy as a couple of drinks.

"Look, Rabbi, I'm only trying to get through the day here."

"You're the only one, not his wife, not his daughter?"

"You want the truth? I went back to bed. After breakfast, I told Ruthie to go on ahead and I got back in bed."

Rabbi Ruderman snorts. But just before he turns away to resume the comfort of those far worthier, Alf notices a glint of a little wetness in his eye. Might be rain. Might not be rain. Christ sake, even the rabbi—

Over somebody's shoulder (Alice Wolpert's?), Alf catches a glimpse of Sarah's face a few bodies away. He waits as she's hugged, grabbed, pawed at. Melba Kuperchmid, Renda Grayboys, Pearl Feldman, Lois Blattner, Trudy Falk, his own Ruthie. They all want a piece of her. Oh Sarah, oh Sarah. And then, upon a signal from Fischer, the engine of the hearse roars to life, and everybody begins to scatter and rush to their cars. And for a moment, Sarah's left alone in the rain without an umbrella, a solitary figure in a black dress, the guest of honor forgotten. It's then that Sarah and Alf look at each other. No need for touch. And it's never been a well-kept secret that Alf loves Sarah, chastely, of course, but unchastely, too. Has since pretty much the day Walt brought her home from Providence a married woman. Walt was nineteen; Sarah was seventeen. But let's table this, as it's been tabled all these years, and just say that here are Sarah and Alf a few feet away from each other in front of Beth El, just loving each other. In grief. They say it's heavy, but there's lightness in it, Alf thinks. The man may have been heavy but—

And Alf alone clocks in at two thirty on a good day. So why's he floating?

Walt could find a joke in here somewhere.

Alf steps closer and pulls Sarah close. She digs her head into his shoulder. There's a reason we've got bodies. In order to hide in someone else's once in a while.

"Where were you?" Sarah says. "You should have seen the rabbi's face when he counted the bearers. It was like somebody stole his wallet out of his vestments."

"In Constantinople. I stopped in hell on the way home."

"You sound like him."

"He was my friend," Alf says.

She releases him. "My chariot—"

And Alf watches the slow procession of cars make their foolish way left on Pearce, heading for 79 North. As she drives by in the Ford, Ruthie reaches over and rolls down the window.

"Need a ride?"

Her hair is up, but a few curly strands hang down past her eyes.

"I knew a guy once said he could always get a date at a funeral."

"Who?"

"Burt Zifrin. Met him at a sales conference. Said it worked every time unless he went with his wife and even then—"

"You're not going to the graveside?"

"Isn't enough enough? Now I got to put him in a hole?"

"Alf, you stood out here the whole time."

The car behind Ruthie gently beeps. It's Al and Mary Wasser, waving, apologizing for beeping, But the hearse, we've got to follow the—

"I'll see you at home," Alf says.

He crumples the paper with the directions, chucks it onto the sidewalk, and walks back up the stairs to the sanctuary. Funny, remove the people, lose the rabbi, and the place does get a little holy. Alf takes a seat amid the discarded programs bearing his friend's name. He listens to the rain beat against the twelve tribes of Israel. Walt's bit was something about camels?

29

100 Delcar Street

Rain-soaked afternoon, another one, Fall River sky the color of old mud. Walt's been gone four months. The sort of day they'd take a drive, maybe see a movie at the mall in Swansea, or a late lunch at Magoni's or the Lobster Pot in Bristol. And she puts on some rubber boots and goes out to the garage, hoists the door, the little rusty wheels shrieking, and sits in the passenger's seat of the Lincoln. She's not waiting. It used to be called waiting. Walt still inside searching for his other galosh.

Is this the plot? The history of Fall River is a man drops dead while zipping his pants, and nobody's even home to hear him fall? She wants a refund. Where does she cash in ten thousand nights? Loneliness, somebody must have said too many times already, is a physical thing. It's in the fingers, the palms. It's in the tightness of your neck because to loosen would be to sink, and the only way to sink, to truly sink (and come back again), is with another, is with *the* other, arms and legs entangled. Funny thing is they never wanted for anything. You could almost laugh. As if they didn't know the money didn't matter. Oh hell yes, it mattered. Still does matter. Now more than ever. Walt said life was 90 percent economics and the rest was inflation. Alf, bless him, paid off the Lincoln so that she could sit in here in her own garage in the rain. She'll sell the house by the end of the year.

Still. Think about their friends, Milt and Pearl, Dot and Lloyd. Yes, even Alf and Ruthie, they said it, too. They'd always say they envied Walt and Sarah, and the whole time secretly (not so secretly) they thanked God they weren't Walt and Sarah. Hand to mouth. Can you imagine? But there are times when polite, saccharine-sweet lies are more truthful than what people hold inside, times when the casual lie *is* the secret. They did envy us, Walt, she thinks. They just didn't know why. They think it was because we were happy. (And happy's nice, happy's terrific, like a Christmas bonus. Let everybody be happy!) But empty pockets? That's a rough pill to… They can't see an inch past their noses. They envied us because we never wanted for anything. Two beds not even big enough for one of us much less two? Walt sold furniture his whole life, you think we couldn't have bought a queen on wholesale?

Because they knew we never wanted for anything.

She waits in the Lincoln. The leather seats have a way of surrendering, of molding to the contours of your body, not at first, but eventually. And eventually, she'll doze a little. The rain pounds on the little roof of the garage. Still, there's life. Even today, in this rain, she's got to pick up a prescription, stop by Ida's (Norm's in the hospital again), and meet the girls at Milt and Pearl's to play bridge at three thirty. Some days, and the man's still fresh in the grave, she forgets to remember him.

30

Sarah

In the spring of 1989, Sarah went with Ruthie Dolinsky to see Don Rickles at the Foxwoods Casino in Mashantucket, Connecticut. She didn't want to see a show. She wanted to gamble. Or at least give some Pequots her money. She'd drawn out eighty-five dollars cash to squander. And last time, didn't she take home twenty-eight bucks?

But Ruthie said it would be good to laugh. When was the last time you laughed, honey?

"I laugh," Sarah said. "I just don't laugh out loud. You'd be scandalized by how much I laugh."

What Sarah meant by this Ruthie didn't ask. She didn't want to know.

But Sarah went along, and at first she hardly listened to a thing Rickles said. Why would she want to? Still, she laughed, out loud, along with the rest of the audience. Ruthie elbowed her if she didn't. Rickles's body was so thin and wiry it was hardly there at all. But his mouth was a gaping horn. Sarah found herself watching him as if for a sign. He seemed the saddest man she'd ever seen. Not angry, his anger was so clearly a gag he didn't even bother to hide it anymore. He stood up there being sad, not mopey, fundamentally sad from top to bottom, and it was almost too familiar. And he wasn't trying to be especially funny, which of course made him funny, except that everybody laughed, as people seem to do, at the wrong time. The time to laugh is just before any punch line, not after, because if a joke is funny, what's funny about it is never, ever the punch line. The punch line is overkill, for dopes who miss the joke. Was it Walt who told her all this? Who else? Who'd bother to concoct such a formulation? But here she was, as if to demonstrate the nontheoretical, practical truth of it, cackling just before the punch line. This confused Ruthie and annoyed the people sitting around them. What? You alone, lady, get the joke? Even so, it wasn't like she was listening to the bits. She was only waiting for that almost imperceptible moment when Rickles appeared to hold his breath. There, right there, that's funny. She watched him, his little fishy eyes, that maw of a mouth open but, for milliseconds, silent. A decrepit comic on his last legs. He said he was starting to get booked at funeral homes. At one point Rickles lay on the stage and did a routine from the grave. Listen, worm, only one of us is getting out of this joint alive. You ever hear a worm laugh? It gnaws at you. Ruthie almost bust a gut.

She knows they talk about her, Ruthie and the others. How she never mentions Walt's name. How in twelve years you could count on one hand how many times she's said his name in conversation. Some of the girls think she's cold. *They always seemed so close. Goes to show you. Now it's like the poor guy never existed.* Others, like Ruthie, say she's being superior. That Sarah thinks her grief is somehow purer because she doesn't say things like what a relief it is not to have to live with Alf's fungus feet. Wouldn't let him near me unless he washed them in Clorox.

Husbands die. That's what husbands do. Most of them from their circle are dead now. Alf passed two years after Walt. Pearl's Milt had a stroke in '83.

Sarah has dated a couple of the sturdier widowers. She went

out a few times with an O'Malley, head of maintenance at the hospital where she still volunteers at the gift shop. And also, twice, a mousy, retired accountant, originally from Fall River, now living in Boston. Slept with both of them. Ted O'Malley was jolly and would call her up at all hours and ask what she was doing. What do you think I'm doing, Ted? It's two in the morning. You lack spontaneity, he told her, and eventually he stopped calling. The accountant, Sandy Edelstein, would drive down to Fall River and spend the night. But he was too scrawny. It was like going to bed with a bag of sticks. She needed a man with more baloney. She didn't think that. Walt thunk that. His body up and left, and it is Walt's body, it must be said, that she still craves. His thoughts? By Christ, didn't she have enough of those when he was around? There were days, weeks, when his talking was like a radio somebody left on in an empty room, when he was only disembodied noise. It's his body she refuses to live without. But try telling this to the girls. I just want his sweat, his beer breath. That's pure? That's being superior? Like Ruthie going to see Alf, she'd like to stop by Walt's grave once in a while, leave a rock, and be done with it. But he died and he didn't die, and she can't go around explaining this to everybody who wants to know why she doesn't say his name in public. He's not hallowed, he's still here, the part I don't want.

And Rickles talks on about how dead he already feels, and the more he talks, the more roaringly alive is that mouth. And Sarah remembers how Walt used to watch him when he was on Carson. He'd call out from the new room, the add-on from the '50s, because they needed somewhere to put a TV, and back then you didn't put a TV in the living room. "Carson's got Rickles. You gotta see this! Sar?" And she'd be doing something in another part of the house. Finishing the dishes, darning a sock (she's never darned a sock in her whole life), or maybe she'd just be sitting on the edge of a bed upstairs, because didn't she have her moments of ponderment? And she wouldn't come. What did she want with that nasty man? But she'd listen to Walt's guffaw. For a bookish highbrow, he sure could laugh at a television. And now she sits, in the dark, watching this sad sack, and Walt nudges her in the synapses and says, Sarah, you gotta live!

Onstage, Rickles is having a coughing fit. Hard to know if it's real or fake. When he catches his breath, he says, "Hell, why not kick it here? These Comanches have already paid me my ducats—"

What the hell did Walt think she was doing? Playing dead?

Yes, he said. And yet you're right, it's a curious thing to ask someone to do. Because how to define live?

See? He won't let up. How could she possibly explain this to Ruthie?

Live! Yes. A verb but, in this instance, clearly a command, an exhortation. Still, quite vague. I mean, I'm no scientist, but take a cell—

You know what, Walt? Go exhort yourself. Us two soldiers nightly foxholed. Remember that? And you deserted, decamped, Splitsville, you took your breath from me, your fingers—

Acknowledgments

A grateful thank-you to the editors of *The New Yorker,* where "My Dead" first appeared; as well as to the *New York Times,* "Allston"; *The Paris Review,* "Ineffectual Tribute to Len"; and *Tin House,* "Maggie Brown." Further grateful thanks to the editors of the following magazines and journals, where stories appeared in an earlier form: *Alta, Arkansas International, Bomb, Conjunctions, Confrontation, Faultline, Guernica, Harvard Review, Kenyon Review, New American Writing, Ploughshares,* the *Southern Review, Zyzzyva.*

The Isaac Babel line that opens the book is from "Childhood at Grandmother's," translated by David McDuff (Penguin, 1994). The line that appears on page 22, "The only defense against man's envy...," is a muddled quotation from Aeschylus's *Agamemnon,* translated by David R. Slavitt (University of Pennsylvania Press, 1997). The Natalia Ginzburg quote on page 187 is from her book of essays *The Little Virtues,* translated by Dick Davis (Arcade, 1989). The Rita Dove lines from *Thomas and Beulah* on page 211 are from *The Selected Poems of Rita Dove* (Vintage, 1993).

Names. Isn't there something very beautiful about a list of names? Think of Genesis. *The sons of Levi: Gershon, Kohath, and Merari. The sons of Judah: Er, Onan, Shelah, Perez, and Zerah (but Er and Onan died in the land of Canaan); and the sons of Perez were Hezron and Hamul.* It makes me think of my maternal grandfather, a furniture salesman who died before I had much of a chance to know him. He used to collect Fall River phone directories. I inherited these heavy bound books. I like to imagine him up in his little office, delighting in the names of his fellow citizens. There's more information in these directories than in our modern, now mostly vanished, phone books. 1945 is here on my desk. *Arthur Rand dentist (Phyllis), Manuel Rapoza printer (Herculana cook), Joseph Raska radio service (Eva trimmer), George Rasmany shoe repair (Anna), Rita Ratcliffe sanitary laundry, John Ratowski grocer (Catherine button sewer)...* I could read this book all day. Name after name, each and every one a story. Don't you wonder about Herculana? In this spirit, here's my own (very) partial list of indelible names of people without whose support this book, among many other more important things, would not exist: Ellen Levine, Ben George, Reagan Arthur, Betsy Uhrig, Nicholas Regiacorte, David Krause, Elizabeth Garriga, Kimberly Burns, Martha Wydysh, Pawel Kruk, Sue Betz, Cynthia Saad, Shannon Hennessey, Pat Strachan, Ian Strauss, Lee Boudreaux, Chris Abani, Andre Dubus, Marilynne Robinson, James Alan McPherson, Tish O'Dowd, Charles Baxter, Vievee Francis, Bill Craig, Sally Brady, John Griesemer, Nelson Mlambo, Yuki Tominaga, Maxine Chernoff, Debra Allbery, Oscar Villalon, Mary Ladd, Rachel Levin, Josh Richter, Jeff Sharlet, Gabe Marr, E. J. Hahn, Paul Griffiths, Charlie Harb, Junse Kim, Anna Lynch, Mike Brown, Kelsey Crowe, Julia Scott, Jason Roberts, Tom Barbash, Riccardo Duranti, Donal McLaughlin, Audrey Petty, Evan Lyon, Michael Parker, Julie Gordon, Alex Gordon, Rob Preskill, Nancy Amdur, Eddy Loiseau, Matt Goshko, Rhoda Pierce, Dan Pierce, Eric Orner, Blake Maher, Rosalie Crouch, Katie Crouch & Phoebe & Roscoe.

About the Author

Peter Orner, a two-time recipient of the Pushcart Prize, is the author of five previous books, including the novel *Love and Shame and Love* and the collection *Esther Stories,* a finalist for the PEN/Hemingway Award. His memoir *Am I Alone Here?* was a finalist for the National Book Critics Circle Award. His fiction has appeared in *The Atlantic, The Paris Review, Tin House,* and *Granta* and has been anthologized in *The Best American Short Stories.* The recipient of the Rome Prize, a Guggenheim Fellowship, and a Fulbright to Namibia, Orner holds the Dartmouth Professorship of English and Creative Writing at Dartmouth College.